THE BAKER'S MEN

POISON TOE PRESS

ALSO BY DONALD LEVIN

THE MARTIN PREUSS SERIES

Crimes of Love

Guilt in Hiding

POETRY

In Praise of Old Photographs

New Year's Tangerine

FICTION

The House of Grins

THE BAKER'S MEN

DONALD LEVIN

A MARTIN PREUSS MYSTERY

Copyright © 2014 by Donald Levin.

ISBN-13: 9780997294118

ISBN-10: 0997294116

Second Poison Toe Press edition published 2016

For Alex and Lauren

How do we forgive our Fathers?
Maybe in a dream
Do we forgive our Fathers for leaving us too
     often or forever
when we were little?
                    —*Dick Lourie*

Prick it and prick it and mark it with a T
And there will be enough
For Tommy and me.
                    —*Child's rhyme*

Sunday, April 12, 2009

1

The man hurried along the sidewalk on the other side of the street with both hands clasped on top of his head. He looked like he was trying to keep his scalp from floating away.

"Hold it, baby," Jared Whalen murmured into his cell phone.

He watched the man lurch past the cooling units of the Foodland, then dodder out of his line of vision. He had parked his scout car in the lot of the Ethiopian restaurant across from the supermarket to make his call.

Burly in his Kevlar and with close-cropped blond hair, Whalen put the cruiser in gear and eased up to the edge of Nine Mile Road in Ferndale. The financial meltdown of the previous year brought a spike in B&Es around Ferndale and neighboring Pleasant Ridge, so they were all warned to watch for anything unusual.

Case in point: this guy.

As he watched, the man continued down the sidewalk, more or less in a straight line.

Seems harmless, Whalen thought, and relaxed. This character might just be a bit tipsy, maybe got over-served at Rosie O'Grady's down the street and decided to walk home. At least he wasn't lit to the point where he was weaving all over the place so he'd step into traffic and become Whalen's most pressing problem.

"What's the matter, sugar?" the woman on the phone said. "Nothing more to say?"

Whalen smiled at the petulance in her voice. He turned his attention from the man on the sidewalk and pictured her pillowy red lips drawn in the pout that drove him wild. He met her last Valentine's Day when he stopped her for speeding on Woodward and one thing led to another. They hadn't spoken all day because her ex never picked up their kids as he promised he would so she was busy with the two girls, but now they were asleep and she could talk freely.

"C'mon, baby," he said, "got lots more where that came from."

He went on with her for another ten minutes until the dispatcher's voice interrupted.

"10-56, 7-Eleven at Nine Mile and Pinecrest. Meet the clerk."

Whalen sighed. 10-56, intoxicated person. The 7-Eleven was four blocks west of where he was parked. Probably the guy he just saw walking down the street. No big deal, but still.

Reluctantly he said goodbye to his sweetheart and told the police radio, "Unit 1267 responding."

He swung the cruiser onto Nine Mile toward the convenience store.

"Did you see him?" Nadine Kotter asked.

"Who?"

"Guy I called about. He just took off."

No one was inside or outside the store. Whalen walked around the side of the building and checked behind the dumpster. Nobody there.

Out front again, he said, "I don't see anybody, Nadine. What's up?"

Standing in the doorway, she sucked the last of her cigarette and backhanded it onto the blacktop. She was a tough-looking woman with spiked hair bleached white and tattoos of roses intertwined among her knuckles on both hands. Whalen liked to stop in to say hello and share a smoke on quiet nights.

"Guy comes into the store and starts mumbling some shit about the bakery." Her words came out in staccato bursts of smoke. "I go, 'Dude, what are you talking about,' and he's all, 'The bakery, the bakery.'"

"Sunday night," Whalen said, "always brings out the wackjobs."

"I know, and this guy seemed pretty jumpy. But then he goes, 'Police.' Then he goes back outside and sits in the corner for a minute, then he's up again and walking away."

"Which direction?"

"Up Pinecrest, that way." She pointed around the corner of the store.

"The thing was," she continued, "his head. It was a bloody mess."

Whalen stared at her.

"I'm serious. Like he took a shampoo in it or something."

"We're talking about a stocky black male, dark sweatshirt and Levis? Walking kind of like he's in a daze?"

"So you did see him."

"Further up the street I did, yeah. There was blood on his head?"

"Uh, hello?" Nadine gave a loose wheezy laugh, like a bag of gravel shifting in her chest. "The whole right side of his face was covered with it."

The right side . . . the side away from Whalen.

"I thought he might have fallen and hurt himself. Anyway he didn't seem right so I called it in. He was sitting over there."

She indicated the metal rack that held propane tanks at the far side of the store.

In the white glare from the overhead lights Whalen saw spots on the ground beside the rack. He swept his flashlight beam over the area. Definitely blood.

A second blue-and-white rolled up and another patrol officer stepped out adjusting the gear on her belt. Gail Crimmonds was a substantial woman with dark hair pinned back and skeptical eyes. Whalen filled her in quickly and asked her to take Nadine's statement.

He jumped into his scout car and wheeled it around the lot and out to Pinecrest.

Thinking: Bakery, blood, police—this is not good.

He went north, scanning the empty sidewalks and pausing at each corner to shine his spotlight down the side streets. The guy would only have a few minutes' head start.

When he reached West Drayton, Whalen figured the guy couldn't have made it this far so he drove back toward Nine. He called Dispatch and asked for assistance to search the neighborhood.

At the traffic light on Nine he took a left and drove east, picking up speed as his unease grew. The only bakery left in Ferndale was the Cake Walk, near the southeast corner of Nine and Planavon. There used to be two but the other one went bust the summer before. Most Ferndale businesses weathered the financial crash but a few, like the other bakery, couldn't hold on and now there were empty stores like missing teeth around the downtown.

He skidded to a stop in front of the Cake Walk facing the wrong way on Nine. The street was deserted and dark except for the lights at Rosie's down toward Woodward.

The front selling area of the store was empty, with bare display counters and shelves. The front door was locked.

He saw a light glowing in the rear so he trotted around to the back of the building. The bakery was the third business off the side street, beside two restaurants closed for the night.

He pulled at the handle of the steel rear entrance to the Cake Walk and the door opened.

He drew his duty weapon and stepped inside. A short corridor from the door to the back room ended at a partition that he couldn't see past.

He heard no sounds except the pounding of blood in his head and the knocking of his heart.

He stood for a moment, quieting his breathing, getting himself ready for what he might find.

He looked into the workroom, lit by overhead fluorescents.

The scene took his breath away.

He struggled to stay upright against the partition. He stood like that until the room stopped spinning.

Then he pulled himself together to call it in.

It was 9:32 on the evening of April 12, 2009.

Easter Sunday.

2

The day had not gone the way Martin Preuss planned.

In the morning he phoned his son's group home and asked them to get Toby ready for their usual Sunday outing. While he was in the shower the landline by his bed rang, and, assuming the group home was calling back, he rushed from the bathroom and punched the answer button before noting the caller's ID.

Mistake number one.

"Martin," a woman's voice said, "hi. It's me."

He grimaced. Exactly who he didn't want to hear from right now.

"Did I wake you? You sound sleepy."

"No," he said. "I've been up for a while."

"So I was supposed to go to my sister's for dinner this afternoon," Emma Blalock said, "but her kids are sick and she cancelled. I thought if you were free we might grab something. Unless you have other plans?"

"As luck would have it, I'm taking my son out today. Sorry," he added.

Not, he thought.

"Oh, I'd love to meet him. Would you mind if I tagged along?"

He couldn't really say no, could he?

Mistake number two.

"Would that be all right? Martin? Are you still there?"

She met them at the Red Robin on John R in Madison Heights. Preuss intended to eat at Joe's Crab Shack, Toby's favorite, where the servers sang and danced around the room. But he didn't want Emma intruding on their good place, not yet, so he decided on Red Robin instead.

Toby didn't mind. He sat in his wheelchair, Tigers cap jauntily askew on his head, gazing around at the restaurant's commotion with nearly sightless brown eyes. His slender fingers were wrapped around a skinny pink rubber rabbit with long bendable arms and legs that one of his aides gave him for Easter.

While they ate, Emma chatted about her caseload with the Oakland County Sheriff's Office. Preuss hated rehashing his own job because it meant reliving events he found hard enough to get through the first time. So mostly he listened and made appropriate one-syllable responses.

Toby, on the other hand, thought Emma's stories of criminal stupidity were hilarious. He squealed with glee at her imitations of their claims of innocence, which made Emma herself laugh.

Which made Preuss reconsider his decision to break it off with her.

Since they met the previous fall when the Kaufman girl went missing, she pursued a relationship with him as energetically as he tried to elude it. She was certainly an attractive woman, slender with a flawless cocoa complexion and wide engaging smile. And she was wonderful with Toby, talking with him and responding to his flirty crooked grins with pats on his shoulder and taps on his arms. She spoke to him as Preuss did, as if the young man understood every-thing, and she included him in the conversation even though he could only vocalize sounds like "Onion" or "Num."

What wasn't to like? Was he really going to find somebody bet-ter?

If only he liked her more.

If only that subtle quality of chemistry hadn't been absent.

If only he could bring himself to tell her.

They ordered ice cream sundaes for dessert. Emma wanted to give Toby a taste of hers, but Preuss asked her not to. Toby wasn't supposed to have anything by mouth because the complications of respiratory problems if he aspirated food were potentially fatal, especially since he was recovering from a bout of pneumonia in January.

After lunch he lifted Toby into his Explorer and Emma leaned in to give the boy a kiss on the side of his face, to his great delight. She gave Preuss a full-body hug and a kiss on the lips—to his great discomfort.

They agreed to talk again soon.

Happy to be alone with his son, Preuss drove back to the group home. They sat together for a long time on the side of Toby's bed. He had his own room that Preuss decorated like any sixteen-year-old's room, with posters on the walls of musicians and concerts they'd gone to: Arlo Guthrie, Judy Collins, the Chieftains, Los Lobos. There was also a photograph of Toby in his wheelchair with his dad meeting Arlo when the singer came out to sign autographs for the fans who hung around after a concert.

Toby couldn't sit up by himself because of his cerebral palsy so Preuss propped him upright with his arm around the boy's shoulders. Toby gradually leaned into his dad as he relaxed from his day.

It was a time of intimacy and they both loved it.

Preuss gave him a kiss on top of his head, and Toby copped a nose rub against his father's chest.

"You're all I need," Preuss said. "You know that, don't you?"

Toby hummed in reply.

Later on Preuss helped the aides give the boy a bath and get him ready for sleep. When they got him into his pajamas, fragrant with strawberry shampoo and rosy from the tub, Preuss laid his son curled like a comma on his side in bed and tucked the covers around him.

He sat in the armchair beside the bed and read aloud another chapter of *Harry Potter and the Chamber of Secrets*. Toby loved being read to, and when he was on administrative leave at the end of the previous year Preuss began the Harry Potter series.

He read while holding the boy's hand in his own. Toby listened carefully until his grip relaxed and he drifted into asleep, snoring gently.

Preuss closed the book and soon dozed off himself, unwilling to leave his son's side but unable to keep his eyes open.

The cell phone's ring jolted him awake at 9:47.

In his sleep-fogged mind his first thought was, *Oh no!* and he was back on the night the troopers told him about his wife's accident.

His head cleared at once when he heard the voice of the night dispatcher calling him in.

Warning him the officer on the scene said it was a bad one.

3

She wasn't wrong.

Martin Preuss looked down at two figures sprawled on the concrete floor of the workroom in the Cake Walk bakery. Both male, one dead, one not. The dead man lay prone with his face turned away almost modestly, as if he were ashamed of the mess made by the hole in his forehead and the bigger hole in the back of his head.

He looked to be in his late thirties or early forties and showed signs of living rough: sunken cheeks, grizzled face now grey with the pallor of death, the smell of stale man-sweat rising off him. On the side of his neck was the tattoo of an American flag surrounding the silhouette of the World Trade Center's twin towers. He wore a soiled green tee shirt that rode up on his back and faded Levis without a belt. His Nike running shoes were so worn there was very little tread on the soles.

One shot, execution-style, and that was it.

The other victim was younger and with long dark brown hair thick with blood. EMTs attended to a head wound.

Preuss looked around at the walls but saw no CCTV cameras. None outside in the parking lot either.

The action of lifting his head at the same time as he turned it brought on a wave of vertigo. He was still having problems with dizziness and headaches months after being clocked on the head by a troubled young man in a burning cabin in the woods of central Michigan. He was fit for duty, but he knew he wasn't as sharp as he had been six months before.

The workroom was a rectangle roughly fifteen feet by twenty, with light brown plaster walls and an ornate tin ceiling painted white. To the right was a metal worktable covered with a steel top criss-crossed by a thousand scratches; straight ahead and on the left wall open metal shelves held baking supplies and pans and trays of various sizes. The wall across from the work table held a row of ovens, all off.

EMTs and evidence techs filled the workroom. The number of people complicated Preuss's efforts to visualize what might have happened. As the senior officer in the Ferndale Police Department Detective Bureau he was situation commander and would lead the investigation.

The head of the department's Evidence Tech Unit knelt by the dead man. Arnold Biederman shook his head and stood, groaning from the audible cracking of his knees.

"We haven't seen one like this for a while," Biederman said. He was an intense man with an unsmiling face as sharp as the blade of an axe.

"Any IDs?"

"Neither one. Dead guy's got thirteen bucks in his pocket. I hear there's a third man."

"He split before anybody could talk with him."

Preuss's cell phone rang and Biederman returned to his work.

Janey Cahill's tense voice. "Hey," she said. "I'm on my way in. What's happening?"

"It's hell on wheels. Two men down, one dead. The injured one looks like an older teenager. No identification."

"Tall kid, good-looking, long black hair?"

"Sounds right."

"Probably one of the owner's sons. He's only fifteen but he looks older. I'm just coming up to Nine, be there in a minute."

He ended the call and took one last look around before leaving the techs to their work and going outside. At the threshold he slipped off his shoe coverings and stuffed them in the pocket of his bomber jacket.

In the parking lot behind the bakery the police chief, William Warnock, stood in conversation with Nick Russo, the chief of detectives. Preuss walked up to them but before he could open his mouth Russo broke off and strode away without looking at him.

Preuss and Warnock watched Russo's wide back for a few seconds, then exchanged a look of gloomy understanding.

"Any idea what these guys were doing here Easter Sunday night?" Warnock asked. He raised his voice against the growl of the two rescue vehicles parked in the alley with lights flashing crazily out of sequence.

"We don't know yet."

Warnock's sad eyes took in the back of the bakery where techs were going in and out. "What do you need?"

"Whoever you can spare. We're short-handed with Tony gone." Tony Tullio was the squad's senior detective until he retired at the beginning of the year.

Preuss looked around, spotted a rangy figure moving around the lot.

"I could use Ed Blair, for starters."

"Where's he detailed now?"

"Narcotics Enforcement. Undercover work, I think."

"Take him. I'll square it with NET. We'll find the money somewhere."

Janey Cahill's F150 roared into the parking lot beyond the yellow tape of the police perimeter. She pulled to a stop and trotted over to the two men.

She nodded to Warnock. "They still here?" she asked Preuss.

He led her into the store. As always she radiated hyper-caffeinated energy no matter what the hour. An FPD cap tamped down her wild hair. As the detective assigned to the Youth Bureau, she went into every situation where a young person was the victim or perpetrator of a crime.

One of the techs handed her a pair of shoe coverings, which she wrapped around her running shoes. Preuss put his covers back on.

Two EMTs were loading the young man onto a spinal board. "Yeah, it's Mark all right," Cahill said. "The owners' son, Mark Lewis. How is he?"

"Stable," one of the EMTs said, "but we'll know better once we get him to Beaumont."

The EMT and her partner lifted the boy onto the gurney and hustled him out to the ambulance.

"What about this one?" Preuss said.

She looked to the older man. "Don't recognize him. Looks like he's lived a hard life."

"Yeah. Though I'm guessing nothing worse than today."

"You interviewed Whalen?" Preuss asked.

Reg Trombley nodded. He stood in the parking lot with the Detective Bureau line supervisor Paul Horvath.

"Anything jump out at you?"

"No, what he told me matches what we see here. Only thing we can't account for is the third man."

"You put a bulletin out on him?"

"Of course," Trombley said. The youngest detective in the department, he was a lean man with skin the color of caramel and model-fine good looks that at this moment were haughty and cold.

"Let's get the techs to the 7-Eleven. Call the hospitals, too, see if he shows up anywhere."

"You got it, Fearless Leader," Trombley said.

Unsmiling, Trombley held his gaze for a moment and then turned and walked away.

Lately everything Trombley said to him had an edge to it. And Preuss specifically told him he hated when people called him Fearless Leader.

They would have to sit down and talk it through. When there was time. One more unpleasant thing to look forward to.

On the other side of the retaining wall at the north end of the parking lot was a row of small Ferndale bungalows. West of the lot stood a senior citizen high rise.

"Ed," Preuss said, "Chief said we could use you on this."

"Good deal."

"Why don't you take a couple uniforms and canvas those houses and the senior residence, see if anybody saw anything."

"Will do." The tall sergeant who reminded Preuss of Buddy Ebsen strode off toward a knot of patrol officers. He started gesturing toward the homes across the street.

"Janey," Preuss said, "can you get in touch with the bakery owners? See if one of them can come here first and tell us who the guy inside is."

"Detective Preuss!"

Gail Crimmonds, calling from the tiny park beside the side wall of the strip of stores across Planavon from the parking lot.

"Better take a look at this."

When he crossed the street she shone her flashlight on a pile of cloth in a heap on the ground.

"Looks like an apron from the bakery," she said. "There's the logo."

In the light from her flash he saw an R. Crumb-style cartoon of a goofily smiling birthday cake wearing a chef's hat and doing a keep-on-trucking strut while holding up a smaller birthday cake on a platter.

"Then there's this," she said.

She shone her light over dark blotches of blood covering the skinny legs of the walking cake.

4

"Yes?"

The boy was eerily self-possessed in the way some twelve-year-olds can be. "Can I help you?" The glass of the storm door muffled the formality of his voice.

Janey Cahill met him before, but the boy didn't seem to place her. She held her shield up and said her name. "I don't know if you remember me, but I talked to your class once."

When he didn't reply, she said, "Mom and Dad home?"

Kenny Lewis looked at her a moment longer, then faded away inside the house. It was a compact two-story bungalow on Earle Street facing Blair Park on the west side of Ferndale. Waiting on the stoop, Cahill turned to scan the dark grounds behind her. Her gaze settled on the utility shed in the far corner. For years area kids climbed the shed to have sex on its flat roof. She herself had been up there a few times back in the day.

A few too many times, now that she thought about it.

"Yes?"

The woman behind the storm door gave Cahill a severe look over black half-rims on a heart-shaped face. She had honey-colored hair cut in a short messy shag and she wore a Red Wings sweatshirt and faded blue sweatpants.

"René Lewis?"

"I am."

"Janey Cahill, Ferndale PD." She showed her badge. "We've met at the middle school?"

"Yes. Hello."

The woman opened the storm door and the two shook hands in the doorway.

"Sorry to be so late. Can I come in?"

"Please," René Lewis said. Cahill stepped into a hall between the living room on the right and a room set up as an office on the left.

"It's never good news when the police come to your door at 10:30," the woman said.

"No. René, is your husband home?"

"He's out with a friend. What's going on?"

"I'm sorry to have to tell you this, but there was an incident at the bakery tonight. A shooting."

René's hand with a large round turquoise ring flew to the winged wheel logo on her chest.

"Mark was there," Cahill said. "He's okay," she added quickly, "but he sustained a head wound. He's on his way to Beaumont right now."

"What happened?"

"We're not exactly sure."

"I want to see him," she pronounced. "Kenny?"

The boy appeared in the doorway from the kitchen.

"Get your coat, please."

"What's going on?"

"We're going out."

"But I haven't finished my science project."

He looked back at a table in the breakfast nook, where a trifold poster stood up with "How To Catch Stardust" printed across the top.

"We have to go. There was trouble at the store. Mark was hurt."

The boy went pale. "Is he all right?" he asked in a small voice.

Without answering, René said, "We'll stop by the bar and pick up your father."

"Why don't you and Kenny go to Mark," Cahill said. "Let us pick up your husband. We need some information from him first anyway. We'll run him up to the hospital after."

She thought about that for a moment, then said, "He's at Mr. Sal's on Woodward."

"We'll take care of him."

"Kenny, where's your coat?"

"I'll get him," Preuss said. "All the uniforms are busy and the reporters are starting to gather. I'd just as soon let Russo handle them."

"This guy'll be easy to spot," Cahill said. "Sunday night at Sal's he'll be the oldest guy in the room. He's in his 40s, a little shorter than you, starting to grow a belly, round face, boyish looks, close-cropped hair starting to go grey."

"Where are you going to be?"

"I'm going to the hospital with René and her other boy."

"Meet you there after I pick up Matt."

On the way to his car he passed Nick Russo with his bull neck and barrel chest bathed in the cold cone of lights from the news cameras.

In his glory.

Mr. Sal's Bar and Grill was an old neighborhood saloon with its original funky bar vibe in spite of the changing demographics in Ferndale. Now it no longer catered to older working-class men trying to drink away their troubles, but to the young and hip who moved into town over the past decade. There were tattoos, piercings, and shaved heads everywhere, along with something passing for music blasting from the speaker system.

Preuss recognized the band: the Wall Street Wankers, a group from Hamtramck, heavy on drums and angry fuzz guitar but light on actual talent.

Only one of two guys in the place could have been Lewis. They were together at the bar, bent over their drinks and chatting up the barmaid. Preuss walked over and said, "Matthew Lewis?"

The man closest to him said, "That's me," and the barmaid faded away.

Janey Cahill's description was dead on. Preuss introduced himself and produced his shield. "Can we talk outside?"

Lewis looked at his companion, then back to Preuss. "What about?"

"Let's talk outside, Mr. Lewis, okay? Bring your coat if you have one."

"Am I under arrest?"

Preuss leaned in close. "It's about Mark."

The secret words. The man jumped up and Preuss led him outside to where the Explorer was double-parked around the corner on East Drayton.

Lewis smelled strongly of alcohol. "Are you okay to talk?" Preuss asked.

"You mean am I drunk? No, but I'm getting more worried by the second."

"There was a shooting at your bakery tonight. Your son was there. He wasn't shot but he was injured in the fracas. Your wife's on her way to meet him at Beaumont. I'll run you up there, but first we need to stop by the store."

"Why?"

"A man was fatally wounded and I'm hoping you can tell me who he is."

Preuss started the car and made a U-turn on the side street. He pulled across the light Sunday night Woodward traffic to make a Michigan left at the median.

"Somebody was killed at my store?"

"He's wearing one of your aprons, I'm assuming he was an employee. Was anybody supposed to be there besides your son?"

"Two guys. Oh god—" He slapped his hands on his head and leaned against the side window.

"Are you going to be sick?"

Preuss pulled to the curb and lowered the passenger window. Lewis stuck his head out and choked back a gag but didn't vomit. He pulled his head inside and nodded to Preuss he was okay.

When they reached the bakery, Preuss parked in the lot behind the store and Lewis rushed into the store through the back door.

What he saw stopped him.

Preuss grabbed him by the arm so he wouldn't enter any further. He pointed toward the body on the workroom floor.

"Do you know who that is?"

"It's Leon Banks. Oh no. Oh, Leon."

Preuss moved him into the small office between the workroom and the front selling area. Lewis sat heavily in the chair behind the desk and Preuss sat in the visitor's chair.

"Leon's dead. Oh Jesus."

"I know this is hard but I need to ask you some questions," Preuss said. "We need to do this now."

"What happened here?" Matt Lewis asked.

"We don't know yet. You said two men were going to be here?"

"Leon and my assistant baker. Eddie Watkins."

"Why were they working tonight?"

"I have a catering job in the morning and they were going to come in to get it prepped. It was really Eddie's job, but Leon said he'd help out. So did Mark. I was going to swing by, too, in a little while."

"Does Leon work for you?"

"No. I let him do odd jobs around the place. I told him I'd hire him, but he never wanted a full-time job. Too much to handle, I guess."

"In what way?"

"Every once in a while he seems a little off. He's an Iraqi War vet. I assume it's PTSD. The demons some of these guys deal with when they get out are pretty rough."

"Did you ever see him get violent?"

He thought about that. "Not violent. But every so often he'd get worked up about something. But it was always all talk, I never saw him act on anything he ever said."

"Does he have any family?"

"He never mentioned anybody. Or friends, either. Far as I know, he keeps to himself."

"Can you think of any reason why somebody would do this to him?"

"Absolutely not. I don't think he even knows another soul in around here, apart from us. He came with a buddy after they got out of the service, but his friend moved on and Leon stayed."

"All right," Preuss said. "The other man is Eddie Watkins?"

"Yeah. Now Eddie's an employee. Another vet. Iraq, like Leon. After he got out, he had a rough time of it too, but I gave him a break, same as I did with Leon."

"What do you mean, rough time?"

"He told me his wife threw him out before he went into the army so he was homeless when he got out. At loose ends, no job, no prospects, that kind of thing. Like too many vets. But he's been try-ing to make a new life for himself. He even went back to school, took some classes at Wayne County Community College."

"Has there been any trouble around the store? Any people you don't recognize hanging around?"

"Not that I know of. I can ask my wife, but I probably would have heard."

"Can you get me whatever information you have on these two guys?"

"I can give you Eddie's employment application. I don't have much on Leon. He never applied for a job, so I don't have any pa-perwork on him. All I know is what he's told me. I think I have his address someplace."

Lewis logged into the computer and scanned through files.

"Sound like you have a thing for vets in trouble," Preuss said.

"Always have. Couple months ago Channel 2 did a feature on me, everything I'm doing to help out vets from Iraq. Did you happen to see it?"

"I usually don't watch the news. Were you in the service?"

"No, but my father was. Nam."

He printed a copy of Eddie Watkins's information. "Most of what I know about him comes from my mother. He died when I was a little boy."

"Sorry."

"He didn't have it easy either when he got home. When he couldn't take it anymore, he stuck a gun in his mouth and blew his head off," Lewis said matter-of-factly. "Left my mother to pick up the pieces. Now there's a whole new generation of damaged vets and their families. And then for Leon to survive a war and come home to this . . ."

"Never ends," Preuss said.

"No. We never learn."

He handed Preuss the printout. "Here's what I have on Eddie." He searched through the top desk drawer and came up with a stick-on note. "Here's Leon's address."

Preuss copied it on the printout. "One more thing," he said. "Does Watkins drive a car?"

"Yeah, an Olds Cutlass Supreme. Big-ass beater from the eighties."

Preuss made a note of it, then said, "Let's go see your son."

5

"Where is he?" Matt Lewis asked.

René Lewis was pacing outside an empty cubicle. "They took him to get x-rays."

"Did you see him?"

"I did but he was so out of it, I'm not even sure he knew we were here."

Matt Lewis and Martin Preuss entered the room. Janey Cahill sat in the corner with a young boy who was focused on the insect whispering of his iPod. Cahill made the introductions. The boy was Kenny, Mark's younger brother. He gave Preuss a cursory nod and returned to his device.

"What are they saying about him?" Matt Lewis asked.

"He has a concussion but they're thinking he won't have long-term damage," René said.

"Thank God," her husband murmured.

"What about Eddie and Leon?" René asked.

"Nobody knows where Eddie is. But Leon's dead, baby. Some-body killed him."

She covered her mouth with a hand and began to sob.

"We're trying to figure out what happened," Preuss said. "We're hoping Mark can fill in some gaps for us when he's ready."

"I don't think we're going to get much from him tonight," Cahill said. "He's going to be out of it for a while. And who knows what he'll remember about it all. But I'll wait with you folks till he's back from x-ray."

The Lewises said they would like that.

René said, "Please find out who did this."

"We'll do our best," Preuss said.

He left the hospital and drove back to the bakery. The tech unit was finishing up and the crowd of police and neighbors had thinned out. Biederman said he'd push to have something for him in the morning.

At this hour the only cars in the lot were police cars. There was no sign of Eddie Watkins's Cutlass Supreme. Assuming he was driving it tonight, he must have made his way back here and driven it off without anyone noticing it, Preuss thought.

He returned to the Shanahan Law Enforcement Complex on Nine Mile and ran the Olds through the state DMV registry. He got a hit on an '88 Cutlass Supreme registered to Shatoya Watkins at an address in Detroit. He put out a BOLO on the vehicle and filled out his incident reports.

When he finished, he called Janey Cahill, who told him Mark was admitted for observation, so was spending the night. René stayed with him while Matt Lewis took the other boy home.

They said goodnight and he took himself home.

Where a message from Emma Blalock awaited him on the answering machine on the counter in the kitchen. The time stamp was 12:14 a.m.

"I heard what's going on down there. I figured you'd be swamped so I'm leaving the message here instead of on your cell. Hope it isn't as bad as it sounds. I'm waiting to see if they're going to call us in for it. Give me a ring when you get home if you feel like it, otherwise I'll talk to you soon."

He played the message again, and erased it. Lately she was insinuating herself everywhere in his life. He didn't want to come home from his worst night in years to find her worrying about his well-being.

He stood in his kitchen with his back to the sink for another few minutes, turning away from Emma Blalock and filling his thoughts with the scene in the bakery. He tried to visualize every element. It was his way of imprinting it in his memory so he could recall it whenever he needed to.

There was nothing dumber than violence, Preuss thought as he remembered the raw, ripe mess of blood and brain matter from Leon Banks. Nor more meaningless. Nor more pervasive anymore.

He wondered, not for the first time, if it was all too much for him to deal with anymore. Over the past months he felt as if he'd lost something vital, whatever it was that let him accept increasing levels of craziness and still keep going. When Tony Tullio retired, Preuss began to consider putting in his own papers. A night like tonight only moved him closer to that point.

He rubbed his face with his hands and kept his fingers pressing against his eyes till the darkness scintillated.

Then he went upstairs and tried to sleep.

Monday, April 13, 2009

6

"He's the senior officer on the squad after you," William Warnock pointed out.

"I don't care. He never should have returned to duty."

Nick Russo sat facing him in Warnock's office. Warnock sipped his tea placidly while Russo glowered out the window at the overcast April morning. The only sound was the clink of the china cup on its saucer.

Russo grew more and more steamed. If Russo weren't such a wild bull, Warnock thought, it would have been enjoyable to watch him get wound up.

Warnock reflected it was pretty enjoyable anyway.

"There's a letter of censure in his personnel file for the way he handled things with the Kaufman case," Warnock said. "That alone will sink his chances for advancement, and he knows it. I think it's punishment enough."

"I don't." Russo cracked the knuckles of his big hands. "He wouldn't even have gotten that if I hadn't pushed for it."

"It's worst than he deserved. He kept things from going completely tits-up. He saved a lot of lives."

"He didn't save that little girl."

"She was alive when he found her. And he was in all the right places at all the right times. Except for some reckless behavior, it was good police work."

"That reckless behavior is exactly my point. Do you really want an officer who takes the kinds of risks he did?"

"Those were unusual," Warnock admitted. "But I want somebody who gets results. So should you."

"I told him straight out I didn't want him back. He doesn't even want to be on the force anymore. You know it as well as I do."

"I don't know any such thing."

"He as much as admitted it to me after my daughter died."

"You can't hold a man to what he says after his wife is killed."

"If he'd been a better man, she'd be alive today."

Warnock sighed. Now we were getting to the heart of the matter, he thought. Russo never forgave Preuss for the accident that killed his daughter after she ran out of the house following an argument.

Warnock held out his arms, palms up. "If things were different, they wouldn't be the same. I wish your daughter were still alive. I wish Tony Tullio were still here. But wishing won't bring either of them back. With the budget as bad as it is, Tony isn't going to be replaced. The fact remains, Martin's the best."

"I want him off the case."

"And then who'd run it? The next senior detective is Bellamy. Seriously?"

"We'll bring in the County again. Or the State. They should be on this anyway."

"Not going to happen. They're in worse shape than we are."

"You mark my words, he's going to bungle this and people are going to get hurt. And I'm not going to look the other way this time when it happens, either."

Warnock sipped his tea. "You didn't look the other way the last time."

"Well, I'm not going to take it."

"That sounds like a threat."

"It's no threat." He contradicted that by expanding his aging bodybuilder's chest in a gesture that put Warnock in mind of a primate showing dominance.

"It's a prediction," Russo said. "He's a loose cannon. He's going to wind up embarrassing the department, and lives are going to be lost."

"I hope you're not going to do something to make sure that actually happens."

"I'm going to be on him like stink on shit, is what I'm going to do. And the first time he mishandles something I'm going to push for his dismissal. And I'm not going to stop until he's gone for good."

"Nick, this really is beneath you."

"I'm giving you fair warning. I know him a lot better than you do. You'll regret leaving him in command."

Russo stood and stormed out of the office.

Warnock thought about telling his chief of detectives not to do anything he himself would regret, but decided to save his breath.

He was pretty sure Russo would wind up regretting everything about whatever he had planned for Martin Preuss. One way or the other.

7

"Both the night clerk at the 7-Eleven and Officer Whalen identified the missing man as Eddie Watkins," Preuss said.

He hadn't wound down enough to sleep until after four and was up two hours later trying to get himself going with coffee. Now his nerves quivered and his mind felt like cotton as he finished summarizing the events of the night before.

He looked at the weary faces of Arnie Biederman, Janey Cahill, Reg Trombley, Hank Bellamy, and Ed Blair, all sitting around the table in the conference room. They didn't look as if they slept much either.

"Anybody have anything to add?" he asked.

When no one spoke, he said, "Arnie, can you walk us through what you have?"

Biederman cleared his throat and stood beside the white board at the front of the room. He passed around a photograph of the storeroom at the bakery, and taped a blown-up version of it onto the white board, along with a series of photos taken at the scene. On the large photo were three rudimentary figures drawn against a worktable. The figure in the middle was represented by a dotted line.

"The dead man was shot in the head by what looks to be a .38 calibre handgun," Biederman continued. "No shell casings on the floor. Heavy GSR stippling, indicating the shooter put the barrel against Banks's head and pulled the trigger."

Trombley whistled. "That's cold. Sounds like an execution."

"Preliminary examination of the blood spatter indicates he was standing in front of the worktable abutting the side wall of the bakery, like so."

With a laser pointer Biederman indicated the figures on the crime scene drawing. "Based on where they were found, Banks was standing on the left, the youngster on the far right. We pulled a bullet from the side wall, here."

He indicated a hole high up in the wall between the figures for the dead man and Mark Lewis.

"We're examining it for blood traces. Banks and the boy were both standing facing away from the wall. We won't have the PM results for a while so we won't know the exact angle the bullets were fired from. But we can make some preliminary assumptions. Reg, do you mind?"

He pulled Trombley to his feet and stood him sideways. Trombley was several inches taller than Biederman. "Reg is about Banks's height."

Biederman held his arm straight out with a finger pointed at Trombley's head like a gun. "Based on the spatter patterns, this roughly approximates the angle of entry. It appears the shooter held his arm out like so." He demonstrated. "Which would make him roughly my height. Around five-eleven. Thanks," he said to Trombley, who resumed his seat.

"No bruises or abrasions on either man apart from the boy's head wound," Biederman said, "which suggests there was no struggle."

"Gail Crimmonds found what we assume is Watkins's apron," Preuss said, "in the pocket park across Planavon."

"We're running tests on that, too," said Biederman.

"So," Preuss said, "it's looking like Watkins wasn't the shooter. If the bullet you pulled from the wall was the one that grazed his head, someone else must have been there."

"That's what it looks like to me. At some point I believe the third man was standing against the table, in the middle of the two other victims."

"Which suggests a fourth person in the room. The target may have been one or all three of them. Or Eddie Watkins was the shooter's confederate, which is why he took off."

Preuss looked at the photo of the scene on the whiteboard. He got up close to it. "What's that?" He pointed to what looked like a tube on the floor under the worktable.

"A rolling pin."

"Maybe it's what Mark got clocked with."

"There were traces of blood and hair on it, which we're analyzing."

When no one said anything else, Biederman said, "I'll leave you all to it. I'll get my report in soon as I can."

"Thanks, Arnie," Preuss said. "Great job."

Biederman dipped his head in appreciation. He gathered his materials and left the room.

"Janey," Preuss said, "what do we know about the bakery owners?"

"René and Matthew Lewis. They opened the bakery about a year ago, good citizens, donate baked goods to school events, support community activities. The boy who got hurt, Mark, never had any run-ins with the juvenile justice system."

"How's he doing?"

"He's stable. René spent the night with him and says he still isn't in any shape to talk to us. I asked her to call me as soon as he's alert enough to talk."

"Anything come up in the canvas?"

Ed Blair said, "Nobody heard or saw anything. Lots of people didn't answer. I'll have the uniforms try again today."

"Anything from the hospitals?"

"Not as of last night," Trombley said.

"Hank, why don't you take over the hospitals. Reg, I'd like you to look into Banks, found out what his story is. Especially if he has any narcotics involvement. Run him through OTIS," he said, referring to the state Offender Tracking Information System. "And trace his movements yesterday."

Trombley nodded. "There may also be a military connection here," he said. "Both these guys are veterans."

"Very possible. Matt Lewis has a thing for veterans in trouble."

"I'll stick with Mark," Cahill said. "He should be in good enough shape to talk later today."

Preuss nodded. "Hank, when you're done with the hospitals, start looking at the bakery owners, see if there's anything there we want to know about. In the meantime I'll look for Watkins. Let's meet this afternoon at four and see where we are."

8

Preuss followed Reg Trombley's narrow back as he returned to his cubicle. When he noticed Preuss behind him he stopped and waited. Even his look was chilly, as though daring Preuss to confront him about something. What was up with this guy?

"Got a minute?" Preuss asked.

Without replying, Trombley continued into his work area and held a hand out to the visitor's chair while he dropped into his own seat behind his desk.

He rested his elbows on the clean surface waiting for Preuss to begin. Preuss's own desk, by contrast, was a tumult of stacks of files, half-filled containers of Tim Horton's coffee, and cryptic Post-it notes whose meanings only he understood.

"I'm picking up tension between us and I just wanted to find out if there's something going on here I need to know about."

"Tension," Trombley repeated, and didn't say anything else though his practiced blank stare was eloquent.

"Reg, we don't have time for this. If you have a problem with me, let's get it out in the open and talk about it."

"I don't have a problem." Trombley's tone said he did in fact have a major problem.

"Then what's with this 'fearless leader' bullshit? And the attitude you're giving me right this minute?"

"I have no idea what you're talking about."

"Come on, man, I thought we were close. Let's talk about this."

"Nothing to talk about."

Preuss stared at him. This was not the Reg he knew, the Reg he thought respected him, worked with him willingly and gladly. Until recently.

"Whatever's going on, if you won't discuss it at least be professional enough to keep things civil till we can work this out. And I don't know about you, but this isn't the way I want to be with the people I work with."

"Fine."

He sat stone-faced, waiting for Preuss to leave.

Before he said something that would bump this up to another level of rancor, Preuss went back to his office.

With a cup of coffee from the machine in the office of Tanya Corcoran, the Detective Bureau's administrative assistant, Preuss made some space on his desk to go through the personnel sheets for Eddie Watkins. His problems with Trombley would have to wait.

Watkins's file was just a few pages of PDFs of his employment application. The handwriting on the application was a scrawl, almost impossible to read in the electronic reproduction. The reference page was blank.

Watkins listed his address as the Journey's End Motor Inn on Eight Mile and Woodward in Ferndale. With no references, Preuss searched his notes from the night before and found the name of Shatoya Watkins, which was the name Eddie's car was registered in. His ex-wife, maybe? Her address was on Marlowe in Detroit.

A recording told him her phone number was no longer in service.

Have to hit this old school, Preuss thought. Wear out some shoe leather.

He connected to OTIS and ran Eddie Watkins's name, but no hits came up. So no connection with the Department of Corrections for the past three years.

He called Janey Cahill's cell but it went right to voicemail. He told her he was headed out to start looking for Watkins and asked her to let him know as soon as Mark Lewis came around.

"I'm not responsible."

"For what?"

"Whatever this guy's done."

"Who said you were?" Preuss asked.

"Just saying. My company is not responsible."

With a sigh Preuss stepped by the overweight Chaldean desk clerk and into Eddie Watkins's unit. The Journey's End Motor Inn was a shabby hotbed residential motel well-known to the Ferndale police, so rejecting responsibility was probably a good idea. At least once a week a call came in about shots fired, fights between residents, or other kinds of public disturbances, or complaints from a citizen about being beaten or robbed by one of the whores of both sexes who lived in these cramped, foul-smelling rooms, or else by their pimps.

Watkins's room was the same as every other one in the long, two-story building: a boxy, twelve-by-twelve unit with water-stained institutional yellow walls and a small fridge and hot plate. The fridge held a pint of outdated milk, a half-jar of peanut butter, and three containers of yogurt. Beside the hotplate was a jar of Spartan instant coffee, a dirty cup from Wayne County Community College, a plastic dish, and a sauce pan.

Men's clothes—work shirts, Levis, tee shirts and and underpants—hung in the tiny bath to dry after being rinsed out in the sink, there being only a rickety, moldy shower stall beside the toilet.

On the bureau was a compact CD player beside a stack of CDs—Miles Davis, Sonny Rollins, Art Blakely and the Jazz Messengers, as well as a handful of other jazz giants. He opened up one of the Miles Davis CDs, *Bitches Brew*. Both discs were well-worn and scratched.

Preuss opened drawers in the single bureau and found only a few shirts and pants with the lived-in look of Salvation Army goods. In the drawer in the nightstand he found a jumbled mix of personal belongings—a shaving cream can with rusted bottom, disposable razors, brush, toothbrush and mashed tube of Crest, bottles of aspirin and ibuprofen, books of matches, coins, miscellaneous receipts, and an envelope containing pay stubs from the Cake Walk. Watkins made $10 an hour.

All in all he found only the sad and impersonal fragments of the life of one of America's transient poor. The only exception was a battered case on the shelf in the closet; Preuss opened it up to find a trumpet, its brass weathered and dented but clearly the most valuable object in Eddie Watkins's life.

He stowed it back on the shelf and hoped Watkins would return to retrieve it.

Outside the room Preuss asked the clerk, "When was the last time you saw him?"

"I don't make of point of studying my guests."

His *guests*, that was a good one. "Have you seen him since yesterday?"

"No. I never see him."

"How does he pay for his room?"

"He leaves cash in an envelope in the drop box in the office once a week."

"Is he paid up?"

"We require guests to pay a week in advanced. They don't pay, they don't stay."

Preuss gave the clerk his card. "He shows up, call that number immediately, all right?"

The clerk put the card in his pocket without even looking at it. "I am not responsible for the behavior of my guests."

"Duly noted," said Preuss, and returned to his Explorer, where he texted Paul Horvath and asked him to put an unmarked car on the place in case Eddie Watkins showed up. In seconds Horvath texted back his acknowledgement.

Preuss sat in the lot for another twenty minutes until a nondescript Ford police interceptor driven by a plainclothes officer wheeled into the lot and parked where he could see the front entrance. Watkins would have to be blind to not recognize this as a police vehicle driven by a policeman, but Preuss walked over and told the officer who he was looking for and what to do if Watkins showed up.

Then he returned to his Explorer and set the GPS for Shatoya Watkins's address in Detroit.

She lived on a dead-end street of pre-Second World War brick bungalows near Hubbell and Plymouth on the city's west side. The home was compact and tidy, though the concrete front steps were badly chipped and the small front yard contained mostly spiky weeds just beginning to awaken in the early spring. Under a wrought-iron park bench on the front stoop a misshapen pie tin overflowed with nasty-looking cigarette butts. Half of the other houses on the street were boarded up.

He pressed the doorbell a few times but there was no response. He walked around to the backyard, where a small plastic playhouse, its reds and yellows weathered to pale shades of pink, leaned precariously in the brisk April wind. As he stood taking in the blank back of the house, he noticed a curtain part behind a barred window of the house next door.

A woman's face glared out at him in a tight fist of disapproval.

When she saw him looking back at her, she pulled away. In less than a minute she was outside, coming across her backyard to stop a few feet from him with the fence between them. She was a heavy woman in a long army overcoat thrown over a faded print housedress. The bitter smell of cigarette smoke hung around her.

"There a problem?" she demanded in an angry rasp. Her face was the color of aged leather.

He showed her his shield, which most likely verified her hunch he was trouble on two legs. "I'm looking for Shatoya Watkins."

"What you want her for?"

"Is this where she lives, ma'am?"

"What you want her for?"

"It's about Eddie."

At Eddie's name, the woman stood straighter and pulled a sour face. "Might should have known."

"Have you seen her today?"

"I see her every day. She live here with her chirren."

"Is she home now?"

"Uh-uh."

"Do you know when she'll be back?"

"Can't say."

"Have you seen Eddie around lately?"

"Hmm. What he done this time?"

"I just need to speak to him. Does he have any other relatives you know of? Someplace else he might go besides here?"

"Not no more, not around here. All his people dead and gone. But you looking for somebody really know Eddie, you see Pastor Rocellus."

"Who's that?"

"Rocellus Gaines. They go way back, those boys. Pastor, he know everything there is to know about Eddie Watkins. Tell you where to find him."

"Thanks."

"One condition."

He raised his eyebrows. He was starting to like this woman.

"You don't bring Toya no trouble. She have enough already."

"I'll try my best."

She fixed him with a hairy eyeball. "You see you do."

The Mt. Zion Church of God in Christ was a yellow brick storefront between vacant buildings in the middle of a block on Michigan Avenue in Inkster, a city near Detroit about twice the size of Ferndale. An awning across the front of the church announced the church name in rough hand lettering above the words "Pastor R.G. Gaines," in smaller script. A safety gate covered the rusty metal front door and the only windows were six vertical slits of glass block, three on each side of the door.

Preuss reached for the buzzer on the doorframe. In a minute he heard the clatter of locks being undone on the other side of the door.

Which was opened by a lanky, painfully thin man whose face formed a terrible scowl when he saw Preuss. Just bringing little rays of sunshine where ever I go today, he thought.

"Rocellus Gaines?"

He gave a wary nod.

Preuss showed his shield and introduced himself. "I understand you know Eddie Watkins?"

"What's the problem?"

"If I could come in, we could talk about it."

"Guess you better," Gaines said, and undid the complicated locks of the gate.

As in most storefront churches, the large room contained a dozen rows of folding chairs on either side of a center aisle. The pulpit was a podium on a raised altar at the far end. Six plush chairs stood behind the podium in front of a mural done by an untrained artist. It showed a forest scene with a waterfall and a sickly-sweet-looking black Jesus standing with open arms among a herd of jungle animals. To the right of the altar an American flag hung limply on its stand.

Pastor Gaines held a hand out to one of the folding chairs and Preuss sat. Rocellus took a seat in the row in front and turned around to gaze at Preuss with a look of deep concern. He was a handsome man with expressive red-brown eyes.

"So," he said, "what's he done?"

"He was involved in a shooting in Ferndale last night."

Gaines shook his head. "Anybody hurt?"

"One man was killed and another was injured."

"And you think Eddie did it?"

"It's not clear. He's disappeared and I'm trying to find him."

"I wish I could say I'm surprised to hear this. But I'm not."

"How do you know him?"

"We run together back in the day. Close as brothers at one time."

Rocellus sighed, his sad eyes lost in a memory.

"Have you kept in touch with him?"

"I haven't seen him since he came home from Iraq. Two years or so, I guess it's been. He came to see me, said the war showed him life was too precious to lose touch with your friends. But I haven't talked to him since."

Preuss showed the pastor a photograph. "Do you know this man? His name is Leon Banks."

"Never saw him before. Who is he?"

"The man who was killed."

"When I said I haven't *seen* Eddie, I don't mean I haven't heard *about* him."

"I don't follow."

"A lot of people from the old neighborhood come to church here now. So I pick up things every once in a while. I heard he might have got himself in a little trouble with some folks."

"What kind of trouble?"

"I heard he took a little something wasn't his and now people are after him to give it back. Not good people, either."

"What exactly are we talking about here, pastor?"

"Maybe money, maybe drugs. Maybe something else entirely. Not sure. This is just what I hear people talking about, you understand. I can't swear to it one way or another."

"You haven't heard anything about who he's involved with?"

"No, sorry."

"No idea? Really?"

Rocellus worked his mouth for a few moments and said, "I had to guess, I could give you a name. Another fella we grew up with. Yummy Hendricks. Rough customer, too, I have to say."

"How so?"

"Yummy, you name it, he's got his fingers in it. Drugs, women, gambling."

"I take it Yummy's a nickname?"

"His given name's DaRhon. But nobody's called him anything but Yummy since we were kids."

"Know how I can find him?"

"He still lives down in Detroit in the old neighborhood. What's left of it, anyway."

Then Rocellus shook his head again. "Poor Eddie. It just goes to show."

He turned to look balefully at the hand-painted image behind the altar.

"Sooner or later, life catches up to you. Can't run away from yourself. Only thing can turn your life around is Jesus."

9

Returning from a cigarette break, in the elevator up to the eighth floor of Beaumont Hospital Janey Cahill reflected again on what a good news/bad news joke it was to be a married single mother.

On the one hand, it meant the responsibility for the boys was hers alone. She had to arrange someone to pick them up and drop them off for all their athletic events, to be there when they got home from their latch-key program, and to watch them whenever she was called out on her off-hours, like last night.

Fortunately her mother was usually available, and if not then Millie next door could help out at a moment's notice. And besides all her standard gender-specific household tasks (cleaning, cooking, laundry), she needed to do the ones her husband Tommy took care of too (lawn, trash, maintenance).

Tommy couldn't find work locally and had to travel to find a job. She knew this was hard on him and the boys. Now he was working near Harrisburg in Pennsylvania, where he found a job as a union carpenter on the construction of a wind turbine field. He lived in a tent like a migrant worker with a couple of other men because the turbines were out in the boonies away from any motels or decent places to stay. The job was steady for now, but the unpredictability of the project's funding meant he could be laid off any time. Then he'd come back to Ferndale and go to the bottom of the union list and who knew when he'd find something else?

On the other hand, she totally loved living away from him, and there was no sense even trying to deny it. She loved living by her own rhythms and those of the kids, without worrying about tiptoeing around the house wondering if she was going to say something to set him off. His temper was legendary in their neighborhood, and even the boys, young as they were, already knew not to mess with Daddy when he was in one of his moods. They could already scope out when one was coming on.

While she felt badly about his situation, she knew they never got along better than they did now. His absence was saving the marriage. She even started to wonder how long she could put up with his being around once this job ran out.

She stepped off the elevator and headed toward Mark's room. You made your bed, her mother used to say when Janey would complain about Tommy. She talked to some of her girlfriends about him because most of them were in the same boat so they could be supportive, and every once in a while she would drop a hint to Martin Preuss.

Usually he was sympathetic, though she was careful not to go deeply into her problems with him. It was more fun to give him advice on how to improve his own life. It was always easier to fix someone else's problems, she reflected. The solutions were so much more obvious.

She paused in the doorway to Mark Lewis's room. He was the only patient in a double room. René was asleep in the chair between her son's bed and the window, which looked out on the Shrine High School athletic field on Thirteen Mile Road. Mark was asleep too. He was free of the cervical collar but a gauze bandage stuck up from his head.

Cahill left them sleeping and stopped at the nurses' station to ask where the vending machines were. The nurse working at a terminal behind the counter directed her down the hall. With a container of yogurt and a Diet Coke she returned to a hard chair in the visitors' area at the end of the corridor. She scarfed the yogurt in about five seconds.

Despite the No Cell Phones sign staring her in the face, she checked her messages and saw one from Martin.

She worried about that man. More than she should, and that was a fact.

Once, a few years after Jeanette died and he had stopped drinking, she came dangerously close to crossing a line with him.

One night they found themselves together in her pickup following a pizza dinner at Como's celebrating Tony Tullio's birthday. She gave him a lift back to the Shanahan where he left his car, and sitting in the darkness of the parking lot behind the station, chatting quietly about Tony's party, she felt an overwhelming urge to lean into him and be taken into his arms.

A moment, ridiculous in retrospect, when her sympathies for his situation merged with her own need for someone to hold her and make her feel wanted in some more significant way than as maker of lunches.

And she was a second away from doing it—might even have started toward him, in fact—but he abruptly said goodnight and left the truck and the spell was broken.

Did he know? Could he sense the distance between them shrinking by a millimeter? Did he see it in her eyes and that's why he left so quickly?

Neither ever mentioned it. Now it was ancient almost-history.

Thinking of that night, wondering still if it had been a narrow escape from a mistake they would both regret or a chance lost forever, she strolled back to Mark Lewis's room.

Where René's back was to the door as she was up and leaning over the bed.

Something was happening.

Cahill stepped inside and René turned toward her. Her eyes shone with tears.

Mark was looking around the room, glassy-eyed but definitely awake.

"Hey, big guy," Cahill said. "Welcome back."

Mark turned his unfocused gaze on her. He made as if to say something, but both women told him to relax.

He tried to pick his head up but couldn't bring it very far and it fell back to the pillow. He looked agitated.

"Don't try to talk," René said. It was the exact opposite of what Cahill herself wanted, but she knew he wasn't ready to say much anyway.

The boy continued to struggle to say something. René leaned toward him and he croaked out a sound.

"What's he saying?"

"He said, 'I'm sorry.'"

10

Leon Banks lived in a house in Hazel Park near the Raceway. When Reg Trombley called the owner, the man said he could meet him there in an hour. Trombley drove over to a tiny diner nearby on John R to get some food in him before the meeting.

Munching a couple of overcooked coney dogs, he reflected on his talk with Preuss earlier. Preuss was right, of course, he was shrewd enough to pick up that something was happening between them. What he didn't know was how much Trombley missed their former closeness. Ever since he joined the Detective Bureau, he wanted only to be as good a detective as Preuss was. Tony Tullio was a phenomenal mentor, but whenever Trombley and Preuss worked together, Trombley felt like he was getting taken to school about how to treat witnesses and suspects, how to be dogged, how to share information with colleagues who needed to know, how to cut through the bullshit to what was key in an investigation.

In Trombley's opinion, how to be the best.

When Trombley was the one Preuss asked to accompany him on the jaunt up to Montrose last year, Trombley was tickled, and even though Preuss wound up with most of the heroics, he, Reg, held his own and came through when needed.

And everybody lived, which was the main thing. Thanks to Reg and Martin working together, they all survived.

But now . . .

He was in a tough spot. He had his principles. If maintaining them meant sacrificing his relationship with Preuss, well, maybe that's what would have to happen. Especially if Preuss wasn't the guy Reg thought he was.

No, he was between a rock and a hard place here and it pained him. And as always the question was, Who to trust? In his heart he knew the only people in the world he could trust completely were his family . . . his wife and two boys were the most precious people in his world. He talked about this Preuss thing with his wife Sandra—his partner and best friend—but all she could say was, Listen to your heart, baby.

If only he could hear what it was saying.

He ordered a cup of coffee and tried, without success, to interrogate his heart.

But it must have lawyered up because he couldn't get a thing out of it.

"George Katsoulis?"

A heavy white man stood smoking on the front stoop of a Dutch colonial. He was a foot shorter than Trombley and twice as wide but the most striking feature was his head—it was extra-large, as though Katsoulis borrowed it from a much taller man.

"Detective Trombley?"

"That's me."

"Come on in."

Katsoulis tossed his smoke into the bushes by the front door and led the way into the house. "There's a separate entrance for the top floor," he said, "but it's easier to get up this way." He had one of those comically nasal white men's voices Richard Pryor loved to imitate.

Wheezing, limping, Katsoulis lumbered up the protesting wooden stairs and stopped, breathing hard, outside a door on the third landing. He stood with his jaw forward, exposing a row of tobacco-stained bottom teeth. Trombley watched him carefully in case he was fixing to keel over.

Instead he withdrew a ring of keys from his pocket and sorted through them. They were all labeled with numbers.

"Those to all your properties?" Trombley said.

Katsoulis nodded and cleared his throat wetly. "Got ten units, couple of them duplexes. Rather be doing what you're doing, though. Used to be on the job when I was younger."

"Oh yeah?" Trombley tried to hide his amazement. "Where?"

"Right here in Hazeltucky."

Trombley knew this town was called that because of all the immigrants from the Appalachians who came to Michigan to work in the auto plants back when the industry was thriving. A lot of them settled in Hazel Park. The nickname grated on Trombley's ears though he knew the southerners would likely have worse to say about him.

"Yeah," Katsoulis said, fiddling with the keyring, "took a bullet in the thigh when I was on a home invasion run one night ten years ago. Shattered the bone and I wound up disabled out. Had to find something to do with myself, so I got into real estate. Good move, I gotta say."

"Even though things are so bad?"

"It'll change. Besides, nobody can afford a house now, but everybody needs a place to live so lots of people are renting. This is the time to pick up properties. Everything's going for a song. Always missed the excitement of the job, though"

"Sometimes it's a little too damn exciting."

"Maybe. Beats prying the rent out of good-for-nothing tenants, trust me on this one. Ah."

He found the right key and got the door open. He stepped inside and called out, "Landlord."

"This guy's never going to hear you."

"Can't tell who might be staying here. You'd be surprised the people I find where they don't belong."

No, I wouldn't, Trombley thought but didn't bother saying.

The place was small, a cheap and dirty remodel from a minuscule attic. He took a quick look around the living room, galley kitchen with few groceries in the cupboard, a tiny bedroom, and a bathroom Trombley could barely fit his lean frame inside.

The place stank of male sweat and dusty air. The living room held a threadbare sofa and no other signs of occupancy except for a stack of books leaning against the sofa and a battered backpack beside the stack.

Trombley gloved up and started to pick through the volumes in the pile, well-thumbed used books with titles like *The Islamic Jihad Against the West*, *Christianity's Last Stand*, *The Coming Nuclear War with Iran*, and *"We Will Bury You": The Islamo-Zionist Conspiracy to Destroy the West (and How to Stop It)*.

A little light reading for an evening, Trombley thought.

He brushed through the pages of a few of the top books. He skimmed a few paragraphs about the on-going Islamic war against democracy written from the paranoid right of the political spectrum.

He looked through the backpack, which held several bundles of tattered spiral notebooks bound together with enormous sticky rubber bands. He separated them and opened the top one. It appeared to be a journal written in a large hasty scrawl, page after page filled with barely legible thoughts.

Trombley sensed a terrible anger radiating from the scribbles. What he could make out seemed connected to the subject of the books . . . the looming conflagration as two civilizations, Islamic and Christian, prepared for their final apocalyptic confrontation, and all the ways the American government was traitorously capitulating to the world-wide Muslim menace. And how the international Zionist conspiracy was behind the planet's current financial meltdown as a way to goad Christianity and Islam into all-out war so the Zionists could step in and take over all the resources of the Christian and Muslim worlds that they bankrupted.

The pages were greasy and wrinkled. As he looked more closely he could see these weren't only feverish journal ramblings. Some of the pages were drafts of letters with salutations to the director of the FBI, the President of the United States, His Holiness the Pope of Rome, and a variety of lesser governmental agencies, including governors, mayors, and police chiefs of states and communities around the country. Two were to the mayor and council president of the City of Ferndale.

With grim foreboding—these could be the rantings of exactly the kind of army-trained wackjob loner who committed a mass shooting, he thought—Trombley searched through the rest of the apartment. No clothes hanging in the closet, and only a few shirts and socks scattered in the bureau in the bedroom.

Most importantly, there were no weapons anywhere, and nothing indicating somebody mixed up in either drugs or mass murder. No stash, no drug paraphernalia, no prescriptions, no plans or equipment for making bombs, no caches of grenades, no ammunition . . . just the ravings of a lonely and deluded man.

Katsoulis sat in the living room, breathing heavily, while Trombley made his way through the apartment.

"Anything interesting?" Katsoulis asked when he was finished.

"How long has he lived here?"

"Couple years now."

"He travels pretty light. Any other renters in the house?"

"It's divided up into two more apartments, both occupied."

"Do you live nearby?"

"Down the street."

"So you wouldn't know about any visitors he might have?"

"Nope, couldn't tell you."

"He ever talk to you about family or friends?"

"Honestly, I never saw the guy, except when I came to collect the rent first of every month. Most of the time he just gave me the money without a word."

"When was the last time you saw him?"

"First of this month, when I came for the rent."

"Where'd he get the money from?"

"He came up with a little of it himself, from where I dunno, and I let him work off the rest of it. He shoveled the snow, kept up the yard. Everything I can't do. Now I gotta find somebody else to do all that."

Trombley nodded absently. Death is so inconvenient, he thought.

"I want to take these journals with me. I'll get you a receipt for them."

"Be my guest. I'll never have any use for them."

"I also want to get the evidence techs in here to give the place a going-over, so I'll ask you to keep everything as it is for now. Afterwards it'll be up to you to dispose of his stuff if nobody claims it."

"How long till I can re-rent the place?" Katsoulis asked in his comical voice. He peered up at Trombley with his big head and strangely juvenile and petulant gaze, like a pouty and moist-lipped child who was unfairly being denied something he wanted.

"We'll let you know when we're finished."

"Kee-rist!" Katsoulis whined. "When'll that be?"

"We'll be done when we're done," Trombley said, and re-wrapped the journals in their gummy rubber bands.

Before he left, Trombley knocked on the doors to the other apartments. The two other tenants were home. The one who lived directly under Leon Banks's apartment was a talkative older woman whose slurred speech and unfocused gaze indicated heavy drinking. But she was clear-minded enough to tell Trombley that she heard Banks upstairs the whole day before, until he left at some point after dinner.

"The floors and stairs squeak something awful," she said, "so I can hear every step he takes. And he's a pacer, always walking around, day and night."

To her knowledge, no one ever came to see him, or at least she never heard any other voices up there besides Banks's, talking to himself.

"He's an odd duck," she pronounced. "Is he in some trouble?"

"Yes," he said, "the worst possible kind."

She stood there wavering in her state of inebriation, trying to puzzle through what he meant. Before she did, Trombley gave her his card, asked her to call him if she thought of anything else, and hurried away.

The tenant who lived below her on the first floor was a basset-faced man who stank of body odor and who said he knew nothing at all about Leon Banks, including that he even lived in his apartment. He said he thought the attic unit was empty.

At the station he called Arnie Biederman and asked for the tech unit to go over Banks's place.

Then he started with the dead man's last known connection, his military service. He began with the Detroit Veterans Affairs Regional Office. The counselor he spoke with said she would look for his records and call him back when she found them.

In a half hour Trombley heard from her. She told him Banks was originally from Asheville, North Carolina, and served two three-year enlistments from 2003 through 2008, with three deployments to Iraq. He received the standard workshops and training to prepare him for the transition from military to civilian life. He was 35 when he left the service and promptly dropped off their radar. There was no record of any family or next of kin.

After the VA, he called the Michigan Department of Military and Veterans Affairs, which told him to contact the Oakland County veterans affairs counselor, who told him there was no record of a Leon Banks ever having contacted them for help with emergency or hardship services.

By the time he got off the phone with them all, he knew little more about Leon Banks.

Sitting in his cubicle he thought back to his examination of Banks's apartment. Those stacks of books . . . where would he have gotten them?

There were two used book stores nearby in Ferndale, one on Nine Mile and the other on Woodward. The owners of both stores remembered Leon Banks because he sometimes came in asking for books about the Islamic threat. Both said they carried books about Islam but never carried materials as inflammatory as Banks wanted.

They both gave the same picture of the man: always alone, barely civil some days and other days overly chatty, talking nonstop about the threat Islam posed to our way of life. Both owners said he claimed to have learned about Islam from serving in Iraq and seeing up close how fanatical "those people" were and how dedicated they were to our destruction. And how the people of this country needed to stand up to the world domination efforts of the Islamic bullies.

"And their Jewish bankers," the owner of the Nine Mile bookstore said, shaking her head at the absurdity of the notion. "Don't forget them. It always comes down to the Jews with these nuts."

Both owners said he made them uncomfortable with his rantings, but neither said they felt at all fearful in his presence. On occasion they both asked him to leave their stores when he went on a particularly loud rant. He always went without incident.

The owner of the bookstore on Nine Mile summed him up: "He always struck me as a very angry and terribly misguided man."

Neither merchant could direct him further. Neither ever saw Banks with anybody else, neither ever heard him talk about any association he might have belonged to or heard about, and neither recollected him ever mentioning knowing another human being. Neither knew where Banks could have gotten those books.

Yet he must have gotten them somewhere, Trombley thought on the way back to the Shanahan Complex. Maybe on the internet?

He didn't remember seeing a computer in Banks's apartment, so he stopped in to the Ferndale Public Library to show Banks's photo around to the librarians. No one remembered ever seeing him using the work stations.

Even if he knew where the books came from, would it bring Trombley any closer to finding out what happened to Banks at the bakery? He doubted it. They were still too much in the dark to rule anything out but it was a stretch for Trombley to see how a loner like Banks could have been involved with the bakery killing in any other way than as the victim. He seemed to have no human contact.

At the station he ran Banks's name through the state and federal criminal history databases, national and state sex offender registries, state and national wants and warrants listings, and anti-terrorism watch lists. Some of these would take a few days to kick back results, but the ones coming back right away were all negative. Except for his military service, Leon Banks lived mostly off the grid. Nobody knew him or knew where he was in the days before his murder.

He walked down to the canteen to get a cup of coffee in preparation for going through the journals, but Paul Horvath collared him. Trombley needed to leave the Cake Walk investigation temporarily to meet an officer at Providence Hospital to speak with a woman about a domestic violence situation.

From experience he already knew he'd be dealing with an abusive husband and his battered wife who likely would already have changed her mind about pressing charges. And nothing he could say would change her mind, so her scumbag husband would be free to beat her up the next time she didn't bring him his beer fast enough.

Just your basic day fighting crime, he told himself, and started for the hospital.

11

"Martin! Christ on a cracker!"

Janey Cahill let her head loll back until she was staring at the tiles in the ceiling. She stood by the elevators down the hall from Mark Lewis's room. Save me from this guy, she pleaded with no one in particular.

"No," Preuss said, "it's not the same thing at all. I've learned my lesson."

"Yeah, that's why you're in Detroit staking out a house by yourself."

He sat in a car on Sheridan Street between Warren and Forest on the east side of Detroit, down the block from the address for DaRhon Hendricks that he found in OTIS. He was about to get out and ring the bell when he saw a black Crown Vic pull up and three big men spill out and rush into the house. He thought it might be wise to hang back and see what was going on.

"I wouldn't call it a stakeout. I'm just keeping an eye on things, trying to see if Eddie Watkins is around."

"Surveilling a building to observe suspicious activity is the actual definition of a stakeout."

"You're so literal sometimes."

"And how conspicuous do you think a white man in an SUV is in that part of town?"

"Relax, all right?"

"I don't have much choice."

"Trust me. What's going on there?"

"Mark is awake. He's not in very good shape but I want to see what he remembers. So far he hasn't said anything. How much longer are you planning on staying with your non-stakeout?"

"I'll wait for a while and see what's happening with the three amigos."

"At least tell the local cops what you're doing."

A sharp rap on the driver's side window made him start. From outside the car a hand the size of a ping pong paddle was holding a gold Detroit PD detective's shield against the glass.

"I'm sure I will," Preuss said, "in the very near future. Gotta go."

"Martin?"

The line went dead.

Suddenly extra jumpy, Janey Cahill spun around when she felt a tap on her shoulder.

René Lewis recoiled, hands up, from the unease radiating off Cahill.

"Sorry," René said. "Didn't mean to startle you."

"Not a problem. What's up?"

"I just wanted to let you know, Mark says he remembers something."

"Can you just give me a minute? I'll be right in."

René retreated to Mark's room and Cahill tried Preuss's number. It went straight to voicemail.

She disconnected without leaving a message. For a few seconds she debated what she should do . . . her immediate impulse was to fly out of the hospital and race to where he was. But she knew the best thing to do was to stay put and trust Preuss knew what he was doing.

In Mark's room, the young man was sitting higher in bed with his mother beside him.

"Mark," Cahill said, "you're looking good."

Mark nodded his appreciation.

"I asked if he remembered anything," René said, "and he told me he has something to tell you."

"Great. I'm all ears."

"I can tell something," Mark said, "but it's not much."

"Anything you can tell us is helpful."

"'So me and Eddie and Leon were getting ready to work when this guy showed up."

"What guy? Did you know him?"

"No."

"Did Eddie or Leon?"

"I'm not sure."

"How'd he get in?"

"He came in through the back but I don't remember anything between the time he showed up and when I woke up here."

"Did this guy seem to know Eddie or Leon?"

He thought about that question, then said, "I don't think so. It's all kind of fuzzy."

"I understand. You said he came in through the back door." She remembered Whalen said the door was open. "Was the door unlocked when you got there?"

"No, I used my key to get in."

"Do you remember if you locked the door after you?"

Mark nodded.

"The door locks automatically," René said. "There's a push bar on the inside so you can get out but nobody can come in unless it's unlocked. We always keep it locked when the bakery's closed, whether we're there or not."

"Okay," Cahill said, "so the three of you were there, and a fourth guy who came into the building through the back door. That's what you're saying?"

"Correct."

"Would you know him again if you saw him?"

"I don't know," Mark said. "My memory's sort of cloudy."

"Can you describe him?"

"He was a white guy, but I just can't remember much more than that. Sorry."

"That's okay," Cahill said. "It might come back to you. So do you remember if this guy was carrying a gun when he came in?"

Mark Lewis thought about it and shook his head. "Sorry. I can't remember."

"Can you remember if he said anything?"

Again he thought, then nodded. "I think he said something like, 'Where's the safe?'"

"Were those his exact words?"

"Yes. 'Where's the safe?'"

"'Where's the safe.' Was that the first thing out of his mouth?"

"Yes."

"Did anybody answer him?"

"I don't think so."

Cahill turned to René. "Do you have a safe?"

"A wall safe in the store office. But we deposit each day's proceeds in the bank after we close so we never keep a lot of money around."

"Okay. Mark, you're doing great. I'm going to ask you something that might make you upset, but you have to try to work with me on this. It's very important. Do you remember him firing his gun?"

"No."

"You remember getting hit in the head?"

"No."

"Do you remember anything after he said, 'Where's the safe'?"

"No."

"This is very helpful. I'm going to let you rest. We'll talk later, though, all right? Once you're rested? Maybe I'll ask one of my colleagues in the department to talk with you, too. Things might start coming back to you."

"Okay."

She patted his arm and gave a gesture with her head to ask René to follow her out of the room.

When they were in the corridor, Cahill said, "I'll give you the name of a counselor you might want to talk to in case he starts to have problems. She specializes in treating children who've been through traumas."

"How will we know?"

"He'll have trouble sleeping, he'll have nightmares, he'll start to talk about how he's worrying about dying, he'll be depressed, have headaches, trouble in school . . . you'll know. Trust me."

"What should we tell him about Leon and Eddie?"

"I wouldn't lie to him, but I'd try to put off the conversation till he's a little stronger. It's going to be tough news to take."

"I don't know if we can put it off," René Lewis said. "He's a pretty smart kid. I'm sure he'll figure it out on his own."

"Maybe so. But sooner or later you'll have to tell him the truth."

12

"Well, well, well," said the man sitting next to him in the Explorer. "Long way from home."

He handed Preuss's ID back to him and half turned in the passenger seat. The two men sized each other up.

With close-cropped hair and smooth dark skin, Alonzo Barber was one of those homely men who carry themselves as if they were handsome. His ears and his nose were too long for his round creased face and his eyes were bleary and puffy. But he wore a gorgeous dark brown suit that looked made to measure for his paunchy body and a chocolate brown shirt and tie that looked hand-painted.

"Am I interrupting something in the Hendricks house?" Preuss asked.

"Why do you ask?"

"Those three big guys who just went inside. They may as well carry sandwich boards saying 'I'm a cop.'"

Barber gave a throaty laugh. "Just paying Mr. Hendricks a friendly visit. What's your business with him?"

"I don't have any. I got his name as a possible connection to a guy I'm looking for, Eddie Watkins."

Barber pulled a stick of gum from his jacket pocket and slowly unwrapped it. He carefully folded the gum into his mouth and sucked its flavor before starting to chew. "Eddie Watkins."

"Yeah. Know the name?"

"Not offhand. Why are you looking for him?"

"He's involved in a case I'm working on."

"That shooting out there last night?"

"That's it."

"Yeah, heard about it this morning. Sounded messy."

"It was. We think Watkins was there when it happened but he left the scene. I want to find him as soon as I can."

Barber nodded. "I feel you."

"I just got some information he and Yummy Hendricks might have some dealings with each other."

"Like what?"

"That's not exactly clear."

Barber nodded. Both men watched the front door of the Hendricks house, a two-story frame structure. Like many streets in this part of the city, Sheridan was lined with single-family homes separated by empty lots where other homes once stood in the better days of the city's past.

"This shooting," Barber said, "ordinarily I wouldn't put something like that past Yummy. What time it happen?"

"Little after 9:30."

"Yeah, a guy who does business with Yummy wound up on life support at Receiving last night. Pretty sure Yummy's behind it. I can place him at a club downtown between 9 and 10 with the guy who's in the hospital."

The door to the Hendricks house opened and the three big men came out, escorting a short slender man in a Kangol cap worn backwards and a short black leather jacket. He wasn't in handcuffs but it was clear he was in their custody.

"That's Yummy?" Preuss said. "The guy in the middle?"

"That's him." Barber laughed softly. "Steady thinking he Samuel L. Jackson."

"Everybody has to be somebody."

"That's a fact."

Barber reached out a hand, which Preuss shook. The palm was big and dry and hard. "All the same," Barber said, "next time you come looking for somebody, give me a holler. Might could save you some time."

"Will do."

"Take care of yourself, my brother."

"You do the same," Preuss said. "We'll talk again."

"No doubt."

13

"So there was a fourth person in the room after all," Reg Trombley said when Janey Cahill finished recounting what Mark Lewis remembered.

It was after five and they were in the conference room going over what they learned that day.

"And it sounds like the motive was robbery," he continued.

"That's what Mark said."

Preuss picked up the note of doubt in her voice. "You don't believe it?"

"I don't know, doesn't ring true. A guy walks in and says, 'Where's the safe'? Sounds like something a villain on TV would say, right? It was me, first thing I'd do after I got there, I'd take their money, which we know this doofus didn't do because Banks still had some on him. Then I'd be like, 'Any other money around here?' First thing out of my mouth wouldn't be, 'Where's the safe?'"

"Do they even have a safe at the Cake Walk?" Preuss asked.

Cahill told them what René Lewis said about their wall safe.

"So what do you think about what Mark said?"

"Far as I'm concerned, it's a place to start. But we need to corroborate it before we put much stake in it."

"Fair enough."

He filled them in on his day's activities.

"So," Trombley said, "if Watkins took something from some dealer, let's say, now he's looking to make it right so he's setting up a robbery at the place he works because that's the closest place he can think of to get some quick money."

"On Easter Sunday night?" Hank Bellamy said. "When other workers are going to be there?"

"Why not?" Trombley said. "The Easter weekend proceeds might still on the premises, no customers around to get in the way. Maybe whoever did it didn't know anybody else would be there. Maybe he didn't know Watkins, maybe he lost his head, showed up lit and forgot why he was there, maybe he thought he was going to double-cross whoever set this up and keep all the money for himself . . . there could be a hundred reasons why things went bad."

"We need to consider this information," Preuss said, "but as of now it's unsubstantiated." He looked through the case folder. "There are too many maybes here. We need to started cutting some of them out. Where are we on Leon Banks?"

Trombley went over what little he found. "From what I can tell so far," he concluded, "this guy's a loner with no friends or connections. I asked Arnie's people to go through his place. I also thought I'd go back to Hazel Park and canvas the neighbors around Banks's house."

"Good," Preuss said. "Maybe that'll tell us something too."

"I also requested a list of soldiers in his unit, see if there's anything there."

"I'm going to head back to the hospital," Janey Cahill said.

"I'll keep working the neighborhood around the bakery," Ed Blair said.

"Hank," Preuss said, "you keep looking into the Lewises' background, right?"

Bellamy nodded.

They sat going over their notes for something else to add.

"We're all exhausted," Preuss said, "but let's keep pushing forward in the directions we're going in, and we'll meet again in the morning."

After they separated, Preuss followed Cahill to Beaumont Hospital, but Mark Lewis was sound asleep, as was his mother, snoring lightly in the recliner beside his bed.

They got what little they could from the charge nurse about the boy's condition, then he left Cahill there and stopped for a hamburger at the McDonald's around the corner from the hospital. As he gobbled down the greasy food he realized this was the first time he had eaten since morning.

It was after eight by the time he returned to the station.

In the Detective Bureau everyone was gone except Hank Bellamy. He was in his cubicle staring at a report on his computer with his hands folded placidly over his belly.

Preuss stuck his head in. "What are you still doing here?"

Bellamy returned the greeting in a miasma of Listerine. Once Bellamy, like Preuss, had been a heavy drinker, but Bellamy had been dry for as long as Preuss. He hoped the overwhelming cloud of mouthwash didn't signal a relapse. Bellamy's wife left him within the past year, so that might have set him off.

Preuss stepped further inside the cubicle to see if he could smell any of the alcohol that seeped through the pores of an alcoholic. The only odor was the sharp mint of mouthwash.

Preuss sat, uninvited, in the visitor's chair. "Are you doing all right?"

Bellamy gave Preuss a sour look. Getting these from everybody today, Preuss thought.

"This your little way of asking me if I'm drinking again?"

"The mouthwash is making me nervous, that's all."

"Not that it's any of your business, but I have a date after my shift. Some people have a life, you know. And since when are you so interested in my life?"

Preuss held his hands up in surrender. "I'm not." He stood to leave. He didn't care for Bellamy enough to put up with this.

"If you must know, she's a nurse. Works the three to eleven. We're meeting for coffee after her shift and I figured I'd stick around long's I'm going to be up anyway."

"Trust me on this, Hank, I don't care."

"I just want to see if I can get a little sum-sumpin again before I die. As it is, I'm going to be working till they carry me out feet first. Damn banks, my retirement won't be worth a dime."

"Maybe things'll come back before you check out."

"And maybe if the pope got married he'd have kids. I heard the city budget's so bad the Council's talking about cutbacks in the department."

"Where'd you hear that from?"

"It's around. People are saying there's going to be a force reduction and it's going to include the Detective Bureau."

"Warnock'd never let that happen."

"Not from what I hear."

Suddenly eager to be anyplace else, Preuss said, "Good luck with that whole getting-something thing. I'll see you in the morning."

"You're so interested, I'll keep you posted."

"I'm already sorry I asked. What I really want to know is if you found anything on the Lewises."

"Nothing so far."

Preuss sighed. That was Bellamy-speak for, I haven't done a goddam thing yet.

He nodded his acknowledgement and left Bellamy and the station behind.

There was only one antidote to this day.

14

Toby sat in his wheelchair angled toward the television in the living room of his group home.

The first *Star Wars* was on, the sequence where the Rebel fighters are trying to fly into the trench on the Death Star to destroy it. It was loud and noisy and Toby watched with great seriousness, mouth hanging open, matching the screams of the characters and the blasts of the laser weapons with his own foghorn cries.

Preuss nodded to the staff sitting around with the other residents, and planted a loud kiss on the side of his son's face. Toby yelled even louder and Preuss thought his heart would burst with love for the boy.

"Up late tonight," he said.

Melissa, one of the aides, said, "We started watching the video before his bath and he was still wide awake so we thought we'd let him finish the movie."

"This guy's a night owl, you know."

"Oh, we know, don't we, T?"

Preuss pulled a chair from the dining room to sit beside his son. He held the boy's hand and felt the youngster give a gentle squeeze . . . something dismissed as a primitive grasp reflex by most of the boy's doctors and one or two members of the staff, who doubted Toby had any control over his movements. But Preuss knew in his heart Toby meant to do it. It was true, there wasn't much Toby could control, and his hands were bent almost double at the wrist from the high muscle tone of his cerebral palsy. But many of his movements were too appropriate to be accidental, and squeezing his old man's hand was one of those.

Or so Preuss thought.

Wishful thinking, the doctors said. So be it. What was to be lost from assuming Toby could do more rather than less?

They sat together watching the climax of the movie, then when it was over and the good guys won (for the time being), Preuss wheeled Toby down the hall to his room and used the electric overhead lift to get him settled in bed. Toby couldn't stand or walk and had to be carried or lifted everywhere, just as he couldn't take care of any of his own daily living activities. Preuss always simply lifted Toby everywhere, but lately his son was too heavy to move as easily.

"And I'm not getting any younger," Preuss said as though Toby were privy to his thoughts. Which he might very well be.

He settled Toby into bed and rolled the boy on his side to ease the lift sling away from him. Preuss raised Toby's pajama top, inspecting his body to make sure there weren't any spots where his skin was breaking down or showed an indication of rough treatment.

There were none. The staff at this house took particular care with Toby. They took good care of everyone, but Preuss's coming every day did a lot to guarantee the staff's special attentiveness to his son. It was a fact of life in a group home, where the staff changed over often because these were relatively low-paying jobs. If they knew the family was watching, they were extra-careful.

Melissa came in to help get Toby settled.

"Now," Preuss said to his boy, "are you going to be able to sleep after all the stimulation of saving the universe?"

Toby beamed up at him with Jeanette's eyes and hummed.

The boy looked so much like his late wife, Preuss could never see him without being reminded of her . . . he had her round face, her Roman nose with the Brandoesque bump at the bridge, her full lips, her wry crooked smile. His other son Jason favored him, with the same long face with high flat forehead and bushy eyebrows.

Assuming he still looked like that, of course; Preuss hadn't seen Jason for years, and wasn't sure where he was. Preuss knew he was released from the jail in Needles, California, where he was confined most recently. The boy was hard to track when he wasn't in detention somewhere. Preuss never heard from him anymore, but he kept tabs on his older son as well as he could through police contacts around the country when Jason and the law knocked heads.

Toby couldn't have been more different. Toby was all Jeanette, except neither his late wife nor Preuss was as good-natured and content as Toby, so happy in every situation. It must be a function of the disability, he thought, and a compensation for the young man being so compromised.

And the main source of his charm. And of the lessons the kid could teach his father, and anyone else who cared to pay attention.

The nurse came in to give Toby his nightly seizure medication, and on her way out she turned the overhead light out. Preuss pulled the armchair next to the bed and sat watching a rerun of *Law and Order* on the TV in Toby's room until his son began to snore.

Preuss gently extracted his hand—no easy task, since Toby's grip was strong, primitive reflex or no—what nonsense, he thought again—and turned off the TV. He put on three Judy Collins disks to cycle through Toby's CD player so he'd have something to listen to if he woke up, and kissed his son good night.

He patted the fragile bird-bones of Toby's shoulder beneath the pajama top and left in a state of peace.

Tuesday, April 14, 2009

15

"Let's go over what we know again," Preuss said. He was more rested than the day before, with a clearer mind.

"I have something to say first," Bellamy said to the rest of the investigative team gathered in the conference room. He ran a knuckle over the thin mustache above his lip.

"I was thinking about that whole safe thing," he said. "Nine times out of ten, these little mom and pop joints, they don't keep their money in a safe because nobody can afford one. They keep their money in a cash box or in a money bag they lock in a drawer or take to the bank every night. So if this guy comes in all, 'Where's the safe?' then he doesn't know anything about how the business works. It shows he's just a random mook who stumbles in off the street."

"If Mark remembered correctly," Cahill said.

"And if he was telling the truth," Preuss added.

"Why wouldn't he tell the truth?" Bellamy said. "It's his family's business."

"Clearly you've never parented an angry adolescent," Preuss said. "But let's assume he's telling the truth. We still don't know who this guy is. Or why the shooting started. Or how he got inside a locked store. Besides, a random crime of opportunity is a possibility, but it's just one of many."

"Yeah?" Bellamy said, testy now. "What are the others?"

Man, Preuss thought, who woke you up?

"First," he said, ticking off the alternatives on his fingers, "it might be something Leon Banks or Eddie Watkins cooked up. Second, it might be somebody who worked there before, who maybe has a grudge against the family. Third, it might be somebody who knows Banks or Watkins who thought this would be a ripe setup. Fourth, the Lewises might be into something we don't know about yet and this is related to that. Fifth, maybe Leon Banks pissed somebody off somewhere along the line, maybe even going back to Iraq, and this is settling an old score. And sixth, it might be something we haven't even thought about yet. At this point all these are possibilities."

When nobody said anything, he looked at Bellamy. Might as well keep pushing. "You said you'd look into Matt and René's background. Where are you on that?"

"No place yet."

"Don't let that go, please."

Bellamy folded his arms but said nothing.

"Reg, is there anything back from Biederman?"

"Nothing useful yet," Trombley said. "About a million fingerprints, but that's to be expected from a working bakery, you got deliveries coming and going all the time. Some footprints in the blood on the floor. It's all still being processed."

"What about Banks's apartment?"

"In the works," Trombley said.

"Walk us through what we know about this guy again."

Trombley recapped what he learned on Monday.

"So no phone to check records on," he summarized, "no bank accounts, no VA benefits since he never enrolled, no associations, no friends, no movements yesterday anybody remembers."

"Do you see him putting something like this together?" Preuss asked.

Trombley thought for a few seconds. "Nothing I've found points to it. But somebody else could have. Banks could have been talking to somebody about the bakery, maybe somebody he ran into on the street, maybe a buddy from the service, and they came up with the idea to hit the bakery. This guy was into some weird shit, trust me on this one, I've read his journals."

He pursed his lips and circled a finger around his temple.

"We just don't know that much about him yet."

"More maybes," Preuss said. "That's all we have."

"The Lewises are barely keeping their heads above water," Cahill said. "Two bad weeks in a row and the business is kaput. Talk about slim pickings. You don't think Banks knew that?"

"He's somebody with no family or friends," Trombley said, "sees conspiracies everywhere, maybe he looks at the Lewises, misunderstands their financial situation, gets jealous of their lives, says something to somebody and the next thing we know there's a robbery attempt that goes terribly wrong."

"So assuming an insider, we have three competing theories," Preuss said. "One, it's an inside job with Eddie Watkins as the link, with possibly somebody from the outside as a supporting player. Two, it's an inside job with Banks as the link, with somebody we don't know yet as the outside player. Or three, it's somebody connected with the bakery, maybe a former employee with a grudge."

"Don't forget the fourth alternative," Bellamy said. "A completely random crime."

"Fifth alternative," Trombley said. "A terror connection."

They all looked at him.

"Just saying, this guy Banks's all about the Muslim conspiracy to take over the world. I don't think we can rule it out. We don't know anything about who he knows, or who knows him."

"You seriously think a Muslim terror squad killed him?" Cahill asked.

"Say he knows some wingnuts from the service who want to fund their paramilitary organization and decide to knock over the bakery," Trombley offered.

"Yeah," Cahill said, "for all the dough."

"Jesus, listen to you all," Bellamy said. "This whole thing screams random crime of opportunity. Some idiot comes along trying doors and blunders into the bakery, tries to stick it up and loses control over the situation and starts shooting. The bad guy's half-way to California while we sit here with our thumbs up our butts talking about Osama Bin fucking Laden."

"I can't remember the last time you were this geeked over a case," Preuss said. "Maybe you should get laid more often."

"From your voice to God's ear."

Preuss thought with a sudden pang of what Jeanette used to say, back in better days. She used to tell people, only half-jokingly, it's been so long since she had sex she couldn't remember who got tied up.

But then the longer they actually did go without sex, the less funny the joke became.

"Whether it's a crime of opportunity or not," Preuss said, "the only witness we have is Mark Lewis until we find Eddie Watkins. We have to get more information about whoever it was came into the store."

"I'll keep working with him, see what I can do," Cahill said.

"Meanwhile, we need to find Watkins," Preuss said. "I'll stay on that. We also need the names of former employees. Or the other vets Matt's helped out."

"I'll see Matt or René at the hospital and get that from them," Cahill said.

"Reg, will you stay on Banks? Hank, why don't you pay a visit to the minister and take a closer look at the link between him and Eddie Watkins, see if we can nail down the connection between them and this bad crowd the minister talked about. Ed, check all their backgrounds, see what they have in the way of a record. If they ran together when they were young, there might be some unfinished business between them."

The meeting broke up and Preuss retreated to his office.

Janey Cahill appeared in the doorway. "Knock knock."

He beckoned her inside.

"What's your gut tell you about this?"

"Inside job," he said.

"Seriously?"

"It's what makes the most sense. I just don't buy a scenario where somebody walks down the alley and randomly tries doors. Somebody wanted to stick up a place, the 7-Eleven's right down the street. Why hit a closed bakery in a block of closed stores on Easter Sunday night?"

"Doesn't sit right with me either."

"I'm not saying it couldn't be random. The other thing is, René Lewis told you the back door to the bakery is locked when they're closed. So there's no way some passing doofus could find it open unless one of the three people who we know were there deliberately left it open."

"Or else made a terribly stupid mistake on the exact wrong night."

"It could happen, but it's too much of a coincidence."

"I don't know about Watkins being the connection, though. If the guy was trying to get his shit together, why jeopardize it with something like this?"

"If he's on the hook to somebody, he might need some quick money," Preuss pointed out.

They sat in silence. Then Cahill said, "How are things going otherwise?"

"They're going."

"Things okay with Emma?"

"Here we go again."

"Martin, she's perfect for you."

"Right, if by perfect you mean completely inappropriate. Why don't you just let me be the lonely, unhappy man I was always meant to become?"

"Dude, you're hopeless."

"Exactly my point. So not to change the subject, but when are you going to the hospital?"

"Probably not for another hour at least. I have to swing by the middle school first."

"Text me when you're ready to go and I'll come with you."

"What are you going to do in the meantime?"

"Something I don't want to do."

She left and he punched in Tanya Corcoran's number on his desk phone.

"Nick in?" he asked. As much as he hated to do it, he felt compelled to update the chief of detectives on their progress.

"Hang on," she said. She put him on hold and was back in ten seconds. "He says he can't talk to you right now."

Ah, he thought.

Reprieve.

Nick Russo, the chief of detectives who was also his ex-father-in-law, would not have anything productive to add, Preuss was certain. All he would do is bluster about what a piss-poor job Preuss was doing, which would do nothing but raise Preuss's blood pressure.

Besides, he thought, what's he going to do, fire me? He's already tried it. Preuss didn't know how much longer he would be able to rely on Chief Warnock's good offices to save him, but he was getting to the point where he didn't care anymore.

He sat staring at the chaos of his desk for another minute, then went downstairs to the canteen. He got a coffee from one of the machines and sat in the empty room with his hands wrapped around the paper container.

At the beginning of the second day, the directions for the investigation were starting to become clear. His instinct told him it wasn't a botched random robbery. Despite what Janey thought, the Watkins link seemed the likeliest, given what they now knew. Though it was true, Banks could have said something to the wrong person, maybe some vet he knew who decided to hit the bakery. Banks could have left the back door open, then was killed to remove him as a witness, as Trombley suggested.

Or else someone had it in for Banks, maybe settling an old score from the service.

His phone double-chimed, announcing a text.

Lately the only person who texted him was Emma Blalock. Sure it was going to be from her, he pulled his phone from his jacket pocket.

It was not from Emma.

The number was familiar, but he couldn't immediately place it. It took a few seconds before he realized who it belonged to.

Shelley Larkin.

A number he hadn't called in almost five months, not since he realized she was never going to respond to his efforts to contact her after she left him the message on his answering machine when he was on suspension. He was in the middle of a difficult and upsetting case, but he and Shelley had clicked, or so he thought. They saw each other a few times, at first because she was putting together an article on it for the *Metro Voice*, the alternative weekly she wrote for. But as they got to know each other their contacts grew more personal and it seemed, at least to him, something serious was about to start.

He remembered one particular late-night phone call when they were both in bed at their separate homes. He could still hear her sleepy voice, low and seductive as they murmured back and forth to each other.

Until she left a message telling him she was seeing someone else, but still wanted to keep in touch with him. Despite the fact that she never returned any of his calls and texts.

And now here he was, in the middle of another complicated case, and Shelley was back again.

Dammit.

He stared at her number on the screen of his phone, then returned it to his pocket.

There must be something about this case that piqued her interest. She must be writing another article and needed some inside information. Otherwise why would she be in touch with him?

He sipped his coffee. He was just starting to get comfortable with the notion that they weren't meant to be. And now this.

So why *is* she getting in touch with me? he thought.

Only one way to find out.

He retrieved the phone and opened her message.

Hi it's Shelley. Thinking about u
and just wanted 2 say hey.

He put the phone to sleep and slipped it back into his jacket.

Dammit to hell.

He dumped his coffee in the trash container and headed out to his car.

16

"Comfortable?" Cahill asked.

Sitting up in his hospital bed, Mark Lewis nodded. On the tray table in front of him was Cahill's digital recording device, its red Record light glowing.

His mother stood at the foot of the bed. Preuss leaned against the window sill. René said her husband was at the store cleaning up. The other bed in the room was still empty so they had privacy. Preuss closed the door and asked the nurses not to disturb them.

"Detective Preuss and I are going to ask you some more questions, and then we'll let you rest."

Mother and son nodded their assent.

She walked Mark through his responses from the day before, confirming they still represented what he thought happened. She asked questions and gave the young man time to gather his thoughts before answering. The interview went slowly.

In every instance his answers were the same as those he had given her.

"Now," she said, "you told me you didn't know if you could recognize the man from the bakery if you ever saw him again. Do you still feel that way?

He thought for a few moments, then said, "I think I'm starting to remember a little about him."

"Excellent," Cahill said. "Does that include what he looks like?"

"Yes."

"Great. What do you remember?"

"I remember he was a white guy. Kind of tall."

"As tall as Detective Preuss?"

Mark eyed him and said, "Maybe a little taller."

"How much?"

"Couple inches."

Preuss was five-ten. So the man was roughly six feet.

"Could you tell how old he looked?"

"I'm not good at guessing ages. Maybe in his thirties?"

"Any distinguishing features? Something you'd recognize if you saw him again?"

"Yeah, he wore dreads."

"Dreadlocks?"

"Blond. Dyed."

"How could you tell they were dyed?

"I could see the roots. They were black."

"How long were his dreads?"

"Down to here." He indicated his shoulder.

"Big messy Rasta dreads?"

"No, more like Lenny Kravitz's."

"So neater."

"Yes."

"What was he wearing?"

"A white hoodie. And sweatpants. Dark blue with a red stripe."

"Good," Cahill said. "Did he have the hood up?"

"At first, but then it fell down off his face. That's how come I saw his dreads. He also had a scar on his cheek. Here." He indicated his right cheek.

"Can you show me how long the scar was?"

Mark drew a finger down the length of his cheek from his eye to a line even with the corner of his mouth and she repeated it for the recorder.

"Anything else you can tell me about him?"

He thought for a long few seconds, then said, "That's all I remember. It happened so fast."

"I know." She patted his arm. "This is very helpful."

He gave a beamish shrug.

"They're saying he might come home tomorrow," René said.

"Terrific," Cahill said. "Bet you can't wait."

Mark shrugged again, this time without much enthusiasm.

"I think he likes all the pampering," his mother said.

"And the hot nurses," Cahill added. It got a sort of smile from the young man.

Preuss said, "Mark, now that you remember so much, can you tell us for sure if you've ever seen this guy before?"

Mark picked at the bandage on his head. "Honey, please don't do that," René said. "Look, he's getting nervous just thinking about this. How much more do you need to go into this right now?"

"I can see it's bothering him," Preuss said, "but this is important. Mark?"

Mark shook his head firmly. "I never saw him before."

"Never saw Eddie or Leon with this guy? He never came into the store, either in the front or the back? Or was waiting for them outside?"

"Nope. Never."

The pressure on her son was clearly making René agitated, so Cahill said, "Can we see you in the hall?"

She led René by the arm away from the door to Mark's room. Preuss followed.

"We have to be sure about this," Cahill said. "That's why we're pressing him."

"I know. It's just that he's been through so much."

"But he's doing well."

"He's doing great," Preuss agreed.

"One of the other things we're thinking about is whether this might be something a disgruntled former employee cooked up," Cahill said. "Is there anybody who used to work for you who might be angry enough to do this?"

"We're such a small operation," René said, "there haven't been many employees, disgruntled or otherwise."

"But there have been some?"

"Just one. About six months after we opened we tried a part-time counterperson. I had an emergency appendectomy and I needed time at home."

"'Tried,'" Cahill said. "Does that mean it didn't work out?"

"No, she wasn't with us long. Maybe a month. She was the daughter of a customer who knew we were looking for somebody to fill in for me. She seemed like a nice kid so we gave her a shot."

"But only for a month? What happened?"

"She quit. One day she told me she was quitting because her schedule at school was conflicting with her work schedule. She goes to Wayne State. It sounded like a white lie, to tell you the truth. I suspected there might have been something more to it, but I didn't want to push the matter. I told her we could negotiate her work schedule, but she said she'd already lined up another job."

"She's been the only employee beside Eddie?" Preuss asked.

"We really haven't been doing well enough to be able to afford someone. What with the economy the way it is."

"Did you use any other veterans? Maybe bring somebody in just for a short time?"

"No, Leon was the only one. But Matt brings baked goods to the VA hospital all the time and does other good things for vets whenever he can. Especially homeless vets."

"If you give us the young woman's name, we'll run it down."

"It's a hard name to forget. Rainbow Moss."

"We'll talk with her," Preuss said, "see what she says. This way we can scratch her off the list."

The pitifully short, useless list that isn't worth shit, he thought.

17

"You're nowhere? Still?"

"No. Every time somebody makes a suggestion, he shoots it down," the man on the other end of the line said. "Meantime he's off chasing some gangbanger in Detroit while the real villain goes free."

"Who's the real villain?" Russo asked.

"Nobody knows because Preuss is off wasting resources and we're getting nowhere."

Russo thought for a moment, staring out the window of his office at the afternoon traffic on Nine Mile.

Then he opened the styrofoam container that held his lunch from the Thai place on the other side of Woodward. He asked for an eggplant dish made as hot as possible. With the phone handset between his ear and his shoulder he unwrapped the plastic cutlery and dug into his meal. He could smell the heat.

He shoveled the delicious soppy mess into his mouth. Divine.

"I told the chief this would happen," Russo said through a mouthful of white rice.

Sweat broke out on his forehead from the heat of the meal. He patted it away with a paper napkin.

"You were right," the other man said. "It's one thing to pursue this line of inquiry, fine, the guy was mixed up with some bad people, I definitely can see it as a possibility. But he's got us all working on it. There's nobody available and no time to work any other theories of the crime."

"You talk to anybody else about this?"

"No way. They're all in his pocket."

Russo thought about that. He rolled the heavy muscles in his shoulders and ate another forkful.

"All right," he said finally, "here's what I want you to do. Write this up. Everything you just told me. What he's doing, what he's not doing, what you think he should be doing, the whole nine yards. For my eyes only. Don't use the email system at the station. You have a computer at home?"

"Sure."

"Then do it on your home computer and let me have it on a flash drive. I want it first thing in the morning."

"You got it."

"I'm finally going to get that sonuvabitch," he muttered. To the man on the other end of the phone, he said, "I won't forget you did this."

"That's my sincere hope, lew."

18

Standing in the north visitors' parking structure at Beaumont Hospital, Cahill said, "Blond dreads and a scar. Sound like anybody we know?"

"Nobody I can think of," Preuss said. "But it does remind me of something."

He thought for a moment and then shook his head. "I'm almost certain I've seen the guy he's talking about but I can't pull up any details."

"Maybe a street person you've seen around town?"

"Maybe. Let's put it through state CHR"—the Criminal History Record System—"and see what comes up. Also liase with the Sheriff's Criminal Intelligence Unit. Have you heard from Hank?"

"Not yet."

"I wonder if he got ahold of Rocellus yet."

"Couldn't say."

They got into his Explorer to get away from the noise of the structure while he called Hank Bellamy.

They spoke briefly and he ended the call with a wry smile. "He's home. I woke him up. Not only hasn't he interviewed Rocellus, but he's taking the day off and Horvath pulled him off the case anyway and put him on an attempted robbery in the Troy lot. Interesting way to solve a case, starving it of manpower."

"We're low on people, Martin, we're all stretched thin."

He gave her a hard look.

"Just sayin'. I'm sure it's temporary. Not everything is because Russo's out to get you."

"And I'm just sayin' it's another way to undermine the investigation. This is a murder, Janey. It takes precedence."

"Hey." She gave him a friendly pat on the arm. "I'm on your side, all right?"

"I'll pick up the rev myself."

"Take Reggie with you, why don't you?"

"I can't imagine I'll need his help."

"Yeah, right, man of God, what kind of problem could he be?"

They both thought of the minister mixed up in the Madison Kaufman disappearance and how much unpleasantness he caused.

"You know he's a good man to have in a pinch. Especially with you on your anti-gun crusade."

After the episode with Madison, Preuss decided he didn't want to be associated with guns anymore so he stopped carrying his service weapon. It had been a long time coming and none of the people he worked with understood it, not even Janey. But firearms caused too much damage, and carrying one only added to the problem. What he saw at the bakery did nothing to change his mind.

He shook his head. "He's a hothead. And I don't trust his loyalties anymore."

"Meaning what?"

"There's some kind of weird thing going on between us."

"What kind of weird thing?"

"You haven't noticed the tension?"

"We're all tense," she said. "It's the case. It's what's going on with the economy. These are tense times, Martin."

"No, it's something more, I'm certain. Until that gets sorted out, I'd rather not partner with him."

"But—"

"End of story."

She sighed. "Whatever. I'll see you later, then. I have a presentation at the high school. Supposed to give a talk to an assembly on alternatives to violence for conflict resolution."

"Are you going to be tied up after that?"

"Probably not. Why?"

"I was going to ask if you could speak with Moonbeam."

"You mean Rainbow? I think I can look for her this afternoon. Who knows, I might even find a pot of gold."

Preuss snorted. "Yeah, good luck with that."

"I've already told you everything I know. I don't know what else you want from me."

Rocellus Gaines sat in the interview room at the Shanahan in a freshly pressed white shirt and cream-colored linen trousers with a sharp crease.

"I just have a few more follow-up details to sort through."

Rocellus raised a hand in a gesture that said, Knock yourself out. He sat perfectly straight-backed in his chair as though his moral fiber starched his spine.

"First, did you remember anything new since we talked yesterday?"

"I've been praying over it, but so far nothing's come to me."

"You'll let me know if something does?"

"I will."

"You told me you and Eddie Watkins are old friends."

"We grew up together. Had us some times."

"Any of those times include run-ins with the law?"

"Once or twice. Hard to be a young black man in Detroit and not bump heads with the police."

Preuss waited and after a few moments Rocellus said, "When I was thirteen. I spent a year in JDF."

"What for?"

"I got caught breaking into a barber shop on Van Dyke."

"A barber shop? You got sent to the Juvenile Detention Facility for breaking into a neighborhood *barber shop*? Seriously?"

Rocellus straightened the creases on his trousers. "Thirteen. What did I know?"

"Was Eddie with you?"

"He was."

"Was he with you in JDF?"

"No. He always did run faster than me. Taught me a lesson, though, I'll say that for it."

"Despite that, you told me you and Eddie were as close as brothers until he joined the army."

"That's true."

"Did something happen between you? You said Eddie wanted to make amends when he got out of the army. That sounds like there was some kind of falling out."

Rocellus clasped his hands on the table and examined them carefully. Preuss could see the minister was considering how much to tell him.

"It might help us find out who did these terrible things last Sunday night."

"You think I'm involved?"

"The truth is, we don't know who was involved," Preuss said. "When we talked you mentioned Yummy Hendricks. How well do you know him?"

"Yummy?"

"Yes. Do you see him much?"

"As little as possible." The tone was sharp and disapproving.

"But you do see him?"

"No, not at all."

"Pastor," Preuss said, "you see him a little, or not at all?"

"I don't see him at all. He's not a man I keep company with anymore."

"But you did?"

"Yes."

"When was this?"

Rocellus shifted again in his chair. "I'm not sure I—"

"Please answer the question."

"Not since we were much younger."

"You and Eddie ran with him?"

"Once upon a time."

"Was Yummy involved in the barber shop business?"

"No, he'd already moved on to bigger things by then. But you have to understand, the past is dead and gone. I haven't talked to the man in years."

Preuss remembered something he once read by William Faulkner . . . the past isn't dead, Faulkner wrote, it isn't even past.

"When was the last time you saw him?"

"I couldn't tell you, sir. Once I let Jesus into my heart, I walked away from that life and never looked back. And that's God's truth."

Preuss stared at him. Rocellus met his gaze with a watchfulness that seemed to cover agitation.

And, Preuss was certain, deceit.

"Rocellus," Preuss said, "I've been at this for a lot of years, and if there's one thing I know it's that everybody harbors secrets. And to be honest with you, sir, I think you have a secret. I think you know something that can help us find out who killed the man at the bakery on Sunday. And what happened to your old friend."

"I hold many secrets," the minister agreed. "The members of my church open themselves to me because they know what they tell me stays between me and Jesus."

"I believe that. I also believe the secret I'm talking about is yours, not theirs."

When Rocellus didn't answer, Preuss said, "If a man did something he'd regret, maybe in a moment of anger, a moment of weakness, I think he'd want to make a full confession. Don't you, Rocellus? He'd want to make a clean breast of it and ask forgiveness from his God."

He let the moment stretch.

"I have many sins," Rocellus said at last, "and much to beg my lord Jesus forgiveness for. But my conscience is clear about how that man at the bakery died."

"I believe you, Rocellus. But you and I both know you're keeping something from me."

Rocellus covered his mouth with a smooth hand and stroked the bottom of his face thoughtfully.

"Do you want to tell me about it?"

"Back before he joined the army, we had a fight, Eddie and me."

"Over what?"

"Oldest problem in the world. A woman."

"Shatoya?"

Rocellus nodded.

"What happened?"

"She came to me for counseling about trouble she was having with Eddie. We were old friends, too, you see. Neither one of us was looking for something to happen. But yet and still . . . something did. Things just . . ."

He couldn't bring himself to finish.

"Nature took its course," Preuss said. "You never plan these things."

"He especially couldn't stand to see Shatoya pregnant."

"With your child?"

"Yes."

Rocellus let that sink in, then said, "The day she told him about it, that was the very day he went down and joined the army. I regret whatever I might have done to cause his pain."

"Sounds like an impulsive guy."

"He's a very passionate man, with great depth of feeling. I was always sorry he couldn't turn that into religious devotion."

"What did your flock think about all this? Their pastor fathering a child by another man's wife?"

Rocellus cleared his throat but didn't say anything.

"Ah, they don't know. You never told them, did you?"

"I did not."

"So as far as they're concerned, Eddie abandoned her and his other children while you took them into your heart. You wind up looking like the hero."

Rocellus wouldn't meet his gaze.

"When he got out of the army and came to see you, and told you he was tired of carrying the anger he was feeling for both of you, you were happy because it meant he was going to keep your secret safe."

"Yes."

"Are you and Shatoya still together?"

"We got married last year."

Preuss said nothing. Rocellus said, "And now you know my secret."

"We do the best we can, Rocellus. Sometimes that's good enough and sometimes it isn't."

But now it starts to seem like you might have a motive for making sure Eddie was going to keep quiet, Preuss thought.

"I have to ask you to account for your whereabouts last Sunday night," Preuss said.

"I thought you said I wasn't a suspect."

"I have to ask everyone. It's just what I do."

"I was at my church. The men's group I run meets there on Sunday nights."

"What time was that?"

"Seven till ten. Fifteen men saw me there. They'll all vouch for me. We stayed afterwards to talk and have refreshments. I didn't get home till after midnight. Shatoya can vouch for that, too."

"What kind of men's group is it?"

"We talk about issues related to living a Christian life. How to be a good husband, how to be a good father, how to take responsibility for providing for your family. And so on."

Don't forget how to break up another man's family, Preuss thought. How to impregnate another man's wife. How to soil a man's reputation. How to drive a man to desperation. And how to lie about it all.

"Got it," was all he said.

19

Walking into the Ferndale Public Library reminded Janey Cahill of the times she used to bring her boys here when they were little for the story times the library offered. Now that they were older they hadn't been here for a while.

She resolved to start bringing them for the young readers programs. Like most kids, they did most of their homework on a computer, and when they weren't doing schoolwork all they did was play video games. Someday soon kids won't know what a book is, she thought, just like most didn't know what an LP record was.

And all the games they played were so violent, that was the other problem. Explosions, killings, dismemberments . . . how could a steady diet of that kind of mayhem possibly be good for young kids? When she was around, she could control their gaming time, but with her working so much they spent more time with their video games than they should.

At a table by the front she picked up a brochure for Tween programs and stuffed it into her shoulder bag. It wouldn't hurt to try, she thought.

The woman at the checkout desk was thick-set, with a head of curly brown hair and the hint of an elaborate floral tattoo peeking out of the neckline of her dress.

Man, do I love this town, Cahill thought. Even the librarians are hipsters.

"Help you?" the woman asked.

"I'm looking for Rainbow Moss." René Lewis gave her the girl's phone number and Cahill spoke with her mother, who told her Rainbow was now working as an aide at the city library.

The woman behind the desk said, "Wait here," and went into an area in the back.

Shortly a young woman came out following the tattooed lady. She was short and well-rounded in a blue hoodie and gray tights hugging every curve. Her head full of tousled black hair was held back by one of those narrow headbands young women wore nowadays. She looked to be in her very early twenties, with a little pug nose and a sulky mouth. A minuscule stud gleamed on her upper lip.

"Rainbow?"

The girl nodded and Cahill flashed her shield. "Janey Cahill, Ferndale Police. Is there someplace we can talk?"

The girl gave Cahill's shield a perfunctory look, and with a flip of her head led them both past a section of shelves holding CDs and books into an unused study room. Her tights were so form-fitting Cahill could see every jiggle of her ass.

Rainbow fell into a chair and slouched across the table, propping up her head as if her mass of hair weighed a ton.

Cahill sat on the other side of the table. "Your mother told me where I could find you," she began. Rainbow regarded her with sleepy-eyed disinterest.

"So you worked at the Cake Walk Bakery for a little while?"

Rainbow gathered herself to sit upright. Got her interest, Cahill thought.

"A very short while."

"A month last year, right?"

"Right."

"Did you hear about what just happened there?"

"No."

"You didn't hear about the shooting last Sunday night?"

"No. Who got shot?"

"A man named Leon Banks. Did you know him?"

"No."

Cahill watched her closely. Usually people who lie have a tell, and a petulant little chippy like this would have to go some to put one over on Cahill. But she wasn't getting a lying vibe from the girl.

"He wasn't there when you were?"

"No. Who is he? Is he all right?"

"No, he's not. He's dead."

"Oh wow. That's sick. Sorry."

"Did you know Eddie Watkins?"

"Oh, yeah. Eddie's a sweet guy, I liked him. Is he okay?"

"He was there too, but we don't know what happened to him. He's dropped out of sight. Did you have much to do with Mark Lewis?"

Rainbow brightened a bit. "Yeah, Mark's cool. Is he okay?"

"He took a bad knock on the head but otherwise he's fine."

"Jeez."

"Have you seen Eddie or Mark since you quit?"

"I haven't seen Eddie. Mark I saw once. He asked me to meet him for coffee after I left. But he's like way too young for me so we just got together the one time. He's sweet, but he's just a kid."

"So you only worked there for a month. What made you quit?"

The girl took a deep breath. Here we go, Cahill thought.

"Look, I don't want to make trouble for anyone," the girl said.

"You won't, don't worry." Cahill adopted the tone she used for talking with the kids she usually dealt with, a warm and understanding murmur to get through the defenses her charges built to keep the world out. "Sounds like something happened."

"Yeah. The guy who owns the place hit on me."

"Mark's dad?"

"Yeah."

Cahill thought about that.

"You know," she said, "sometimes these older guys say something that makes you think they're coming on to you when really they're just trying to be cool in their own stupid way."

"He grabbed my ass in the back room. Clear enough?"

"Okay," Cahill said, "that'll do it. Was it just the one time?"

"If it was just once, I could have overlooked it, like maybe it was just one of those things you said. But it happened three more times. I'd come into the workroom to ask him a question about an order and while we were looking over the order slip he'd, like, lean into me and sort of rub up against me. And then the last time he came up behind me and I could feel his boner right through his apron."

She gave a mock shudder. "If I'd had a meat cleaver in my hand, we'd be having a different conversation right now."

"Good thing he's a baker and not a butcher."

"For real."

"Did you tell anybody about it?"

"No, when that last thing happened I just quit."

"You didn't tell René?"

"No. She asked why I was leaving and I made up some bullshit about my school schedule. I just wanted to get out of there and get on with my life."

"Did you tell anybody else? Your parents, a boyfriend?"

"No, I just wanted to put the whole thing behind me."

"What about Mark? Did you say anything to him?"

"I never mentioned it. Who wants to hear their dad's a dick?"

"Not many people," Janey Cahill had to agree.

20

Before anyone said hello, he heard children screaming in the background.

One infant howling, an older child crying, a third child shrieking so bloodcurdlingly loud he couldn't tell if the sound came from a girl or boy, a youngster or an older kid.

He was about to hang up when he heard a flat, disinterested, "Hello." The word was surprisingly calm given the chaos in the background.

"This is Detective Martin Preuss from the Ferndale Police Department. I'm calling for Shatoya Watkins."

"Shatoya Gaines," the young man said.

"Yes."

"She not home."

"Who am I speaking with?"

"This her sister Monique."

"Do you know when she'll be home, Monique?"

"She don't come home till after she finish work."

"And when is that?"

"Six o'clock."

According to the helm clock on his desk it was 4:35. The clock was about five minutes slow.

"Where does she work?"

"Northland."

By the time she left the big shopping center at Greenfield and Eight Mile in Southfield, it would take her a half hour to make it home to the bungalow on Marlowe. Then she would plunge into the tumult of the house he heard behind the voice of the young woman on the other end of the phone. It would be better if he could speak with her away from the house.

"Can you tell me where she works at Northland?" he asked.

The women's shoe department manager at Macy's pointed Shatoya Gaines out to him. She was ringing up a customer at the register, a full-figured, dark-skinned woman almost as tall as Preuss, with plump arms and a strikingly pretty face with large round eyes.

He waited till she finished with her customer and then stepped forward. He introduced himself and asked if he could have a few words.

"Oh yeah," she said as though expecting him, "Lexie told me about you."

"Lexie?"

"The lady who lives next door. She said you came looking for me the other day."

"I did. She was very helpful."

"She's a character."

"She is indeed."

"She told me you were asking about Eddie."

He nodded. "Can we go someplace to talk?"

She told her manager she needed a short break and led Preuss back behind the curtain from the selling floor into a large storage space containing a warren of shelves stacked with hundreds of rectangular shoe boxes. The smell of leather was strong and sweet.

The aisles were narrow so they walked single file. "There's a break room for employees," she said over her shoulder, "but it's pretty noisy. And filthy. When I take my breaks I go back here."

At the end of the aisle was a tiny room the size of a closet with two battered bridge chairs and a card table. Taped on the door jamb was a hand-lettered sign: "Shatoya's Office."

"Little joke," she said.

They sat in the two chairs. "Did you find Eddie?" she asked.

"Not yet. Any idea where he might be?"

"I haven't heard from him in a while. Is he in trouble?"

"He might be. There was a shooting at the bakery where he works in Ferndale. A man was killed and two others, including Eddie, were wounded. He witnessed it. And he might be in danger himself."

"Do you know who did it?"

"Not yet. That's what we're hoping Eddie can help us with."

"We aren't in touch very often. We're not really part of each other's lives anymore. I'm not sure how much you know."

"Rocellus told me a little."

She smoothed her skirt across her lap. "I'm guessing he didn't paint a very positive picture of Eddie. Rocellus and Eddie used to be really tight but they're not anymore. And I hate that I'm the reason. I felt so bad for Eddie, I really did. I didn't mean to hurt him. He took it so hard when Rocellus and I got together, it just broke my heart."

"Rocellus said when Eddie got out of the army he wanted to patch things up?"

"He did. He was really a changed man when he got home. He had a plan for his life, he wasn't angry anymore. But by then Rocellus and I already made plans for a life together. When Eddie first came to see me, I think he just wanted to, you know, make amends."

The subject pained her, it was clear. The more she talked about Eddie, the more her glow faded, as if her ex were siphoning it off.

"After he came to see me when he got out, he disappeared for a long time. I didn't hear from him again till a few months ago."

"When?"

"Right after the beginning of the year. He got this idea in his head that Erica—that's our older daughter, mine and Eddie's— should go to Catholic school. He didn't like it she was in the Detroit public school system. He thought she wasn't getting a good enough education. I told him it was a nice idea but there was no way we could afford private school tuition for both the girls. He told me he'd find a way to get the money."

"Did he say how he planned to get it?"

"No. Tuition for Catholic school in Detroit is expensive. I said, 'Eddie, it's over three thousand dollars to send just one of the girls.

Where we gonna find that kind of money?' I told him I wouldn't take it if he was going to do something illegal, so don't even go there. He told me he wouldn't do anything illegal but he'd find the money somehow."

"Rocellus seemed to think he was back with his old crowd."

"I don't believe that. The Eddie Watkins I saw when he got out of the army wouldn't fall into his old habits. I just know he wouldn't."

"Maybe so, but if he needed some quick money . . ." He left the thought unfinished.

"I don't believe it."

"Did you ever hear if he got the money?"

"No, I haven't heard from him. Not since we talked that last time."

She was quiet for a moment. "I hope he didn't go and get himself in trouble for this."

"So do I," Preuss said.

She glanced at the tiny watch on her wrist. "I better get back on the floor."

"Thanks for your time. This was helpful." Preuss gave her his card. "If he gets in touch with you, or you find out where he is, could you call me right away? I really need to talk to him."

"I will." She put the card in the pocket of her skirt. "Now you have me worried."

"You probably should be."

"I'll make some calls. I'll let you know what I hear."

21

He stopped at the group home to kiss sleeping Toby goodnight, then went home and made a scalding hot pot of tea to accompany Steve Earle's *Transcendental Blues*.

He sat on the sofa sipping his drink and letting the music wash over him while he thought about the day's events.

Eddie Watkins's outlines were growing sharper, and as they did Preuss's sympathy for the man increased. Home from war, aimless, trying to escape his former life, betrayed by his wife and former best friend . . . it seemed as if all the traps life can put in a man's path caught him at once.

At the same time, what Preuss learned from Shatoya put a spin on things that didn't look good for her ex-husband. If Eddie needed money to send the girls to private school, that could be the motive they were looking for to connect him to the events at the bakery, if it was a robbery, which he still wasn't convinced of. And if someone else actually did it at Eddie's instigation—maybe one of the bad crowd Rocellus talked about—that might also explain why Eddie ran.

The more he learned about Eddie Watkins, the more the investigation pointed to him as the inside man.

When the last track on the CD, "Over Yonder," ended he didn't feel like he could get to sleep yet even though he was exhausted. He strapped on his wine red Les Paul Classic, fired up the practice amp, and played slow blues for another half hour, feeding the sinuous lines right into the center of his brain through earphones.

Then, still restless, he wandered into the kitchen to stack the dirty dishes from the sink into the dishwasher.

He turned the dishwasher on and as he did a terrible thought struck him.

The next day was April 15.

He never finished his taxes.

He sat down at the dining room table to think about what that meant. He would never be able to work his way through them by the end of the day tomorrow with everything else that was going on. His only option was to take an extension.

Upstairs, in Jason's old bedroom now fixed as his office, he pulled out the tax materials and printed copies of the federal extension from his Turbotax. He didn't think he needed an extension for the state taxes because he didn't think he would owe anything. He never did owe taxes, and usually got a refund.

It was too late to worry about it anyway. He printed up several copies of the federal extension form and put one in an envelope addressed to the federal Internal Revenue Service Center in Fresno.

He wandered into his bedroom and collapsed on top of the blankets, still in his clothes. The green digits on the cable box under the television set said 3:24 a.m.

A headache wrapped itself around the top of his head. He told himself again he needed to get more exercise. He needed it not only for stress relief, but to ward off the heart trouble that was hereditary in his family. His father died of a heart attack at 58, not all that much older than Preuss himself was. His uncle was even younger when he died of heart failure.

Preuss rarely thought about his father, and when he did he was no longer overcome by the choking anger that gripped him in his twenties and thirties. He guessed this was progress. He wasn't the worst father Preuss had ever run into (the guy he arrested a few years back who held a blowtorch to his infant son's feet was far and away the worst) but his old man was bad enough. He was one of those people who should never have had children. Both Preuss's father and mother should just have looked after each other's narcissistic needs instead of ruining the lives of their kids.

He put his arm behind his head and closed his eyes. His father used to be a professor of history at Michigan State University who thought Preuss was employed below his capabilities as a policeman and never let him forget it. Especially when the old man was drunk, which was often.

Even his mother thought so . . . once his mother, who was a professor too but of English, said to him it was too bad he never made anything of himself like their friends' son, who got rich as a stockbroker by riding the junk bond bubble. This after he was promoted to the Detective Bureau.

After he joined the Ferndale Police, he rarely heard from either of them and made no effort to get in touch with them even though they lived an hour away in East Lansing. And he never saw or heard from his brother Dennis, whose drug problem put the final nail in the airless coffin that was Preuss's family. Preuss thought Dennis disappeared from the face of the earth until his father's funeral, when his mother told him his father stayed in touch with Dennis all along, sending him money and several times traveling around the country to visit him.

It was painful but not unexpected to learn his father had money and time and concern for Dennis, but nothing for Martin.

And still Dennis never bothered to show up for their father's funeral.

When his own son Jason took off, Preuss thought it was droll how his son was duplicating both his and Dennis's pattern, putting distance between himself and his father. But Jason was more like Dennis in making sure his father always knew where he was so he could send money. Preuss never asked his father for a cent.

Over the past few years Jason had been out of touch, but he kept tabs on the boy's whereabouts.

Just as his father kept tabs on Dennis.

What a family, he thought.

And then there was Toby, sweet, beautiful Toby, who, out of all of them, seemed to know intuitively what it meant to love and be loved unconditionally. Toby showed how unimportant everything else was next to that.

Toby would be asleep at this hour. And Jason? Where was he now? Still on the West Coast?

He would be twenty-one now. Just beginning his life, if he were a normal young man. Preuss didn't know what his older son was like nowadays, but he sensed he would be like many of the men Preuss saw on his job: wiser than their age in street-smart ways but younger in maturity, less able to think about other people beyond using them as tools for their own selfish ends. Thinking they were adults, but without a family to polish the rough edges and give them models of behavior and love, even young men were just children.

He kept thinking about his sons until sleep pulled him in just as dawn lightened the sky and the birds began to stir in the trees.

Wednesday, April 15, 2009

22

A house near the beach.

More like a country manor than a cottage, with three full luxurious floors. Preuss sat on a sofa on the top floor with his arm around Toby. They were the only two people at home. The floor plan for the living room where they sat was open and airy. His son's wheelchair was nowhere in sight as Toby sat dangling his feet in his immaculate brown and white casual shoes.

Preuss heard the wind sighing through the trees surrounding the place. He stood and walked out to the porch that wrapped around the upper story. From there he could see Lake Huron, calm and mirror-smooth on the other side of a sand dune. He realized he had seen this house before, with Jeanette and Jason and Toby when the boys were around five and ten. They stayed at the cottage Jeanette's parents rented, but it was near this large home and they promised themselves they would stay here someday.

And now he and Toby were here. If only Jeanette could have lived to see it.

"It's a beautiful sight, isn't it?" said a woman's voice.

He looked down the length of the porch and saw Jeanette leaning her elbows on the wooden railing, gazing out at the clouds gathering over the lake.

She gave him a long look, then smiled.

Yes, he thought, watching her, there's the amazing smile I remember, wry and crafty, with that captivatingly charming crooked incisor.

As he watched her, he realized he was looking at Shelley Larkin, not Jeanette.

"It is a beautiful sight," he agreed, and they both knew he wasn't talking about the landscape.

He drifted toward her over the rough floor boards of the porch.

He heard Toby's deep voice calling him. Except his son was using words, not his usual sounds.

"Hey, Dad, come look at this!"

Preuss went inside the house and saw a flock of black birds, maybe a hundred, swooping around the room like an animated dark cloud. Toby was standing up watching them. He clapped his hands. "Dad," he said, "isn't this cool? How'd they get in? And what's the matter with the mama bird?"

He was about to tell his son he didn't know how they got in, it was a mystery, just like how the boy was speaking and standing and clapping his hands.

Off in the far corner of the room the phone began to ring. It was an ancient black Bakelite desk model with an old-fashioned ring, brrrrinng brrrring brrrring.

He walked over to the phone and stood gazing at it. He couldn't bring himself to pick it up . . . then after a few more rings he reached down to answer it, but it wasn't where he thought it was going to be.

He looked around but the phone was nowhere in sight. But why? Where? How?

He popped awake and looked around, his heart pounding crazily.

Nothing was where he expected it to be . . . not Toby, not the airy living room, not Jeanette or Shelley Larkin, not the birds swooping and diving overhead.

It took him several seconds to realize he was in his own bedroom in his house in Ferndale, not in the manor on the lake.

His room . . . his cell ringing on the nightstand . . .

Abruptly it stopped. He fumbled to pick up the phone and didn't recognize the number of the missed call. The time was 8:19.

He lay back, dopey from lack of sleep and sick to his stomach, as always when he woke in the middle of a dream. Most of his mind was still back in the house with his son, who was talking, and walking, and seeing things, and pointing, and saying his name . . .

The message tone sounded on the cell.

Shatoya Watkins, telling him where he could find Eddie.

The address on Riopelle near Eastern Market in Detroit was in an area that used to be a hub of industry but now was mostly burnt over. Graffiti covered every vertical space of the remains of a party store on the ground floor of the lone building still standing on the block surrounded by fields where factories and warehouses used to be. In the distance he saw the office buildings of downtown Detroit, with the columns of the GM Building pointing like a finger into the sky.

An apartment appeared to be intact on the second story of the party store. At least there were still shades on the windows.

He tried the door at the side of the store. The glass on the top half of the door was long gone and the opening covered with tattered plastic sheeting.

The lock was punched through so the door opened easily and he went up a flight of narrow, creaking wooden stairs.

The stairway gave off the sweetish smell of wood rot and wound up to a second-floor landing in front of an ancient door painted a shiny brown. He put his ear to the wood but heard nothing.

He knocked, and when there was no response he tried the knob. It turned and the door opened into a living room with a massive furry sofa and two bridge chairs. Clothes and empty beer cans and bottles were strewn everywhere. The place stank of old food.

He walked through the apartment but found no sign of Eddie Watkins, or anyone else. He paused at the window at the end of the living room and looked out on a vast vacant lot across the street. It probably held a manufacturing facility in the days when Detroit was prospering.

He wondered for the thousandth time how this city could ever come back from the brink it had gone over.

As with most vacant lots in Detroit, this one was a dumping ground for tires, mattresses, and other urban trash. In the center of the lot he saw crows circling what looked to be a pile of old clothes. For a second he thought about the birds in his dream.

As he looked more closely at the pile, he felt a prickle of dread on the back of his neck.

He took the steps down two at a time and crossed over to the vacant lot. He kicked through the trash and early weeds to the pile of clothes he saw from the window. The birds scattered into the sky as he approached.

In the clear spring sunshine he stood looking down on what was left of Eddie Watkins.

"You're spending almost as much time in the D as I am," Alonzo Barber said.

He showed a gap between his two front teeth when he smiled. He wore yet another tailored suit, this one charcoal with a subtle light gray pinstripe and a necktie the color of his suit with small polka dots of varying degrees of gray.

"Going to have to get you one of those Special Detective badges."

Preuss stood with him watching the small army of technicians collecting evidence and plainclothed and uniformed cops around the perimeter they established. The ME's assistant, a light-skinned man named Charles Robinson, knelt beside the body of Eddie Watkins with a thermometer stuck under the dead man's faded blue Lions sweatshirt. Preuss met Robinson a few years before, on another case with a Detroit connection when a father and son team pulled off a series of home invasions in southeast Ferndale and the son wound up shot to death in a drug house in Detroit.

Eddie Watkins lay face-up with the top of his head missing.

"Some heavy firepower, looks like," Preuss said. "I'm guessing it's not the same weapon from my bakery shooting."

"What was that?"

"Thirty-eight."

"Yeah, way too much damage here for that."

"Though he was shot close-up, too."

"They weren't playing with this guy, that's for sure."

Barber pointed his chin toward the apartment over the abandoned party store. "That where you thought he was?"

"Yeah. Belongs to a cousin of his, according to his ex-wife. She found out from an aunt."

"His ex, she the one sent you here?"

"She called me this morning to give me the address. Her name's Shatoya Watkins. Or Gaines, I guess it is now. She remarried after she divorced Eddie."

"Well, we'll pay her a visit," Barber said, "see what she has to say about all this."

"I'd guess whoever shot up the bakery came back to finish the job, except for the different weapon."

"Yeah, I'd say so too. But you never know."

The ME's assistant got to his feet with difficulty.

"What's it look like, Charles?" Barber asked him.

"Hard to tell since he's been outside. But considering the weather I'd put time of death last night, around midnight. We'll know more when we open him up."

"Lots of blood out here," Barber said. "This is the crime scene."

Preuss considered it. "I was thinking Eddie or somebody connected to him was responsible for the killing at the bakery. This might have been to keep him from talking."

"Death'll do that," Barber said.

"He also witnessed what happened. Does this look like Yummy Hendricks's work?"

"I wouldn't put it past him," Barber said. "He's still in the pokey so he couldn't have done it personally. Yummy usually has his bro-hams do his dirty work for him anyway. Thing is, Yummy, he's the kind of guy, he wanted Eddie dead he would have buried him on Belle Isle or someplace over in Windsor. We'd never find him."

"Unless he wanted to send a message. Whoever did this didn't care if we found him or not," Preuss said.

"These knuckleheads, they're not criminal geniuses. I find it doesn't pay to get too subtle trying to get inside their heads. Won't find much there."

Preuss agreed.

Out of three people in the workroom of the bakery, one was killed at the scene, now one was killed afterwards.

And Mark was the other person there that night.

If Eddie was killed because he was a witness to whatever happened, Mark wasn't safe either.

Nearby a gaggle of television news reporters were primping for their stand-ups. One had already begun; Preuss heard, "The latest brutal murder in the City of Detroit."

He walked away from them and called Cahill.

She answered immediately.

"Where are you?" he asked.

"At the high school. You won't believe what's going on here."

"Right about now I'd believe anything."

"This morning a kid told one of his teachers his dad was waiting for him out in the parking lot with a gun. Dad's in custody and now we're dealing with the fall-out for the kid. We're trying to arrange emergency placement for him."

"No relatives?"

"None we can find."

Preuss thought about Stevie Matuzik, abandoned by his parents, unable to be controlled by his uncle, at the mercy of his rages and needs.

"Evidently the boy's been a tad rebellious, been doing too well in school."

"Yeah, I hate it when that happens."

"Dad wanted to teach him a lesson so he drove to school this morning and waited the whole day for him so when school was out he could make his displeasure known."

She sighed. "I love it. So what's up?"

"I just found Eddie Watkins."

"Seriously? How is he?"

"Minus a large part of his head."

"Oh man."

"Do you know where Mark Lewis is? I'm suddenly very worried about him."

"Last I heard he was still in the hospital. Give me ten minutes and I'll find out."

He disconnected and started walking back toward Barber in the vacant field but Janey Cahill called back in less than a minute.

"Mark's home," she said. "They released him this morning."

"I want to swing by their house, make sure he's okay with my own eyes."

"I'll meet you there soon as I can get away."

23

"He's downstairs," René Lewis said, "playing video games. Usually we don't let him play those for hours on end, but I thought we could make an exception after what he's been through."

"How's he doing?"

"Fine." She looked from Martin Preuss to Janey Cahill, who had just gotten there when he arrived at the home on Blair.

"You asked me the same thing on the phone," René said. "What's going on?"

"I'm afraid I don't have good news," Preuss said. "Eddie Watkins turned up this morning. He's been killed."

Her features dissolved into a mask of agony. "Oh, poor Eddie."

"We don't exactly know how this is related to the bakery," Preuss said. "We were thinking Eddie might have been involved in some way in what happened last Sunday, but things just got a lot more complicated."

"I've been trying to think what could have brought this on," René said, "but everything's been fine. Business has been okay, not great but okay, all our creditors are happy. We haven't poisoned anyone. Who can get this angry at a bakery, for Pete's sake?"

"Maybe it doesn't have anything to do with the business," Preuss said. "Everything else in your lives going okay?"

Cahill caught his eye and gave an infinitesimally small shake of her head, which he couldn't interpret.

"Yes," René Lewis said, "everything's been going as usual."

Part of the basement was set up as a rec room, with a big-screen television connected to a shelf of electronic devices, surrounded by shelves full of DVDs and CDs. Mark Lewis was on his back on the sofa working the controls for a video game featuring a first-person shooter maneuvering through the back alleys of what looked to be a city in a mid-eastern desert country. Periodically figures clad in flowing robes with scarves obscuring their faces leapt out of hidey-holes with guttural growls. Mark was firing a variety of lethal weapons at them. When he connected, the figures would disintegrate with a sharp cry that sounded very much like "Allah!"

"Hey, Mark," Preuss said from the stairway. "Okay if I come down?"

"Sure."

"Feeling better?"

"I guess."

"You look a lot better."

Mark swung his feet over the side of the sofa and sat upright to make room for Preuss. He wore Levis and a faded red tee shirt with the large lascivious tongue of the Rolling Stones' logo. A gauze bandage was still taped to the crown of his head.

Preuss dropped onto the cushion beside him and the boy paused the game with the controller.

"When did you get home?"

"This morning."

"Are you going to stay home for a while before you get back to school?"

"They said I should stay home for the rest of the week and then see how I feel on Monday. Depends what's going on with this." He raised a hand to his head. "No soccer for a while for sure."

"Yeah, you don't want to monkey around with head injuries. I got a concussion back in November and I'm still not a hundred percent. I don't know how these hockey players and football players do it when they go right back out to play after a hit in the head."

Mark nodded.

"So have you thought any more about what happened?"

The boy shrugged a boney shoulder.

"Nothing else come to you?"

"No. Sorry."

"That's okay."

Mark was a few years younger than Toby, and Preuss thought again about the differences between where Toby was in his life and where a kid like Mark was. For all Mark's abilities and promise, there was a spark to Toby, a joy, that seemed missing in Mark. Any number of things could explain it: the pain meds he was on, what he just experienced, or something else going on in the household.

Janey Cahill threw him an odd look before . . . Who really knew what tensions there were in the heart of a family?

Then again, Toby was the happiest, most sociable person Preuss knew. Preuss long ago concluded that for all his limitations, Toby innately understood about what was truly important.

After a few moments, Preuss said, "If you do think of anything, or anything out of the ordinary happens, would you tell your parents right away? Or Janey Cahill. You have her number, right?"

The boy nodded earnestly.

"And 911 if it's an emergency."

"Okay."

Preuss nodded to the television screen. "Mind if I watch for a second?"

"Go ahead," Mark said, and unpaused the game. Before he could react, the first-person avatar was immediately massacred by terrorists who slaughtered him in a flurry of bullets and a billowing mist of brilliant red blood.

Janey Cahill walked him to her pickup parked across the street from the Lewis home. The day was turning into a balmy spring afternoon, with a sodden hint of the explosion of the season still to come.

Seated in the cab she let down a window and lit a cigarette. She blew the smoke out the window and he waved away the smell with an exaggerated gesture.

"Don't give me a hard time," she said. "I'm not in the mood for your righteous anti-tobacco bullshit just at the moment. I was dying for a smoke in there."

"And now you're dying for one out here."

She took another deep drag and let it out slowly. "The sweet, hot taste of freedom." She held up the cigarette. "Behold my right as an American."

"Is this a great country, or what?"

"That's what I'm saying."

When she took in and got rid of another lungful of smoke, he said, "What were you trying to tell me in there?"

"When I talked to Rainbow Moss, she told me the reason she quit was because Matt came on to her."

"How'd it make her feel?"

"How do you think it made her feel, Dr. Phil?"

"I'm asking if she seemed angry enough to mastermind this whole thing to get back at him."

"She claimed she just wanted to put the whole episode behind her, and I believed her. Thing is, it makes us look at Matt in a whole different light. If he's coming on to one young woman, are there others? And what else is he into? Did he piss off the wrong person about something?"

"It doesn't seem like adultery is enough to provoke a double murder," Preuss said. "It'd have to be something worse. Something with big money involved."

He told her what he learned from Shatoya Gaines.

"So Eddie might have been squeezed for cash," Cahill said. "That's starting to sound like a motive."

"That was my thought, too. And remember what Rocellus said about Watkins taking something that didn't belong to him and bad people wanting it back."

"So maybe he's being squeezed from both ends. Worse and worse."

"There also might be a link between Matt Lewis and Eddie Watkins that goes beyond Matt's good intentions. I asked Bellamy to check into the Lewises. What do you bet he hasn't done it yet?"

Cahill snorted. "That's not a bet I'd take."

24

Back at the Shanahan nobody knew where Hank Bellamy was.

Preuss was neither surprised nor annoyed. Bellamy had a reputation as a hump so he was just being himself. Rather than keep trying to locate him, Preuss got to work finding what he could about the Lewises, which is what he should have done in the first place.

There wasn't much information. Janey Cahill represented them as good citizens, and so they seemed. He would need a subpoena for their bank records so that would take a few days, if the judge even approved it. But aside from their operators' licenses and their food license he could find no contact with the legal or correctional systems.

There especially didn't seem to be any connection between Matt Lewis and Eddie Watkins or Leon Banks outside of the bakery. In fact, there was so little linking Lewis and the two veterans that Preuss began to wonder how the three men met at all.

He called Matt Lewis's cell and asked him that question directly. Lewis told him a friend of his (the guy Lewis was having drinks with at Mr. Sal's last Sunday, as it turned out) was a career placement counselor at one of the Wayne County Community College campuses and he put Watkins in touch with Lewis when he discovered Watkins's interest in baking.

As for Leon Banks, Lewis said he just happened to wander into the store one day, looking for a place to keep warm during a cold Michigan winter afternoon.

Preuss got the name of Lewis's friend and called him. The man said he was on his way into a meeting but he could speak with Preuss after that.

An hour and a half later Preuss shook hands with a short, pale, portly man with thinning ginger hair and a wispy Van Dyke that seemed crayoned on. His office in a corner of the Academic Administration Building on the northwest Detroit campus of Wayne County Community College was bright and cluttered with files and books on taking standardized career aptitude tests. On the walls hung the kinds of posters about the power of teamwork and positive thinking that Preuss could never take seriously.

The man's smile was pleasantly bland as he said, "Cheery."

Before Preuss could sort through all the possible snappy replies that formed in his head—"That makes one of us" being the one that rose to the top—the short man gave him a wry grin and said, "Dick Cheery. I like to introduce myself that way. Helps break the ice with students."

Cheery moved file folders off a chair so Preuss could sit down. Preuss explained what he was after.

"Sure," Cheery said, "I met Eddie last spring. I knew Matt was getting ready to open a bakery and it seemed like a perfect match. So I arranged for them to meet."

"How did you come to know Watkins?"

"He was taking some classes here and came to see me about finding a job. He told me he was an Iraqi War vet and got a part-time job on campus in the cafeteria. He took to it and said he wanted to look into the food industry as a career."

"How do you know Matt?"

"We're old friends from MSU. Couple of old social work majors. He was an addiction counselor for a while and then decided what he really wanted to do was open a restaurant. He did that for a while and then he decided to open the bakery. I drifted into career counseling. We go where we're called," he added, sounding like one of his posters.

"Matt worked with addicts?" That got Preuss's attention . . . if he worked with addicts at one point in his life there might be some narcotics involvement after all. At the least it opened a window into the criminal world that might be significant.

"Yeah. Evidently his father came back from Viet Nam with a major habit so Matt gravitated toward it."

"How long did he do that?"

"Not long. I think he figured out pretty quickly it's not the best population to work with. Addiction is a disease of relapses and he had a hard time feeling like he was making progress with his clients. Myself I think he was trying to resolve some issues with his father— you know, like by healing others he was trying to heal his father. When he realized it was too late to help his father is when he took his life in another direction entirely."

"Did Eddie Watkins ever have any drug problems to your knowledge?"

"None I'm aware of."

"What about Matt . . . any run-ins with the law?"

"Never."

"No problems or proclivities you know of? Drugs, gambling, anything else? Women, maybe?"

"Well," Cheery said, and paused. Preuss waited. "Matt's honest as the day is long. But I have to say, he always was a bit of a ladies' man."

"Has that ever gotten him into trouble?"

"Oh, nothing he couldn't talk his way out of." Cheery chuckled.

"When was the last time you heard from Eddie?"

"Actually, the time he came to see me when I told him about Matt. The only other time I saw him was when the news did a story on him. I'm responsible for that," Cheery said.

"In what way?"

"I called up a reporter I know at Channel 2 and told her about all the good things Matt's doing for returning vets. So they decided to do a story on him, focusing on Eddie. Other than that, I haven't seen or talked to him. Eddie, that is. I see Matt all the time."

Cheery frowned. "Is Eddie okay? How's he doing?"

"Not well, I'm sorry to say."

Toby's smile.
Nothing better.

Preuss leaned over the recliner in his son's room and planted a noisy wet kiss on the boy's cheek, which set Toby off in a paroxysm of happiness. He wagged his head back and forth and opened his mouth wide and made a humming sound that modulated into a happy chirp. When he smiled he lit up the room.

No, that's not right, Preuss thought. He lit up the world.

He leaned across the chair again and said into Toby's ear, "I don't know what I'd do without you. I love you so much."

Toby beamed again. He understood exactly what his father was telling him, Preuss was certain of it.

He pulled a chair beside Toby's and took the boy's hands in his own. He thought of all the different doctors who examined Toby and tried to test his capabilities, and all the times they told him Toby had few. No higher order thinking, they told him. No vision to speak of. His movements were mostly primitive reflexes unguided by Toby's volition, they insisted. He would never be able to express himself . . . would never talk, never understand what was said to him, never express thoughts he didn't even have to begin with.

To listen to them, Toby was your basic potted plant.

But anyone observing him, and not even for an extended period, would know the experts were wrong. Toby knew so much more than they gave him credit for. He knew where he was, knew who was with him, knew what was happening around him.

He was especially sensitive to the emotional storms that raged through the house when Jeanette was alive. He would scream and cry as soon as Preuss and his wife would start in on each other, and when their other son Jason would jump into the fray, Toby would get hysterical.

But it wasn't just anger Toby responded to. By being so loving he stimulated love from everyone around him, and he thrived on it. And no one seeing the sadness radiating from him after his mother died could possibly doubt he not only knew what happened, but responded to it in ways that were clear and incontestable. It was true he didn't respond in words, because he didn't have the ability to articulate words. But he could vocalize whatever was in his heart, and his vocalizations were as expressive as any vocabulary.

His facial expressions, his body language, the hums and whines and murmurs he produced . . . all were as communicative as anything a boy like Mark Lewis could produce. No, Preuss was certain the experts were wrong about his son. And so he rarely believed anything they said about him.

Sometimes the people you expected to know the most knew the least, he thought as he sat with his son watching the hundredth rerun of a *Law and Order* episode until Toby's eyes finally fluttered closed for the night.

Preuss turned the TV off and sat for another hour, letting the sights and sounds and troubles of the day flow out of him in the tranquility that surrounded Toby, even in sleep.

As always when he left, Preuss was perfectly at peace.

It was the last peaceful night he would have for a while.

Thursday, April 16, 2009

25

"There you go, hon."

The server at Club Bart's on Woodward placed his order of scrambled eggs with onions and a side of tomatoes in front of Martin Preuss. He didn't often stop for breakfast, but he didn't have time to do any shopping in the previous week so there was nothing at home to grab in the morning.

Besides, this morning he felt the need to be taken care of. Without anyone in his life to do that for him, this morning he settled for the impersonal attention of the young woman who served him with half a shaved head, colorful animal tattoos running up both arms like sleeves, and a bead ring piercing her septum.

He peppered his eggs and was about to dig in when his cell phone rang.

Janie Cahill.

He pressed the answer button with his thumb and said, "Good morning."

"Mark's gone," she said without preliminaries. "René just called to let me know."

"Define gone."

"Gone as in missing, as in nowhere in sight. As in now you see him, now you don't. She went in to check on him this morning and he wasn't in his room or anywhere else in the house."

He looked down at his breakfast, now mostly irrelevant.

"I told her we'd be right over," she said.

"Meet you there."

Two scout cars and Janey Cahill's pickup hemmed in the Lewis bungalow across from the park.

Preuss let himself in the front door. A uniformed officer, Paul Vollmer, was taking information from René Lewis in the kitchen.

Preuss nodded to him and followed the sound of Cahill's voice upstairs.

She was going through what Preuss assumed was Mark's bedroom with another uniformed officer Preuss didn't know. The room was small with limited wall space taken up by posters of soccer players. Preuss looked closely at the autograph on one and thought he could make out the name of Carlo Avezzano, who was apparently the captain of the U.S. men's team. The name didn't mean much to Preuss, but then he didn't follow soccer. Or any other sport.

"René said she got Kenny up and ready for school," Cahill said, "and when Matt took him to school around 7:30, she went to peek in on Mark. That's when she realized he was gone."

"So nobody knows when he actually left the house? Or how?"

"Apparently not. He left this."

She handed him a note in an illegible scrawl.

"Please, what language is this in?"

"I had to ask René to translate for me. It's definitely Mark's handwriting. It says, 'Mom and Dad, I need some space so I have to get away for a little while. Don't worry, I'm fine. I'll call you.'"

"What did she say about it?"

"She's worried sick."

He looked into the closet. There were no gaps where clothes seemed to be missing. "Did he take anything?"

"She says just his cell phone and backpack. I asked her about clothes but it's hard to tell." She indicated the piles of clothes on the floor. It was impossible to differentiate between dirty and clean.

"Does she have any idea where he went?"

"No. She called the buddies she knows. But you can't know everyone your kids know."

"You checked everyplace in the house? Basement, attic, garage?"

"Every nook and cranny. She called Matt and Kenny but she can't get through to either of them. Matt didn't answer and Kenny can't use his phone during school."

"Has Mark ever done this before?"

"She says never. Says he's always been a good boy."

At the mention of the phrase Preuss remembered a television show from a long time ago, called *Juvenile Court*. It was an early reality show before there was such a thing, featuring real judges but local teenagers playing kids involved in the juvenile justice system with actors playing their parents. The first words out of the mouths of the mothers were always, "He's a good boy, judge," no matter what the crime.

"Even if he really is just taking a time-out, he picked a pretty damn awful time to bust out of here," he said.

"René tried his cell but he didn't pick up."

"I'm going to head over to the bakery and have a chat with Matt. Are you going to stay here?"

"I am. I'll call you if he turns up."

"He's not going to turn up on his own," Preuss said. "We're going to have to find him."

He stopped in the kitchen.

"René, did you tell Mark about Eddie?"

"I did. I thought he deserved to know. He and Eddie were close."

His face must have betrayed how he felt because she asked, "Was that not a good thing to do?"

"When did you tell him?"

"Last night, after you left. He came upstairs and asked me if you said anything about Eddie. I wasn't going to lie to him."

"No," said Preuss. "But I have to tell you, I don't see this as a good thing. Knowing Eddie was killed after seeing Leon killed might have got him thinking he's next on the list."

"Do you really think somebody's after him?"

"I'm afraid there might be."

26

The front door to the Cake Walk was locked.

When he peered through the window, Preuss saw no activity in the store. A hand-lettered sign on the window read:

TEMPORARILY CLOSED
UNTIL FURTHER NOTICE

He banged his key-ring on the heavy metal frame of the door, then on the plate glass. It brought no movement inside.

He stepped back and looked up and down the street. Nine Mile was mostly empty at this hour, except for some activity down by the coffee shop on the other side of the street, closer to Woodward.

Standing on the sidewalk he called Matt's cell but it went straight to voicemail. He left a message asking for a return call as soon as Matt got the message.

He ended the call and a man came out of the tobacco specialty shop next to the bakery and said, "Hello, my friend."

His name was Amad Yousef and he was on the board of directors of the Downtown Development Authority and the community center down on Livernois. Preuss knew him from community events. He was an emigre from Syria who embraced the opportunities of his new land with a convert's zeal.

They shook hands. "I heard banging," Amad said. "How's life treating you, detective?"

"Like I said something bad about its mother."

Amad threw his head back and laughed.

"I know just what you need. Do you have time for a coffee?"

"A quick one, sure."

He followed Amad into the store. Smoking specialty shops like this one were exempt from the state antismoking law, so anyone could smoke any of Amad's cigarettes, pipe tobaccos, and cigars inside the store. An exotic and sweet mixture of aromas hung in the air. It was pleasant but Preuss knew it would cling to his clothes, hair, and skin all day.

Amad led him to a coffee station at the rear of the store and poured out two small cups of coffee from the hissing and sputtering coffee machine. The dark potent brew would keep Preuss sharp for the rest of the day and night. And maybe into the next week as well.

Amad invited him to sit in the lounge chairs by the machine. He was in his middle thirties with short black thinning hair and a complexion the color of weak tea, as though his hide were being tanned from the air in his store.

They drank their coffee in silence. It was as strong and bitter as Preuss expected.

Then Amad said, "So you're at the bakery because you have a sudden urge for a croissant?"

Preuss shook his head. "I'm looking for Matt."

"I haven't seen him yet today. He used to come over for a cup of coffee in the morning when he got in, but, well, he hasn't for a while. And that killing last weekend . . . how awful."

"We're working hard on it."

"You don't expect these things to happen in Ferndale. The city yes, but not here."

"Violence is general everywhere, unfortunately."

He shrugged. "Why should this country be any different from anyplace else in the world?"

"It's the truth."

"It was a robbery, I assume?"

"It's not clear at this point."

"I'll tell you something, my friend. It all comes down to greed. If you look at what's happening in this country and then what happened next door, it's all the same. Greed, enforced by violence. Can you tell me I'm wrong?"

"You're not wrong."

"You bet I'm not. Greed and violence, sanctioned by all our political and economic systems."

Amad's tirade hung in the air as they sipped their coffee.

"Have you see Matt recently?" Preuss asked.

"I don't see him much nowadays. He not only hasn't been coming over for coffee, he hasn't been opening at ten for a while now. He used to be so punctual, and lately not so much."

"When has he been opening?"

Amad gave an elaborate shrug. "Sometimes 10:30, sometimes not till closer to 11. His baker comes in early to make the goods, but Matt hasn't been showing up till later."

Amad bent a little closer, though there was no one else in the store. "I don't want to tell tales out of school, but if I wanted to talk with Matt, I'd try Mr. Sal's."

The bar where Preuss found Matt on the Sunday night this all began. "At this hour of the day?"

"I happen to know he's been spending a lot of time there. And yes, at this hour."

"All due respect, Amad, how do you know this?"

"I'm a member of the Downtown Development Authority. Matt's on it too, along with Sal Bartoli, who owns the bar. Matt hasn't been showing up to the weekly meetings. Sal and I talked about it at the last one. That's when he told me."

Amad took another sip of his coffee. "He said Matt is turning into one of his best customers."

27

As Preuss entered the tiny foyer of Mr. Sal's Bar and Grill, a blast of hot air from the overhead heater surged over him and made him gasp.

Inside he made a fast visual sweep of the room. The bartender, a lean young man with long wiry hair done up in a Samurai's topknot, stood with his back to the door as he restocked the bottles behind the bar.

The only other sign of life was an old man alone at the far end of the bar. He sat staring into the glass of beer in front of him as though wondering how the rest of his life fit into such a small space.

But no Matt.

The bartender turned when Preuss approached.

"Morning," he said. He wore a faded grey tee shirt under a leather vest. Preuss recognized him as the lead guitarist of one of the local bands though he couldn't place either his name or the name of the band.

"Morning," Preuss said. "Martin Preuss, Ferndale PD." He held up his shield. "You are?"

"Danny Green."

Preuss sat on a bar stool and Danny Green automatically threw a napkin in front of him. "Get you something?"

"No thanks. I'm looking for Matt Lewis. The guy who owns the bakery on Nine where there was a shooting last Sunday? I hear he's a steady customer."

"I know the guy. Yeah, he spends a lot of time here. He's usually in by now but he's late today."

"This about when he usually shows?"

"Yep. Sometimes end of the day too. He's got a . . ."

The young man hesitated.

Danny killed a few seconds by pouring himself a cup of coffee from the carafe behind the bar. He held it up and raised his eyebrows but Preuss waved it away.

"You were saying?"

After a thoughtful sip, Danny said, "I don't want to get anybody in trouble."

"Don't worry about it, Danny. I just need to find Matt."

"He's got like a little thing for one of the servers. Girl named Shay."

"Is that so."

"Yep. You want to find him, he'll usually be sitting at the bar, chatting her up."

"And she's not scheduled to work now?"

"No, she is. She should be here but I haven't heard from her. Don't know where she is."

Preuss slid his card across the bar. "If Matt comes in, tell him to call me right away? It's important."

"Will do."

Preuss raised a hand in thanks and left.

The bakery was still locked with no sign of Matt Lewis. Preuss called Janey Cahill at the Lewis home and she told him Matt called René.

"Did he say where he say he was?"

"He claimed he was out looking for Mark."

"'Claimed he was'?"

"Whatever."

"So he hasn't heard from Mark either?"

"He says no."

"All right," Preuss said. "I'm headed back to the station. I'll get a missing child alert out on Mark."

At noon there was still no news and Preuss went down to the station canteen to buy a cheese sandwich from the machine. As soon as he put in his money and the food dropped he remembered how awful these were, but it was too late. He brought it back to his office where he nibbled on the stale cheese and threw the soggy bread away.

The helm clock on his desk made him remember what he thought about at Toby's the night before . . . sometimes the people who were supposed to be the experts knew the least.

Like parents, he thought.

What was that old saying? It's a wise father who know his own child?

How wise was Matt, he wondered. Was there someone else who might know more about Mark Lewis than either Matt or René?

That line of thought led him to one person in particular.

At precisely 2:40 a wave of middle school students poured out of the low building on Pinecrest. Bobbing like a cork in that wave was Kenny Lewis, already with his buds in his ears and his iPod in his hand.

The boy spotted Preuss and immediately start walking in the other direction, against the tide.

Except he bumped right into Janey Cahill standing behind him. She put out her arms to corral him so he couldn't avoid her. Behind her stood Mr. Simmons, the middle school counselor.

There was no means of escape. With an arm around the boy's narrow shoulders, Cahill steered him toward the car where Preuss was standing.

Preuss opened the passenger door for him. "What's up, Kenny?"

He drove them to the Taco Bell at the corner of Nine Mile and Pinecrest and got Kenny two vegetarian tacos and a Coke. "I'm a vegan," Kenny explained.

Preuss handed the food to Kenny sitting beside him, then parked the Explorer at the back of the restaurant lot. Kenny ate his food in silence, seeming very small in the SUV.

In his looks the boy favored his mother with his heart-shaped face and olive skin. He had clear hazel eyes that accounted for the otherworldly vibe he gave off, and a cleft chin Preuss knew probably earned him the nickname "Buttface" in the cruel world of children.

When he finished his meal the boy squeezed the wrappings into a tight ball.

"So Kenny," Preuss said, "doing okay?"

"I guess."

"Pretty awful, what happened at the store?"

"Uh-huh."

"Have you talked to your brother today?"

"No."

"When was the last time you saw him?"

"Last night."

"How'd he seem?"

Without answering the boy concentrated on compressing his trash into an even smaller ball.

"Reason I'm asking is, after you left for school this morning your mom went in to check on him and he was gone." The boy gave no apparent reaction. "He left a note saying he needed to get away for a while. Did you know about that?"

"No." In a small voice.

"Do you know where he might be?"

"No."

"There's no place where he goes to get away?"

Kenny murmured something, and Preuss said, "Excuse me?"

"I said I don't know."

From the back seat Cahill held her hand out and Kenny deposited the trash ball into her palm. She handed it to Preuss.

"Detective," she said, "why don't you be a good citizen and throw this in the trash container?" She gave Preuss a barely perceptible head feint toward the building.

Dutifully he took the wad of trash and stepped out of the car. He dropped it into the receptacle beside the restaurant door, then went in to use the rest room. He dawdled, giving Janey time to speak with the boy. He checked his messages at the station and texted Trombley and Blair to ask if there was any progress. Of course there was none.

When he got back into the car, Cahill said, "Kenny, please tell Detective Preuss what you just told me."

The boy mumbled something unintelligible.

"Say that again so I can hear it?" Preuss said.

"I know where he is," the boy murmured, louder this time.

Preuss looked at Cahill. "Truth serum in the pop?"

"Kenny needed to get this off his chest." To the boy, she said, "Tell him what else."

Kenny said, "He's pretty sure somebody's after him."

He looked straight at Preuss now. His wide-set eyes were pained.

"He thinks somebody wants to kill him."

28

The deserted building near I-75 held the offices for an electronics supply company that went out of business a few years ago. A crop of leggy weeds was already poking through the asphalt, plants tough enough to sprout in the cold weather.

Martin Preuss waited beside the Explorer in the parking lot. They agreed it would be less threatening if Janey went in with Kenny to bring Mark out.

His cell rang.

He expected it to be Janey but it was Alonzo Barber.

"Yummy was arraigned at noon. He's already out on bond. Just wanted you to know."

"That was fast."

"Revolving door, okay? I asked him about your Eddie Watkins and he said he doesn't know anything about what happened."

"There's a shocker."

"Yeah, but I believe him. He was upset when I told him. Seemed genuine. Said they go way back together. Boyhood friends. I don't think he was involved. He said he'd check around, see what he could find out."

"Better get another one of your Special Detective badges ready."

His phone clicked with call waiting, then chimed with a text.

"Damn," he said.

"What's the matter?"

"Sorry. There's a situation here needs my attention."

"Better get to it. I'll call you back if I hear anything else."

They disconnected. Janey's text read *Better get in here*. Just as he read it she appeared in the door leading into the building and waved him over.

"He's not here," she said. "We looked everywhere and can't find him."

Inside the battered building he heard Kenny yelling his brother's name.

"Kenny?" Preuss called. "Where are you?"

"Up here."

"Where's here?"

"On the second floor." Kenny's voice came through holes in the ceiling but Preuss couldn't pinpoint where.

"Keep talking so I can find you."

"Take the stairs and go straight when you get into the hallway. I'm in a room on the left."

Preuss moved slowly through the wreckage of the building. He smelled the dampness of the sodden vinyl tiles beneath his feet, the acrid odor of animal leavings, and the sour smell of wet, crumbling plaster.

In the office where Kenny directed him, he saw the youngster on his hands and knees on the floor under a table. Someone had recently been here—a cleared area in the rubble held empty food and drink containers from the 7-Eleven.

"I think I found Mark's cell phone," Kenny said.

If it was his phone, then things were really not good, Preuss knew. Kids don't go anywhere without their cells.

Kenny backed out from under the table with a rectangular piece of dark metal in his hands. "No, I thought it was, but it's just this piece of junk."

He tossed it aside. "This is where he goes." The boy appeared to be near tears. "He's in trouble, I just know he is."

Preuss looked around. The space was so messy it was difficult to tell if there had been a struggle. But Mark's Big Gulp cup was still upright, and the room didn't have the look of a fight.

He called Janey on his cell. "Where are you?"

"Looking around the basement."

"I'm going to give this floor another once-over, but it doesn't look like Mark's here. Let's meet outside in fifteen minutes."

He looked into every office and behind every door, but there were no signs of Mark Lewis.

Outside Kenny sat in his Explorer while he walked the perimeter of the building. He called Dispatch to send patrol officers to search the area. If anybody saw Mark Lewis leave the building, he wanted to know about it.

Preuss, Cahill, Kenny, and René sat around the dining room table in the Lewis home.

"Why don't you give his number another try," Cahill suggested to René, who punched in the numbers on her own phone. She put it on speaker so they all heard Mark's line ringing, and then Mark's recorded voice.

"Hello? Just kidding . . . I'm not here. Leave a message and I'll call you back."

At the sound of the tone, René said, "Mark, honey, it's me again. Call me as soon as you get this, okay? We love you, sweetie. Please let us hear from you. We're worried."

She disconnected the call and shook her head.

"Do you know how to access your cell phone records?" Preuss asked.

"No, I always wait till the bill comes."

"Let's go online and get his calls and texts for the current cycle," he said. "We can see who he's been in touch with."

She asked Kenny to bring her tablet and went to their Verizon billing pages. The screen showed the numbers for all the calls, text messages, and data for the current period for Mark's line. Several of the numbers were calls and texts Mark made and received earlier that day, including several calls to and from a number with a 517 area code.

"Recognize this one?" Preuss asked René.

"No."

"Kenny?"

Kenny shook his head.

Preuss called it. A message said, "Hi, it's Shay. Leave a message and I'll call you back."

He disconnected. "Either of you know a young woman named Shay?"

René and Kenny both said no.

"I think I do," Preuss said. He found the number for Mr. Sal's and called it. It rang ten times before Danny Green answered.

"Hey, detective," Danny said. "Forget something?"

"Danny, did Shay ever come in?"

"No, man, she never showed. Never even called. I called her. I told her she was fired. If she's not gonna be reliable, I can't use her."

"What did she say? Did you talk to her?"

"I never got her. I left a message. She never called back. I couldn't get anybody else to come in, and now I have to wait tables on top of tending bar. I had a bad feeling about her but Sal wanted her, so . . . ."

I'm starting to share that feeling, Preuss thought.

"Is this her number?" Preuss read off the phone number from the Lewis's phone bill.

"That's it," Danny said. "Shay Kelley."

"If you give me her address," Preuss said, "I'll get out of your hair."

When he disconnected, Preuss called the station and asked Paul Horvath to send him Shay Kelley's DMV photo. In a few minutes his phone chimed with a text and he opened to see a photo of a striking redhead with ghostly pale skin and eyes so blue they seemed to disappear.

It was the barmaid at Mr. Sal's who was talking with Matt and his buddy on Sunday night when Leon Banks was killed at the Cake Walk. The woman Matt Lewis spent so much time going to see at Sal's.

But what was she doing in contact with his son?

"Is he in there?"

"Yeah," Cahill said, "I can see him in the back."

Preuss accelerated around the corner and left the Explorer in a No Parking zone with his Ferndale Police Department Business sign on the dash. He pounded on the locked back door until Matt Lewis opened it. Preuss brushed by him with Cahill in his wake.

In the store room where it all started, Preuss turned and said, "Tell us about Shay Kelley."

Lewis stood stunned, as though Preuss slapped him.

"Don't even bother, Matt. Just tell us what's going on here."

"What's going on? I don't understand.

"Start with who she is."

"She's—she's a waitress at Sal's."

"And what else do you know about her? What's she to you?"

"Nothing," Matt said. "What's this—"

Preuss slammed his flat hand down on the metal top of the work table. The sound was sharp as a gunshot in the low-ceilinged room. "We don't have time for this. What's she to you?"

"Okay," Matt said. He took a step away from Preuss's anger. "When I go to Sal's, if she's there we shoot the breeze. We've gotten friendly, that's all."

The dark look on Preuss's face showed he wasn't satisfied, so Matt amended it to, "Okay, we've seen each other a few times."

"Outside the bar?"

"Yes."

"So what does that mean?"

Before Matt Lewis could answer, Preuss's phone rang. He checked the caller ID and handed the phone to Cahill. "Can you take this? It's Ed." She turned away to take the call.

"Are you having an affair with her?" Preuss demanded.

"No! We're just friends."

"I don't care if you are. All I'm interested in right now is how she knows your son."

"She doesn't know Mark. I've told her about my children, but that's all."

"Then why is he getting phone calls and texts from her?"

"What are you talking about?"

"There are a dozen calls and texts to and from Shay Kelley on Mark's cell phone."

Matt sputtered as he tried to comprehend what Preuss was telling him.

"That's impossible," he finally got out. "Mark doesn't know Shay. Why would she call him?"

"Where's your phone?"

When he didn't seem able to process the question, Preuss got into his face and shouted, "Where's your phone!"

He pulled it from his pocket and showed it to Preuss.

"Call her."

"What—?"

"Call her and ask her where your son is."

"I'm not going to—"

Preuss put a hand on Lewis's shoulder and pulled him close.

"Call her on your cell phone and ask her where your son is. I'm getting tired of you, Matt. Your son could be in trouble and you don't seem to understand that."

Cahill insinuated herself between the two men and pushed Matt Lewis backwards.

"Martin," she said, "take it easy."

"All right," Matt said, "I'll call her."

He took a step back from Preuss and punched in a number.

"It's going to voicemail," he told them. After another moment he said, "Shay, hi, it's me. Listen—"

Preuss missed the rest of what Matt Lewis said because he was already rushing out the back door.

"What did Ed want?" Preuss said back in the Explorer.

"He found somebody who thinks he saw Mark."

"When?"

"Couple hours before we got over there. You okay?"

Preuss wheeled the SUV around the parking lot behind the bakery just to be doing something. He pulled over on the side street and took a breath.

Without answering her he called Blair's cell. "Hey," he said, "what do you have?"

"I talked with this guy who works across the street from the building," Ed Blair said. "Plumbing contractor. Said he was loading his truck and happened to look up to see a boy he thinks was Mark. He was sitting in a car waiting for the light to change at the corner."

"Please tell me he saw who the kid was with."

"He said the driver was a girl. She was the one who caught his eye, then he looked at the passenger to see what kind of guy was with a babe like her."

"He give a description?"

"All he said was, she was a redhead. And a fox."

"Where are you now?"

"Still over behind the building on Nine."

"We think he's with a woman named Shay Kelley. I'm going to text you her DMV photo. See if this guy recognizes her."

"Okay."

"Did he notice the car they were in?"

"Just said it was an older model, maybe gray. Wasn't concentrating on the ride. Or the direction they went. He turned away to finish loading the van because he was late for his run and when he looked up again they were gone. He's back so I'll show him the photo and see what he says."

29

Shay Kelley lived in the massive red brick apartment building that took up the entire corner of Planavon and Breckenridge in Ferndale. Preuss leaned on the buzzer beside the hand-lettered slip of paper with her last name on it but got no response.

At the bottom of the list was a button that said *Manager* in a thin shaky script. He pressed the buzzer and in another minute he heard through the intercom the sound of a phone being taken off the hook. A woman's voice said, "Yes?" The voice sounded old and strained.

"Is this the apartment manager?"

"Yes?"

"Ferndale Police. Could you come to the door, please?"

Shortly a woman in her sixties trudged down the lower hall inside and loomed behind the glass door of the building's entrance. She wore a floral dress and had highly permed gray hair and the lined, desiccated face of a long-time drinker who hardly ever saw the sun. In one arm she carried an aging miniature poodle, with hair as curly as its mistress's and dark tracks flowing from rheumy eyes. She held the dog with its paws folded primly over her beefy arm.

Preuss held his shield up to the glass.

She opened the door and he introduced himself and Cahill.

"And you are?" he asked.

Her free hand went to her hair automatically to pat it down and Preuss realized it was a wig. "Shirley Orlechowski." Her voice was soft with an unobtrusive Southern accent.

"We're here about one of your tenants. Could we step inside?"

She stepped aside and allowed the two detectives to enter the building.

"We're looking for Shay Kelley," he said. "We're trying to find a boy who went missing from his home this morning and he might be with Shay. We can get a warrant to search her premises, but it would be faster if you would agree to let us in."

"But I think she's at work," the woman said.

"No, she's not. We just checked with her employer. She didn't go in today."

As she thought about his request, which she was clearly not happy about, Janey Cahill said, "A boy's safety may be at stake. We're fighting the clock here, ma'am."

"Oh," the woman said again, and sighed. Preuss caught the unmistakeable odor of gin wafting his way.

"He's just fifteen," Preuss said. "He's part of a larger police investigation, and we're concerned he's in danger."

Cahill pulled the photo of Mark from her purse. "This is him. Have you seen him around?"

Shirley Orlechowski held the photograph very close to her face. "No." She looked down at her dog as if she were going to ask it but handed the photo back.

"Could we see her apartment?"

She thought again.

"I guess it would be all right," she said at last.

She led them up the stairway to apartment 302. She paused to catch her breath, then rapped on the door. "Miss Kelley? It's Miss Orlechowski. Are you there, Miss Kelley?"

When there was no response, and no sound from the apartment, she said, "You'll have to wait here till I get my key."

"Thank you, ma'am," Preuss said.

She returned to the stairs and slowly made her way down.

"Look at Joe Friday over here," Janey Cahill said. "'Yes, ma'am,'" she intoned in a deep voice, imitating Jack Webb's flat delivery from *Dragnet*. "'Police investigation, ma'am. Time is of the essence, ma'am. Just the facts, ma'am.'"

"Sometimes you need to play on their stereotypes of the po-pos. How are you even old enough to remember *Dragnet*?"

"I'm old enough to remember we should have a warrant for this," she said.

"Fresh pursuit. I'm getting more nervous about this boy by the second."

In a few minutes the landlady came huffing and puffing down the hall.

"I'm really not comfortable doing this," she said. She tried to negotiate the key into the top lock on the door to 302 while balancing the dog. It was a deadbolt lock; there was also a lock in the handle. She smelled more strongly of alcohol, as if she just took another quick hit of hooch to steady her nerves. "My tenants count on me to respect their privacy."

"I know they do, Shirley," Cahill said. She reached out and laid a gentle hand on the woman's arm. Her own life bordered on chaos constantly, Preuss thought, but Janey Cahill had a way of coming across as the caring, sympathetic woman she was at heart.

"Under the landlord laws of the State of Michigan," she said, "you have the right to enter a tenant's apartment in the event of an emergency situation where safety might be an issue. And a boy's safety is at stake here."

"And you think Miss Kelley knows something?"

"We're certain she does."

She fit the key into the upper lock and turned it to undo the deadbolt. Then she got the key into the lock in the door handle and turned it. She pushed the door open and stood back as Cahill motioned her away from the door. The two detectives entered the apartment, Cahill with her hand on the weapon in her belt holster.

From the look on her face, Shirley Orlechowski seemed to realize just then this was not television but a very dangerous episode of real life.

She and her pet backed away down the hallway.

30

The front door opened into a wide blank wall. To the right was a closet, and around to the left of the wall was a combined living and dining area. A doorway opening to the right led into a small kitchen, and an archway to the left off the living room led back to the bedroom on the left and a minuscule bathroom on the right. The wall at the end of the living room was mirrored, which enlarged the sense of the size of the room, and gave Preuss and Cahill's reflections back to them as they stood poised to do a closer examination.

A pile of blankets was bunched up on the end of the sofa and a bed pillow was on the floor.

"Houseguest," Preuss said.

Next to the sofa was a duffel containing men's clothing. It was what a young man would wear, workout pants and plaid shirts, tee shirts for rock bands, wrinkled hoodies and Levis.

He lifted a ragged tee shirt with a Metallica Pushed Boris skull and held it to his chest. "Does this look like something Mark Lewis would wear?"

"No," Cahill said. "It's huge. He's a slight kid."

"All the clothes are like this. They're for a much bigger guy than either Mark or Matt."

He replaced the tee shirt in the duffel and continued looking around. The kitchen cupboards held simple food for cooking and eating quickly, soup and macaroni and cheese and cans of tuna. The refrigerator was empty except for a carton of eggs and a container of orange juice. There were no personal items, no photographs or mementoes of trips or friends and family anywhere.

He remembered Reg Trombley talking about the state of Leon Banks's apartment, like this one more a transient residence than a home. Like Eddie Watkins's unit, this belonged to someone who was just passing through on her way to someplace else.

"Martin, in here."

He followed Cahill's voice to the bedroom, where she had laid out an array of receipts and tickets on the bureau.

"Look at these," she said. Most of the receipts were from local restaurants, though a few were from Florida dated the previous fall in the name of Siobhan Kelley.

"I'll call Reggie," she said, "see what he can find out about her."

"Also ask him to run Shay Kelley and Siobhan Kelley through the state CIS and also OTIS."

While she was on the phone with Trombley, he went through the receipts.

She disconnected. "He's going to do it now. See, he's not so bad."

"I never said he was bad. What I said was, I don't trust his loyalties anymore. Look, men's clothes in the closets, there must be a man in her life besides Matt. Do you see any receipts here with men's names?"

"No, but there's a business card with a Florida address."

She handed it to him. It was a card for a Sears store on PGA Boulevard in Palm Beach Gardens. The name on the card was Leo Steinberg, a sales rep in Appliances.

He punched in the numbers on his cell. It went to the main store line, then he followed the directions to reach Appliances. After seven or eight rings the phone was answered by a man with a heavy Spanish accent. Preuss asked to speak with Leo Steinberg.

"Leo is not working today. Can I help you with something?"

"No, thanks," Preuss said. "I'll try back. Will he be in tomorrow?"

"I think so. You can try."

Preuss ended the call and laid the card on the bureau.

She gathered up the receipts and miscellaneous papers and put them back in the pile where she found them.

They took a final walk through the small apartment. "I don't see anything helpful here, do you?" he asked.

She shook her head. "No trace of Mark, anyway."

"I think a little chat with Shirley might be in order."

31

Shirley Orlechowski appeared relieved to see them exit the apartment without carrying anything away.

"You can lock up now," Preuss said. "Thanks."

She hurried forward and pulled the door closed and locked the upper lock. She stood back as though trying to separate herself from the entire episode.

"Did Shay sign a lease? Or fill out an application?"

"Both."

"Could we take a look at them?" Preuss asked in what passed for his most charming voice.

As they followed Shirley to her apartment, Cahill's look told him all he needed to know about what she thought of his charm.

"Does she live here by herself?" Cahill asked while Preuss looked over the rental application in Shirley Orlechowski's apartment. The place had the same layout as Shay's, though it was as neat and old-lady fussy as the young woman's was impersonal, with doilies and antimacassars covering every horizontal surface. In a corner of the living room stood the file cabinet that held Shay's folder.

"Yes," the manager said.

"Does she ever have any male visitors?"

"Well, my apartment's on the first floor, so I wouldn't know unless somebody complained about her."

"And nobody has?"

"No, she's a model tenant."

"But have you ever seen her with any men? If you ever bumped into her in the hall, or even just going in and out of the building?"

She shook her head. Not a hair on her curly wig wavered.

"This application is dated December of last year," Preuss said. "That's when she moved in?"

"Yes."

"Her references are all in the 517 area code, central Michigan. Is that where she's from?"

"Yes, though I can't remember where."

The line for previous residence was blank, but there were a few names put down as references, all from a restaurant chain in Jackson.

"Did you call her references?"

"No. She seemed like such a nice young woman. And the numbers were all long distance calls. I thought I'd just take a chance on her. Was that wrong?" She looked to Cahill.

"You did what you thought was best," Cahill said.

"Ann-Marie Nicastro," Preuss said. "She's listed here under Recommended By. You know her?"

"She lived in the apartment before Miss Kelley. Nice girl. Miss Kelley showed up one day and said Miss Nicastro told her the apartment would be open because she was getting married."

"Do you have a forwarding address for her?"

"I always get one so I can send their security deposit to them. Would you like it?"

"Yes please."

Still holding her dog, Shirley Orlechowski looked through her file cabinet for the information.

"Poor girl," Shirley said. "Miss Kelley, I mean. I felt so sorry for her. She moved here all by herself without a job. She said she needed a place to stay right away."

"Did she say why she came?" Preuss asked.

"Told me she was moving to get a fresh start. I didn't ask, though I assumed it was a man problem."

"Why?"

She looked to Cahill again, this time not for validation but to enlist her into a compact of female solidarity. "Anytime a woman needs a fresh start," Shirley said, "it's usually because of some damn man."

"Shirley, honey," Janey Cahill said, "you told the truth about that."

"Siobhan Kelley," Reg Trombley said, "born two fourteen eighty-six at Allegiance Hospital in Jackson. She has a driver's license registered in that name."

He sat with Preuss and Janey Cahill at the small conference table in Preuss's office at the Shanahan complex.

He passed around a copy of the driver's license photo Paul Horvath sent to Preuss.

"Clean record except for some minor traffic violations," Trombley continued. "In the Michigan SOS database there's a vehicle registration for a 2002 Toyota Camry in the name of Siobhan Kelley Kulhanek, residence in Jackson, Michigan."

"Kulhanek," Preuss said. "Husband? Good work," Preuss said. "Let's get a bulletin out on her. You didn't find anything connecting her with the Lewises beyond her relationship with Matt?"

"Nothing so far."

"And nothing connecting her to Eddie Watkins, either?"

"No."

"He was starting to emerge as the focus of the investigation," Preuss said. "Till he got killed and Mark ran off."

"If Mark is on the run because he's scared whoever killed Banks and Watkins is after him," Trombley said, "that still doesn't mean Watkins wasn't involved."

"True. But he was starting to look like somebody with a reason to stick up the place."

"He still might have."

"All the more urgency to find Mark," Cahill said.

"Let's ping their cell phones," Preuss said. "Also let's get Shay's phone records, all incoming and outgoing calls and texts. Can you work on that?" he asked Trombley.

"Sure. The parents gave permission for the boy's phone?"

"Correct. We'll have to find out who Shay's carrier is and work through a court order. Exigent circumstances."

"Might take a few days," Trombley said. "I'll get started. We got a couple hits from the CHR, guys with scars and dreads. Do you want me to run those down, too?"

"I do. Send me pics and I'll run them by Mark once we find him. Biederman's crew find anything useful in Banks's apartment?"

"Nothing worth mentioning. No prints besides his own. Guy's turning out to be a real cipher."

32

Ann-Marie Nicastro lived on the top floor of a two-family brick house on Cambourne between Woodard and Livernois in Ferndale, not far from where Shay Kelley lived. And close by the street where Madison Kaufman's mother lived. Preuss heard her husband Stanley was still in jail but she filed for divorce.

He hoped the Lewises weren't headed toward the same end. How much did René know about Matt's escapades? As always, it was impossible to tell what went on inside other people's marriages.

In a neighborhood of single-family homes, this block was unusual for all the two-families. Preuss parked at the curb and rang the top bell of a two-story arts-and-crafts style house, the kind called four-square for its even right angles. The bottom flat had a concrete pad for a porch but the top floor porch was open with a wrought-iron railing.

He rang the bell again and heard someone yell, "Who is it?"

Preuss stepped back and looked up to see a bare-chested young man leaning over the top railing. He was hugging himself against the nip of the day.

"Whaddaya want?" the young man said.

"I'm looking for Ann-Marie."

"Whaddaya want with her?"

Preuss held his shield up for the young man to see. "How about I come up and we talk about it?"

He was a tall man in his twenties, taller than Preuss and skinny though he was starting to thicken through his waist. He had a long nose and rubbery mouth, with hair cropped almost to the skin of his head. Except for the piercings on his nipples, he looked remarkably like Neidermeyer in *Animal House.*

The living room of the flat was plain, with two gray overstuffed love seats taking up most of the space. Preuss perched on the edge of one of them and the young man sprawled all the way back in the other. The room was so stuffy and warm it gave Preuss a momentary wave of dizziness. No wonder the guy was shirtless.

"So you're looking for Ann-Marie?"

"She around?"

"No, she's working a double shift today. She won't be home till tonight."

"What does she do?"

"She's an ER nurse at Providence."

"And what's your connection to her?"

"Husband. Vince Mullen."

He leaned forward with a hand outstretched.

Preuss shook it and said, "Do you know a woman named Shay Kelley? Or Siobhan Kelley? She's living in Ann-Marie's old apartment."

"Annie-Marie knows her. She met her at Sal's. Shay took care of us and the girls stared chatting and hit it off. We've seen her a couple times since then. Though after Ann-Marie went on nights we stopped hanging out at Sal's and lost touch with her. Pretty sure Ann-Marie hasn't seen her either."

"So you wouldn't know where I could find her?"

"She's not at the apartment? She took it over when Ann-Marie left to move in here."

"No."

"Did you try her husband?"

"That would be someone named Kulhanek?"

"Yeah. Though maybe he's her ex-husband, now that I think about it. From the way she talked about him, it seems like they're not together anymore. He seemed pretty controlling so he might have some idea where she is."

"Controlling how?"

"You know, always wants to know where she is and what she's doing. She told us he used to beat the crap out of her. She wound up in the hospital once with a broken jaw and he went to jail for like ten minutes for it. Anyway, he seems like a kind of freaky dude."

"Do you know his first name?"

"I think it's something like Dave. Or Dan. Or Don. Something with a D. Maybe Dick?" He shrugged a skinny shoulder. "Can't remember, sorry. I think she said he lives around Jackson."

Preuss made a note of the information.

"The way she talked about him, Ann-Marie and I could never figure out why she stayed with him as long as she did. Ann-Marie said she thought maybe Shay got off on it, you know? Like she hated it and loved it at the same time."

He scratched absently at his scrawny bare chest and Preuss waited for him to say something more.

But all he said was, "Like I alway say, whatever floats your boat."

He couldn't get Vince Mullen's inane phrase out of his head as he gazed at the helm clock on his desk, the one his son Jason gave him when he was promoted to detective. Preuss didn't know anything about sailing, but for some reason Jason thought he would enjoy the clock. Now every time he looked at it he was reminded of his son, wandering, out of touch and angry, somewhere in the country without any guiding helm of his own.

Nine p.m. already. No wonder he was so beat.

He sat for another hour, adding notes to the case file and then rereading it from beginning to end. When he got up to the information about Shay's possibly ex-husband, he paused.

Had she moved down to Ferndale to get away from him, as the apartment manager suggested? Or was he the one who was staying in her apartment?

Another mystery added to the growing list.

He sent an email to Reg Trombley:

*Reg, please confirm the whereabouts of Siobhan Kelley's current
or former husband, last name Kulhanek, first name possibly
starting with D: David, Daniel, Donald etc., residence possibly
the one on Siobhan's registration. Also check for a domestic
charge filed by Siobhan Kelley with a jail stay. ASAP, please.*
Thanks,
Martin

Everything about this case was infuriatingly vague . . . they
didn't know who the principles were, they didn't know how they
were related to each other, they didn't know where they lived, and
most importantly they didn't know where to find them.

The indisputable realities were that two men were dead, and
Mark Lewis and Siobhan Kelley both disappeared at exactly the
same time. It was reasonable to assume the deaths were connected,
and that Mark and Siobhan were together, whatever their relationship might be . . . but even if he found them, would he be any closer
to knowing who killed Leon Banks and Eddie Watkins?

Maybe not, but it would keep Mark safe. Mark was always key
to understanding the events at the bakery, and with Eddie Watkins
dead it was even more important that they find him.

He closed up his office and trudged outside, where he sat in
the Explorer in the parking lot, too tired even to lift his arms to turn
on the ignition. He watched the traffic on Nine Mile, which was
hopping with a constant flow of traffic and the occasional drunken
shout. It was Thursday, the unofficial start to the weekend and a
busy night for the bars and restaurants in town. Ferndale evolved
into a hot night spot destination over the past ten years—to the great
dismay of some older residents.

He let his head fall back against the seat and closed his eyes,
exhausted but willing himself not to fall asleep. Just as he was starting to nod off he heard a woman's voice shout, "Hi, neighbor!"

He opened his eyes and looked around. There was no one in
the vicinity, but the shout combined with his dozing brain to make
him remember they didn't have an important bit of information.

He thought Ed Blair would still be awake. Blair's wife's cancer had recurred and they were bracing for another round of surgery and chemo so Blair was too tightly wound to sleep lately.

He punched in the number on his cell. As he suspected, Blair was still up and answered immediately. Preuss asked him to find out where Shay Kelley lived before she moved into the apartment on Planavon.

"Check with the motels around the area," he suggested. "It would have been sometime before the end of last year, November or December." He reasoned Shay would have moved into the area before she started work at Mr. Sal's and taken over Ann-Marie's apartment. If she took a motel room, she might have gone back to it with Mark.

"Will do. I'll get started now."

"You could wait till the morning."

"Not sleeping anyway. I might as well be useful."

"Al right. Give my love to Debby."

"You bet."

"Stay strong," Preuss added.

"Trying as hard as I can."

Friday, April 17, 2009

33

"Here's the forensics report for the bakery scene."

Tanya Corcoran handed him an envelope. "Arnie just dropped it off. Said he also loaded a copy in the case file online. The tox screens won't be available for another month, as you know."

"Thanks."

Preuss took the envelope from her and put it under his arm. He was feeling good; he had just stopped by Toby's house in time to see him loaded onto the bus for his school, happy and smiling and enjoying being alive.

As soon as the bus aide got him locked down in the school van, Preuss climbed in and gave his son a continental kiss on both cheeks. Toby's head swiveled on his neck as he followed Preuss's face swinging from one side to another.

Tanya held out another manila envelope. "Something else," she said. "From Nick. I need you to sign a delivery receipt." She handed him a form that confirmed he received the enclosed material.

There goes my mood, he thought.

"A receipt, seriously? What is it?"

"Martin, please. Just sign."

He scrawled his name on the appropriate line. "Why do we have to do this?"

"You mistake me for someone who's in charge. I do what I'm told."

"Nick told you I need to sign for this?"

The instant he said it, William Warnock appeared behind him. "Detective," he said. "Busy?"

Without waiting for a reply, he said, "Come with me."

It was not a request.

Warnock led the way through the building and out the front door. They crossed Nine Mile at the zebra crosswalk leading to the 43rd District Court and strolled west toward Woodward. Neither man spoke. Preuss still carried the two folders Tanya gave him.

Warnock turned into the coffee bar on the ground floor of a new loft complex on Nine Mile at the corner of Bermuda, across the street from the library. It was sleek and shiny and very much an attempt at continental elegance. How things were changing in Ferndale, Preuss thought.

"What'll you have?" Warnock asked him. "My treat."

As they stood in a short line, Preuss examined the menu, which was a lot more multilingual than it needed to be for a place where you bought a cup of coffee.

Warnock ordered a caramel macchiato latte and turned to Preuss.

"Same for me," Preuss said. "Make mine nonfat."

"A nonfat caramel macchiato? Why bother?"

But Warnock ordered it for him, and as the young tattooed barista began the fixings for it, Preuss said, "Since when do you go for the fancy stuff? I thought you were a tea kinda guy."

"Usually. My daughter got me hooked on this."

"You know there's like 800 calories in it?"

"What can I say? I love it. Besides, I don't do it every day. Are you hungry? They have sandwiches, muffins. Pick something."

"Are you going to have anything?"

"No, the latte will do me for now. But get what you want."

"I'm good."

They took their drinks to a corner table in the narrow shop. There was nowhere to go to get privacy as they huddled around the table with their backs to the room.

Warnock took a sip and smacked his lips in glowing satisfaction. "Whoever invented this drink deserves a Nobel prize."

Preuss tried his but it was way too sweet. He warmed his hands around the paper container and waited.

"How's your boy?" Warnock asked.

"Doing well. They're putting on a spring pageant at his school, so he's in the middle of getting ready for it. He's playing a flower. They're going to dress him up in this amazing costume with a big daisy hat."

"I bet he loves it."

"He does."

"Though as I recall, he pretty much loves everything."

"He does indeed."

"Lot to learn from that child."

"I'm trying."

After a pause, Warnock asked, "How's the case coming?"

"Developing complications."

He caught Warnock up on the latest, and how he was managing the department's scant resources.

"Sounds like things are under control."

"Except for the part about my wandering witness. That's worrying me." He explained about Mark's disappearance.

Warnock took a deep breath, let it out, and gazed morosely at Preuss. He pointed the top of his head toward one of the folders on the cramped table.

"You know what's in there?"

"One of them is Biederman's report."

"The other one."

"No idea."

"They're the latest charges Nick Russo filed on you."

"Ah, the other shoe."

"He's written up an extensive report of your many failings."

"Such as?"

"Incompetence in investigating the bakery killing. Misuse of department resources. Dereliction of duty in keeping your superiors informed. Disregard of department regulations. Just a few of the highlights."

Preuss opened the envelope he signed for. Sure enough, it was a copy of a disciplinary report.

"Dereliction of duty? Is that even a thing?"

"It's a thing, all right. Your lieutenant's been camped out in my office every morning this week complaining about how you're mishandling the investigation. When he figured out I wasn't going to do anything about it, he filed those. He wants you relieved and disciplined."

"Just like last time."

"Except now he wants you gone from the force. And Martin, he's got somebody in your squad feeding him his information."

"There's a snitch in my squad?"

"Evidently."

"I tried to talk with him but he said he didn't have time to see me. Why doesn't he just read my case report? It's in the folder online. I update it every day, all he has to do is read it."

"He's not so much interested in what you're doing as what you're not doing."

"I don't follow."

"Apparently he feels like you're taking the case in the wrong direction."

"Trying to find out who killed two men is the wrong direction?"

"There are a few theories of the crime Russo thinks you're not pursuing, based on what he's hearing."

"Since when are you involved at this level of the investigations?"

"I'm seeing this as a personal issue between two of my senior officers." The hotter Preuss grew, the calmer and more zen-like Warnock became. "It was one thing when he was coming to my office and blowing off steam. I could put him off. But now the papers are filed, the complaint is in the system, and the process has to work itself out. I pulled strings for you last time, I can't interfere again."

As Preuss thought for a moment, Warnock took another sip of his drink and smacked his lips. Glad one of us is enjoying this, Preuss thought.

Then he caught himself. Warnock was on his side.

"So what's the next step?" he asked.

"The first step has to be that you wrap this up soon. Once the case is closed, these charges lose most of their substance."

"I'm trying, Bill. You don't think I'm trying?"

"I know. You're entitled to union representation, and you're also entitled to legal counsel. Both of which I recommend. Here's where the timing is a bit elastic. The agreement gives you thirty days to get counsel lined up. Because you're in the middle of a murder inquiry, nobody expects you to drop everything and find a lawyer. But you have to make the appearance of taking this seriously. You also have the right to answer these charges in writing, if you chose, so you can buy yourself some time there, too."

They sat for another few moments in silence.

Then Preuss said, "I can answer them all right. But within the space of six months I have two complaints filed against me. It doesn't look good even if this bullshit"—he picked up the folder with Russo's papers and dropped it contemptuously—"is thrown out like the last one."

"The last one wasn't thrown out. You had a reprimand inserted in your file. But if you solve the murder, it's likely most of this will be dismissed. But you can't count on it."

Warnock scratched at his lips with a paper napkin. "I also want to let you know you need to settle this vendetta with him. You don't clear this up, he's going to bring you up on charges every chance he gets. And there isn't much I'm going to be able to do for you."

"There's no way to rein him in?"

"I've tried."

"What if I file harassment charges against him?"

"It'll be seen as a reprisal. It'll make you look worse."

"You and I both know I'm doing exactly the right thing and the members of my unit will swear to it."

"Not all of them," Warnock said. "The other thing you need to do is find out who's working against you."

Preuss took a long hot drink from his cardboard cup. "I think I already know the answer to that one."

Preuss headed straight for Trombley's cubicle, but the young detective was nowhere in sight. It was just as well . . . Preuss would almost certainly say or do something he would regret.

Tanya Corcoran said Trombley came in but rushed out on a call to an armed robbery at the Convenience Market on Woodward. Preuss returned to Trombley's cubicle and scrawled *What are you up to?* on a Post-It Note and stuck it right in the middle of Trombley's computer screen.

For a moment he felt about Trombley the way Russo felt about him.

That stopped him. He forced himself to calm down.

He removed the Post-It and crumpled it into his pocket. He replaced it with another on which he wrote, *We need to talk. See me. MP.*

Back in his office he saw Trombley sent him a terse email response to his request. He found Siobhan Kelley's ex-husband; the man's name was Brian Kulhanek, with the same address in Jackson as the one on Siobhan's registration. When Trombley ran his name he discovered multiple convictions for assaults, including one on Siobhan.

He tried Janey Cahill on her cell, but the call went to voicemail.

Still annoyed after talking with Warnock, he gave in to the urge to get as far away from Ferndale as he could.

34

Preuss set his GPS for Brian Kulhanek's address in Jackson, a mid-sized city in the center of Michigan about eighty miles from Ferndale. An hour and a half later he pulled up in front of a house on North Walker.

He was considerably calmer than when he started out. Warnock was right, of course . . . this had to work its way through the system now, and once it did Preuss knew he would be cleared.

And regardless of what the chief counseled, he was going to file a harassment charge against Russo once the case was over.

The down-at-the-heels neighborhood just outside Jackson's downtown area was filled with dilapidated houses like Brian Kulhanek's, a sad one-story home wrapped in dingy vinyl siding that might have been new when Carter was in the White House.

He stood on the front stoop and rang the bell. Curtains behind the window in the door parted and an old face appeared, wrinkled as a dried apple and gazing at him through the glass with a combination of fear and disgust.

He held his shield up. "Police. Open the door, please."

"What?"

"I'm a police detective. I'm looking for Brian Kulhanek. Does he live here?"

She shook her head violently. "No here."

"Does he live here?"

"Yah, but he no here."

"Do you know where he is?"

"Vork."

"Excuse me?"

"Vork! He at vork!"

"Can you open the door please, ma'am? I need to speak with you."

She shook her head. "He not home."

"I get it. Would you open the door please?" He held his shield up again. "Police."

She stood back and let the curtain fall into place. He was about to knock again more forcefully when he heard locks being undone. The door opened a few inches on the safety chain. In the long slice of the opening her thin face loomed. She was almost two feet shorter than he was, stooped over in the black dress of the old country like a crone in a fairy tale.

"Are you related to Brian Kulhanek?"

She shook her head. "Branko mahdder. Branko."

"You're Branko's mother?"

"Yah, Branko."

Whoever the hell that was.

"But Brian Kulhanek lives here?"

"He *vork*," she said again, as if Preuss were the dense one. "I tell you true."

"I understand that, ma'am. But does he live here? That's what I'm trying to find out. Does Brian Kulhanek live here?"

"Police, yah?"

"Yes, police."

"Show badge."

He sighed and handed it over to her outreached hand. She examined it and gave it back with a puckered expression, as if she smelled something bad.

"Do you know Siobhan Kelley? Brian's ex-wife?"

"You talk Brian. He not here. He vork," she said, and brought her hands together and separated them quickly, in the universal gesture for gone.

"What time does he get home?"

She held up five fingers.

"Five o'clock? I'll come back then. You tell him, okay?"

She shrugged.

"Sorry I bother you. I come back," he said, and realized he was starting to speak the same kind of broken English she used.

Without another word she closed the door in his face and went through an elaborate routine of relocking it.

Still smiling, Brian Kulhanek said, "That's me. How can I help?"

His voice was incongruously high for a man his size. He was massive, in his early twenties with a deep barrel chest in a Megadeath muscle shirt that showcased his hairy biceps ringed with Maori armband tattoos.

He was smiling broadly when he stepped out of the red Firebird with another young man who was even taller than Kulhanek, all leg and shoulders and curly black hair. Now, as Preuss held up his shield, Kulhanek's smile was just as wide.

"I'm looking for Siobhan," Preuss said.

Kulhanek's smile never faded. "What's she done now?"

"Do you know where I can find her?"

"Sorry, I don't have any idea."

"When was the last time you saw her?"

"Tell you the truth, it's been a while, I know that." He turned to his friend. "Can you remember the last time we saw Shay?"

The other man, who was hanging back, now stepped forward.

"A couple of months ago, wasn't it?"

"I'm sorry," Preuss said, "you are?"

"Branko Nikolov. I work with Brian." He reached out a large flat hand that Preuss shook.

"The older woman in the house is your mother?"

"Yes."

"So was that the last time you saw Shay?" Preuss asked Kulhanek. "A couple of months ago? Not since then?"

"Yeah," Kulhanek said, "I guess it was."

"And you haven't seen her since?"

"Correct."

"Have you heard from her?"

"No sir."

"So you don't know where she is right now?"

"Sorry, no idea. Can I ask what this is about?"

"I need to speak with her about an investigation. It's pretty urgent."

"Have you talked to her mother?" Branko Nikolov asked. "She might know."

"No. I didn't know she had one."

"Everybody has a mother," the tall man said with a smile.

Preuss turned his attention back to Kulhanek. "Do you know her mother?"

"Yeah. She's as crazy as her daughter."

"What's her name?"

"Roberta."

"Last name Kelley?"

"No, it's Shepherd."

"Do you know where I can find her?"

"She's in a nursing home. I don't know the name of it but it's someplace in northern Oakland County. Brandon Township, I think it is."

"Brian, where were you last Sunday night?"

"Easter Sunday? Right here. Watching TV with Branko and his mother."

To Branko, he said, "You'll vouch for that?"

"Sure. We spent a quiet night. Watched some DVDs."

"Both you and your mother live here?"

"Yes. Our home was foreclosed last year and we had to move out. Brian said we could stay with him as long as we wanted."

"Nice of him," Preuss said, looking at Kulhanek, who shrugged and waved off the compliment.

"Yeah, he's a good guy."

"Thanks, dude," Kulhanek said.

Sitting in the Explorer outside Brian Kulhanek's house, Preuss used his phone to search nursing homes in northern Oakland County. There was only one nursing home in Brandon Township. When he called, the receptionist told him a woman named Roberta Kelley was indeed one of their residents.

35

By the time he found the place, outside the village of Brandon Township, it was after the dinner hour. The charge nurse at the nurse's station directed him to room 264 on the skilled nursing unit.

How lucky Toby was to be in a group home and not an institutional setting, Preuss thought as he walked the hallway of the long-term care wing. The corridor was one spine radiating off the center nursing station at the North Oakland Rehabilitation and Care Center.

He and Jeanette spent many nights worrying what would happen to their boy once they were gone. They dreaded the thought of Toby abandoned in an institution, cared for by an endless stream of low-paid workers with no devotion to the residents beyond a paycheck.

They thought that would only be an issue in the dim, unimaginable future. Nobody seriously plans for what could happen with a drunk driver in the dark of a Michigan night.

A drunk driver who walked away from the crash that left Preuss's family shattered.

He walked past a glum aide filling a cart with dinner trays. On some trays the food was barely touched and on some the plates seemed licked clean. Tonight's meal was either a slice of mystery meat congealing in a muddy brown sauce, which most left untouched, or a spaghetti dish that seemed to be a bigger hit.

The door to 264 was open, the doorway blocked by an older woman sitting in her wheelchair. She looked up at him eagerly and asked, "Where do I go?"

Before he could answer, she repeated, "Where do I go?"

"Where would you like to go?"

"Where do I go?"

She searched his face, then finding no answer she barreled past him into the corridor. "Where do I go?" she asked the aide who was collecting trays.

The young dark-skinned woman in short tight braids looked like she barely knew where she should go herself. Without answering she turned and went into another room to collect more trays and the woman in the wheelchair took off down the hall.

The other woman in 264 lay in the bed by the window. Her relative youth surprised him. He guessed she would be in her late forties, younger than most of the other residents by several decades. She was long and cadaverously thin, with boney arms and large hands. Her auburn hair hung in lank strands around her face. Her gaunt face focused attention on her eyes, which were wide-set and as dark as huge bright buttons above a snub nose.

She watched the TV that hung on the wall. A plaster cast on her right arm ran from the wrist to the shoulder. A light blue thermal blanket was bunched at the foot of the bed. The thick tubing of a catheter snaked from under her gown to a urine collection bag hanging on the bedrail.

Preuss stepped further into the room. "Roberta Kelley?"

At the sound of his voice, she turned her head. It took a few seconds for those immense eyes to focus.

"Yes?" Her voice was weak and breathy, soft as the voice of a woman decades younger.

"Can I come in and have a word with you?"

She raised a languorous hand with slender fingers, elegant even in the slight gesture. They reminded him of Toby's except they weren't contracted.

He entered her half of the room and stood beside the bed. She smelled of baby powder and urine.

He introduced himself. "Can I impose on you for a few minutes with some questions?"

She muted the television and he pulled the visitor's chair up to the side of her bed. He closed the curtain separating her bed from her roommate's. It wasn't much privacy but it gave them the appearance of being alone.

"It's about Siobhan."

"My girl." A tired smile.

"I'm trying to get in touch with her but she seems to have disappeared. I'm wondering if you know where I can find her?"

She processed this with difficulty. "Disappeared? I don't understand."

"She hasn't shown up to work, she hasn't been to her apartment. Nobody seems to know where she is."

"Is she in trouble?"

"She may be with a boy who's a witness to a crime in Ferndale last week."

"A boy?"

"He's fifteen."

"What would Siobhan be doing with a fifteen-year-old boy?" She blinked a few times as though to see through this murky business more clearly. "I'm sorry, they just gave me my medicine, it makes me a little spacey."

"Do you have any idea where your daughter might be?"

"No, I haven't seen her for over a week. I thought she'd be here for Easter but she never came. I hope nothing happened to her. Did you check at Ronnie's?"

"Who's Ronnie?"

"Her brother. My son. She's been staying with him since his girlfriend took sick. The big C."

She tried to rearrange herself on the bed, getting the one free stick-thin arm under her to push herself up, but she couldn't get a purchase on the rumpled sheet.

"Let me help," Preuss said. He stood and released the side rail to get his hands under her armpits. "On three . . . one, two . . ." On three he gently boosted her up so she was resting higher on the pillow, which he fluffed up around her head.

She fumbled for the bed control. He found it for her and she raised the head of the bed. He lifted the side rail back in place.

"Better?"

"Thanks. You should get a job here. You're better'n the ones they got."

"Not so good?"

"Terrible. That's how I got this." She raised her casted arm.

"What happened there, if you don't mind my asking?"

"One day last month I had to use the toilet, and I rang and rang for help but nobody came. I'm wearing diapers but they were already full. When I couldn't hold it any more I gave up waiting and tried to get out of bed on my own. I wound up losing my balance and fell out of bed and broke my arm. Plus I shit all over myself anyway, and pulled the catheter out."

"Yikes."

"This was a better place, they'd have more aides and they'd take better care of us. But beggars can't be choosers."

She tried to pull the thermal blanket up but couldn't reach it. Preuss retrieved it and spread it over her.

"Thanks."

"So your son, does he live nearby?"

"Not far. In the town.

"Brandon, you mean?"

She nodded. "He won't be happy to see you, I'll tell you."

"Ronnie's had some run-ins with the law?" This was starting to get very interesting.

"Don't get me wrong, he's a good boy."

He's a good boy, judge.

"But he got into some trouble when he was young. He was slow, you know what I mean? The other kids wouldn't ever leave him alone. You know how cruel kids can be. He'd put up with it until he couldn't. He spent some time in the county boys' home. And he went to jail a few times for bar fights and things like that. I tried to keep him in check."

"When was the last time you saw him?"

She squinted, as though trying to see through the haze of her brain fog. "When Siobhan was here. They both came to see me at the same time."

She turned her head toward the window. It was pitch dark outside. All she would be able to see was her own reflection, and whatever her memory was bringing back to her.

"They'd do anything for me, my kids. I did my best, but what could I do, a single mother with MS? It's been rough, I won't lie," she said. "My mother died when I was a little girl and I was shuffled off to my aunt and uncle's."

"Sorry to hear it."

He flashed on Jeanette again, another mother dying and leaving behind grieving children. He imagined Jason saying much the same thing as this woman . . . my mother died when I was younger. And I had to stay with my father, who's a jerk.

"That's the breaks," she said. "You play the hand you're dealt."

"All we can do."

They were both silent.

Preuss said, "Roberta?"

But she had fallen asleep.

He tiptoed from the room, leaving her to what small portion of repose she could find in her troubled life.

Ronnie Kelley lived in the country outside Brandon Township, in an old farmhouse made of clapboard weathered gray by time and neglect.

Preuss stopped the Explorer in front of the house. A light burned behind curtains on the first floor, but otherwise all was dark.

He walked up to the covered porch. The doorbell was missing so he knocked. The woman who came to the door looked like someone out of a Depression-era photo by Dorothea Lange—bone-thin and hollow-eyed with a prominent clavicle ridge above her sweatshirt.

He showed her his shield. "I'm looking for Ronnie. Is he home?"

She shook her head sadly.

"Do you know where he is, Miss—?"

"Claire Smith. He's my fiancé."

In other words, Preuss thought, she's the unmarried mother of one or more of his children currently cohabiting with him.

One of those children peeked around her mother's legs. She looked to be around four. Her face was the miniature image of Claire's, with the same grave affect.

Claire cupped her hand around the girl's head. "This is Mary Grace."

"Hi, Mary Grace," Preuss said. The child disappeared behind her mother.

"Claire, do you know where Ronnie is?"

She shrugged a thin shoulder. "He said he was gonna stay with his sister down near Detroit, I don't know where exactly. I haven't heard from him in a couple days."

"How about Siobhan? Have you seen her?"

"No, not her either. You looking for her too?"

"Yes."

He showed the photo of Mark Lewis. "How about this young man, have you seen him?"

She shook her head.

Preuss gave her his card and asked her to call if she heard from either Ronnie or Shay, or better yet ask them to call. She said she would.

Standing at his car, he looked over the house one more time. Oakland County was one of the richest counties in the country but there were still pockets, like this, where the money didn't reach.

He noticed the curtains twitch over the front window and Mary Grace stuck her head up to the window.

As he watched, the little girl lifted a hand in a solemn and cheerless wave.

It sent a chill down his spine.

Saturday, April 18, 2009

36

Saturday dawned chilly and damp but by the time Preuss showered and dressed in his navy blue turtleneck and Levis, the rain stopped and the day promised to be unseasonably warm. He checked in with the Lewises, who still hadn't heard anything from Mark. He reached Janey Cahill at a cross-country meet with her two boys, but she didn't have any news either. Things were at a momentary standstill.

He stood at his kitchen counter drinking coffee and looking out at his sodden back yard. Maybe he really wasn't taking the investigation in the right direction, he thought. Maybe Russo was right and somebody else would have better luck running it.

As if that thought weren't depressing enough, he thought about the little girl from the night before and another wave of sadness swept over him for all the lost children . . . Mark, Siobhan, Ronnie . . . and Jason, Madison Kaufman, and all the rest . . .

At least one child wasn't lost. He roused himself to call Toby's house and asked the staff to get him ready to go out in two hours. He needed his Toby fix. Melissa, the aide he spoke with, told him she'd make sure he was up and dressed.

He went to the station first and caught up on the case reports Janey Cahill and Reg Trombley filed the night before. He could see who accessed the case file, and noted Nick Russo's name was conspicuously missing. Of course, Preuss thought, why let actual fact interfere with what you'd like to think?

Tanya Corcoran was in her office, putting in a few extra hours to compensate for time she wanted to take off later in the week. He handed her a list of names and asked her to print out DMV photos of everyone on the list.

He parked under the under the portico in the driveway of the group home and found Toby sitting up in his wheelchair in the living room, sound asleep. His second sleep, Preuss called it, because Toby usually woke early but then when he had his seizure medication he often fell back to sleep.

He gave the boy a loud, juicy kiss on the side of his face and Toby stirred, picked his head up while fluttering his eyelids, and then let his head roll back toward his chest, still asleep.

The characteristic movement made Preuss laugh. He delighted in this child. He would never make the honor roll, or even say his father's name, but every gesture, sound, and expression elicited the fiercest kind of love from Martin Preuss.

He settled Toby's Red Wings poncho over the boy's head and around the wheelchair, and loaded him, still asleep, into the Explorer. They headed toward the Big Boy on John R. By the time Preuss lifted him back into his wheelchair in the restaurant parking lot, Toby was awake and gazing around with those beautiful brown eyes. How much he was able to see was uncertain, but when he looked around like this he seemed to take everything in with an appreciation bordering on the reverential.

When they entered the clatter of the restaurant, Toby brought his right arm up, put the back of his wrist to his mouth and yelled with his deep foghorn voice.

My name is Toby Preuss, and I'm here! Let's get this party *started*!

His son was between feeds so Preuss didn't have to worry about hooking him up to his pump just yet, though the house nurse hung it on the back of the wheelchair loaded with his liquid food in the event they stayed out long enough for the boy to need another feeding. Preuss gorged on an unusually big brunch: a Western omelet, bacon, hash browns, orange juice, and endless cups of coffee. He was ravenous and on edge so he kept shoveling in the food.

They sat at a table at the rear of the restaurant, packed as usual on Saturday. Preuss rolled Toby up to the table in his wheelchair. Preuss gave him the red rings he liked to hold because they were exactly the right size for his tight hands.

As always when he was in the middle of an investigation, Preuss described what was happening for the boy. It gave him a way to put his thoughts in order about the events of the cases, and he assumed Toby understood everything so it gave them something to share. Though his son couldn't say what was in his mind, his every thought was visible on his face because he was unable to dissemble. Considering how most people lied to him throughout the day about almost everything, talking to Toby was unfailingly comforting.

When he got to the part about Mark Lewis disappearing, Toby said, "Ohhhh," and furrowed his brow. He gazed around the room slyly as if Mark might be hiding behind the breakfast buffet.

"I know," Preuss said. "On top of the two other killings, the main witness disappearing is very upsetting. I'm worried, too."

Preuss told him about his visit with Roberta Kelley, and how afterwards he swung by Ronnie's house.

He described what Roberta told him about all her hardships.

"Isn't it sad?" Preuss asked. "You know what it's like to lose your mother, don't you?"

"Mmmm."

"And you also know what it's like to not be able to walk."

"Humm."

"But you have your old dad here to take care of you. And I'll never leave you. I promise."

Toby gave him one of his crooked grins and with both hands brought his rings down approvingly on the table top.

They stayed out longer than he thought they would.

It turned into a gorgeous spring day with the temperature in the low 80s. Preuss decided to take advantage of the weather by going to the Madison Heights Nature Center off Thirteen Mile Road in Madison Heights, not far from the Big Boy.

The center was a small wooded area criss-crossed by walkways, with a cabin containing educational exhibits in the middle of the park. By the time they got there it was time for Toby's lunch, so Preuss started the pump for the formula feeding and pushed the boy around the park.

Whenever his son got chilly, as he did sometimes when they walked through an extended shaded area, they went into the cabin to warm up. Preuss wheeled him close up to each display and talked about what it showed . . . tanks of turtles and reptiles, exhibit of birds, explanations of native Michigan wildlife.

He let Toby feel the stuffed birds, opening the boy's contracted fingers and running them along the texture of the feathers and beaks and claws. After he felt it, his hands turned to fists again that worried his right ear.

"Gotta itchy ear?" Preuss asked. Preuss rubbed the delicate helix of each ear—elf ears, he called them, for their pointy tips— and kissed them. "Feel better?"

Preuss got him back home an hour late for his afternoon seizure meds. He told Toby and the staff he would return around seven to take him to the bar where he was performing in the evening with the Flynns, the band he sat in with. He hadn't played with them for a few weeks, and he promised the leader he would be there tonight.

The house staff said they would have Toby bathed and dressed and ready for a night on the town with his father. An aide always went along to stay with Toby while Preuss performed so it was a night out for whoever accompanied them, too.

After he kissed his son goodbye (noting the boy's forehead was a bit warm and sweaty, which he put down to his sitting in the car), he drove by Shay Kelley's apartment. When there was no response to Shirley Orlechowski's buzzer, he called her on his cell. She told him she hadn't heard a thing from Shay since the last time he talked with her.

"Any word?"

René Lewis looked up at Martin Preuss standing in her door-way, her face lit with hope and expectation.

"Unfortunately, no," he said. "But can I come in?"

"Sure. Want some coffee?"

"Great, thanks."

"Latte okay with you? I was just about to make myself one."

"Fine."

She left him in the living room. He heard the sound of water running and the small domestic clinking of coffee preparation. There were no other noises in the house except music playing softly from the kitchen. Joan Baez, singing "There But for Fortune" from one of her early albums. An old Phil Ochs song about the role of luck in our lives. Whether we wound up in prison, on or off the streets, on or off booze, some things were certainly up to random chance, he thought. Terribly bad luck brought Madison Kaufman into harm's way last year, for example, and a chance misalignment of cells was responsible for Toby's condition. So the blind chance of the universe was a powerful force.

But was everything random? Had chance sent a random thief to the back door of the Cake Walk? The closer he got to the heart of the matter, the less likely that seemed. Fortune may have operated in some other ways here, but the Cake Walk killing did not feel to Preuss like a random crime of opportunity.

René came back into the living room with a tray containing two mugs with perfectly formed layers of foam.

"Thanks." He took one of the mugs and, indicating the music, said, "Early Joan Baez. Nice."

She sat on the sofa across from his chair. "Yeah, I'm just an old hippy, what can I say."

"I'm sort of an old hippy myself. When it comes to music, anyway."

"It's hard to think of a police detective being an ex-hippy. I always think of you guys being the conservative types that faced off against hippies on picket lines. That just a stereotype?"

"No, cops do tend to be conservative on the whole. The job is about maintaining order, don't forget. People who want to maintain order tend not to deal well with disruption in their world views."

"Is that how you are?"

"About some things. Not everything. Some change you just can't stop. And some forms of order shouldn't be maintained if there are better alternatives."

She took a sip and watched him over the rim of the cup.

"I guess it depends what you mean by 'better.'"

"Most people who get into this business do it because they genuinely want to help people. But too often 'serve and protect' means preserving the interests of the people in charge, the ones who make the laws, to the detriment of everyone else."

"You don't sound like a cop."

He gave her a wry smile. "That's what some of my colleagues say."

"Do you like being a policeman?"

When he didn't answer right away, she said, "Sorry. I don't mean to pry."

"You're not," he said, but still didn't answer the question.

"What else would you have done besides being a policeman?"

"I don't recall having a lot of options at the time. My ex-father-in-law's a cop and he's the one who convinced me to join."

"What about now? You must have more options."

"If I didn't have to worry about making a living, I'd probably be a musician."

"Aha. What's your instrument?"

"Guitar."

"There's still time. You're not too old to have a second act."

"First I have to ring down the curtain on my first act. How about you? Is the bakery your dream job?"

"Hardly. The store is my husband's dream, not mine."

"So what's yours?"

"I make jewelry," she said. "I don't know if I'd call it my dream, but it certainly is my passion."

He pointed his chin at the ring on her wedding finger. "Your work?"

"Yep." She held out her hand to give him a better look. It was a substantial piece, with a large blue stone he didn't recognize in an ornate silver setting finely wrought with Celtic knots.

"Nice work."

"Thanks. I also do necklaces and bracelets."

"Do you sell much of your stuff?"

"When I can. During the summer we work art fairs, selling bread and pastries, and I always bring a selection of jewelry. Usually I'm too busy at the store or keeping the house together to concentrate on selling. What spare time I have, I use for making it."

"What's happening with the store?" he asked.

"We're still fighting the insurance company about covering all the cleaning. There's really too much for Matt to do by himself, and I can't help because I need to stay close to home in case we hear from Mark. My husband's talking about remodeling, making it into a different place than it was before all this happened so we can put it all behind us."

"Like what?"

"Nice little cafe, maybe."

"Doesn't sound like you think that's such a good idea."

"Well. It means means fighting with the bank as well as the insurance company. And nobody's making any loans at the moment. We have a small emergency cushion, but really, we can't afford to change direction right now. We have to get our little crime scene bakery up and running pretty damn fast or we'll lose the house."

She sighed. "*Crime Scene Bakery*. Maybe that's what we should call it."

"Speaking of which," he said, "we're moving in a couple of directions to find Mark. We're looking closely into the background of the young woman we believe your son is with."

"The barmaid?"

"Yes. Yesterday I spoke with people who knew her, including her mother and her ex-husband. I wanted to run some names and faces by you, see if they mean anything to you. Maybe we can find a connection with Eddie or Leon."

"Whatever you think will help."

"The first is Ronnie Kelley."

He had asked Tanya to print up DMV photos but she made copies of their entire licenses including the photos instead. He laid a copy of Shay's brother's license on the coffee table. He was a handsome young man, clearly from the same gene pool as his sister, with red hair and fine-boned features though his dull, suspicious eyes lacked the spark of intelligence in Shay's. Roberta Kelley said he was slow and Preuss could see it in his face.

"Who's he?" René asked.

"Shay's brother. He might be involved somehow."

"In what way?"

"I'm not exactly sure. But their mother told me Shay was staying with him before she moved to this area, and there was evidence of a man living in her apartment who I think is Ronnie. He seems to have lived a troubled life."

"Was he the one who killed Leon?"

"It's a possibility. Have you ever seen him? Or heard the name?"

"No, sorry."

"How about Brian Kulhanek?" He laid the photo of Kulhanek beside Ronnie's.

"Who's he?"

"Siobhan's ex-husband."

"No, I don't know either of these guys."

He put the photo back into his pile.

"Wait," she said, "who's that?"

He saw there was a photo of Roberta Kelley in the pile. He hadn't meant for Tanya to print out her photo but her name must have been on the list he gave her.

He showed the photo on her license to René. "Shay and Ronnie's mother," he said. It was a photo from the last time she held a license, seven years ago.

René took her time examining it. Her demeanor changed subtly as she focused on the picture, as though the photo drew her in. "Who is this woman?"

"Her name's Robert Kelley. She's in a nursing home near where her son lives. I spoke with her yesterday. She couldn't direct me to Shay but she did put me onto Ronnie. We have to consider everything. Sometimes people and events are interconnected in ways we can't even imagine."

"And it's your job to find those connections."

"It is."

"See, you do bring order out of chaos."

"Sometimes it feels more like uncovering the chaos hidden inside an apparent order. Do you know her?"

She ran a hand through her shaggy hair and shook her head.

"Sorry I can't be more help."

He drained his coffee and stood. "Thanks anyway. Everything brings us a little closer to your son. And the solution to the murder."

"Spoken like a true optimist."

"I'll be in touch."

His phone chimed with a text. For a hot second his hopes rose that it would be Shelley Larkin again but it was from Ed Blair.

Checked area motels, no sign of Shay Kelley staying anywhere or anytime.

He texted his thanks and continued back to the Shanahan. At least they knew a few more places where Shay wasn't.

Thought the ever-optimistic Martin Preuss.

37

"Change of plans," Toby's aide Maria said. "He's got a slight temp. They don't want him to go out."

Preuss followed her down the hall in the group home to his son's room. Toby was in bed with the covers over him. A faint sheen of sweat clung to his forehead. His eyes were open and dreamy and he lifted his head and gave a twitchy little smile as he realized his father was there.

Preuss rubbed his son's shoulder, said, "Not feeling so good tonight?" He leaned over and kissed the side of the boy's face. It was moist and warmer than it had been earlier in the day.

"How do his lungs sound?"

"Not sure," Maria said. "Wait here, I'll get Connie."

She left him alone with Toby and went off to find the respiratory therapist, who swept into the room in another minute. She was a breezy woman whose chest and upper arms were covered with elaborate floral tattoos.

"How's he doing?" he asked.

"His temperature's slightly elevated, but his lungs are clear, no rattles, no rales. But I don't think it's a good idea to take him out. We don't want this to turn into anything. Especially with the pneumo in January."

"No. It's better if he stays put."

She listened to Toby's lungs for a moment with her stethoscope, and nodded. "Still sound good."

"Okay. I'll check back with him later."

"You're playing tonight?"

"Yeah."

"He'll be sorry to miss it," she said, and patted Toby's arm. She left him as the alarm sounded on the ventilator in another resident's room.

Preuss reached down to hold Toby's hand. He felt the faint pressure as the boy squeezed. "I'm sorry you'll miss the show, too, honey. I'll be back to say goodnight later on," he promised.

Then bent to give the child another kiss.

His bandmates were already at Dino's, the Ferndale bar where the group was playing, when he got there at 9:30. It was the shank of the evening as far as the band was concerned. They would just be getting ready for the first set of the night and would play through closing time. All the band members asked where Toby was.

The Flynns were a Celtic punk group. On nights when they were in the groove they put on a wild, irrepressible show on Dino's low bandstand crowded with a dozen musicians and their horns, drum kits, guitars, even a concertina.

Preuss didn't have time to stop by his house so he didn't have his own guitar with him but he borrowed a twelve-string from Brendan Flynn, the leader of the group. It was a fabulous Taylor he played a few times before and loved, an acoustic electric that seemed to play itself. Though he was the Flynns' rhythm guitarist, Preuss pulled out the fingerpicks he always carried with him in his pocket and played fingerstyle. He loved the difficulty of it and the instrument's rich sound.

They ended their second set just after midnight with an original song by Brendan Flynn called "Nine Mile Moan," a long, free-form blues number that brought the members of the audience to their feet. Ordinarily Preuss loved playing with this group because it removed him from the stresses of his job, but tonight this new song, with its minor chords and anguished lyrics, the heartbreaking lament in the voice of the lead singer, Brendan's wife Molly, as she pulled the words up from some tormented place inside her—all dragged him right back into the world where he spent his days. It was a place where lonely and isolated men were killed in cold blood, where children went up in smoke, where the disasters caused by random chance cut through people's tidy lives like scythes.

They usually did three sets, but he was so wiped out after the second that he decided he wasn't going to stay for the last one. Sipping an iced tea he made the rounds of the room during the break between sets, saying his goodbyes.

He was exchanging hugs with Brendan and Molly when he felt a tap on his shoulder.

He turned to find Shelley Larkin looking up at him with a shit-eating grin on her face.

"Hi," she said.

She leaned closer against the din of the room. "I thought I might find you here."

She said something else he couldn't hear. Brendan and the other musicians began drifting back to the stage for the next set. He decided to stay on. Now he didn't want to leave.

So he played the last set, watching Shelley Larkin among a group near the bar in the packed room, standing out as though she was in the spotlight.

He watched her sway her shoulders to the music. She clapped. She snapped her fingers. She brought two fingers to her mouth and gave a lusty whistle through them when each song ended.

Above all she watched him as he played, watching her. Her presence made it harder to lose himself in the music . . . she kept summoning him back to the heat and beer fumes of the room, away from the place where the music took him.

She came up to him again while the band packed up after the last set.

"You're terrific," she said.

"Thanks."

"I had no idea you were that good."

"Now you know."

"I thought you were going to be a hobbyist, but man, you got you some chops."

He thanked her again and they stood looking at each other.

"What are you doing here?" was all he could think to ask.

"I'm with friends. We're celebrating a birthday."

"What?"

"I said we're celebrating a birthday."

"I can barely hear you. Do you want to go outside?"

She nodded and he walked her out into the cold spring night air, a plunge into icy waters after the boozy warmth of the room.

She seemed a bit tipsy. They stood there grinning at each other as if they were both high.

She was just as he remembered, he thought as he stood looking at her—dark and slender with a line of square studs on her ears and a crooked top incisor that broke his heart all over again. But her most striking features were her eyes, deep-set and intense, almost black, with a downward slant at the outer edges that gave her an air of perpetual sadness, even when she smiled.

It's her, he thought.

After months of trying to convince himself the world did not want them to be together, here they were in each other's orbit again. She sought him out.

He thought he was over her. After she told him she was seeing someone else, every day he would tell himself, Okay, it's just as well, she's too young anyway. I miss her and it's bad today but it'll be a little better tomorrow.

And the next day when it wasn't better, he'd say to himself, Okay, this is how it is for today, but wait till tomorrow because it's bound to start getting better tomorrow.

Just as he needed to be strong to get through the day without drinking, he needed to get through a day without emailing her, or texting her, or calling her. At first he gave in to the temptation to reach out to her after the pressure built up. He believed if he could only phrase his message properly, put the right words in the right order, she would realize she wanted to see him.

And each time she never responded and he resolved never to contact her again. Until the pressure built up the next time and the cycle started again.

Finally he got it . . . it just wasn't going to happen with her. But now here she was. Standing so close, feeling the warmth radiating off her, looking into her face, inhaling her scent (a light lemony-lilac), he felt himself falling for her all over again.

Without thinking he reached out and put his hands on her shoulders. The bones were slender, fragile as a bird's, exquisite.

"I missed you," he said.

She smiled at him but didn't say she missed him back.

But she said the next best thing.

"How's Toby?"

Brownie points accrued. Anyone who knew what Toby meant to him was automatically ahead of the game.

But then he knew she was smart. It was part of her attraction. Smart and crafty, knowing the best way to get what she wanted.

"Same as ever," he said. "He was going to be here tonight, so you could have met him. But he came down with a temperature and couldn't come."

"Oh, sorry I missed him. I still want to meet him."

"That can be arranged."

"I hope he's okay."

"Me too. He developed pneumonia in January so I'm worried about his health."

"I hope he'll be okay."

"He will be."

Then he said, "I didn't think I'd see you again."

She cocked her head and seemed to think for a moment.

"Martin, I'm sorry about before. Deeply sorry. It was just bad timing."

"Don't worry about it."

"I've been thinking about you a lot. I read about that murder and figured you were involved with it."

"It's my case."

"Thought so. I texted you the other day because you were on my mind."

"I got it. I didn't know how to respond so I haven't yet."

"I figured. I also figured you'd be busy."

"It's a messy one."

"It sounded awful."

Standing watching her, he realized he'd been waiting for this moment. He'd pretended to himself that he was over her but really this what he was waiting for.

Against his better judgment he allowed his heart to float in possibility.

"So," she said, "is the famous Detective Preuss close to solving it?"

He tried to think of the right words to answer with—again the right words, he thought: the right magical words to make it all happen with her.

Before he could say anything, the door to Dino's burst open and a tall young woman with a paisley bandana around short spiky hair stuck her head out.

"There you are!" she said to Shelley. She gave Preuss an unfriendly look.

"I'm just talking with a friend," Shelley said.

No introductions.

"We're leaving out the back. You ready to go?"

"Almost."

"Hurry it along, okay babe?"

She gave Preuss another look—this one proprietary: don't even think about it, dude, it said; she's taken—and pulled her head back inside like a turtle.

"My friends are leaving," Shelley said. "Gotta go."

"Okay."

"It was nice to see you again."

"Likewise."

It was an awkward moment, when both seemed to be waiting for the other to do something.

Before he could speak the words he wanted to say—Can I see you again?—she gave him a quick peck on the cheek, her hands resting lightly and momentarily on his chest.

Then she raised a hand in farewell and disappeared inside.

He stood rooted to the sidewalk, watching the door as if he could discern her afterimage.

Thinking: What the hell?

And then: I see, said the blind man.

Sunday, April 19, 2009

38

He awoke at 4:00 a.m.

He padded into the bathroom, then stood in the doorway to his bedroom looking at the cold, empty bed. It was too empty, too depressing to return to. He shrugged into his heavy terrycloth robe and went downstairs.

In the kitchen he made a pot of coffee and stood leaning against the counter, staring into the backyard with a steaming cup in his hand. The house, like his bed, was frigid; the temperature outside dropped overnight and his thermostat was in the night mode, which kept the house at a steady fifty-eight degrees. The window in the kitchen was a drafty double-hung so it was even colder standing in front of it.

He watched gauzy flurries drifting down outside. Their airy delicacy reminded him of the feel of Shelley Larkin's shoulders.

She was the last thought in his mind before falling asleep and the first thought on awakening.

Standing at the sink he told himself, Now I'll have to get past this all over again.

I'm too old for this, he told himself. Nothing even happened between them. Why did she have this kind of hold over him?

It was her eyes, he decided. That perpetual downward cast of sadness was what got to Martin Preuss, defender of the defenseless, protector of the vulnerable, empathizer with the doleful.

Yeah right, he thought bitterly. That must be it.

He shook his head, hoping the action would dislodge thoughts of her from his mind as though they were physical objects.

Way too old.

He finished his coffee, left the cup in the sink, and showered, dressed in an FPD tee shirt and a plaid overshirt and Levis, and went to Toby's.

His son was sound asleep. The boy's temperature was slightly higher than the night before. Preuss sat beside Toby's bed for over an hour, during which time the respiratory therapist and nurse on duty both checked on the boy twice. His lungs were still clear, the RT said, and they gave him Tylenol for his fever.

When he got up to go he kissed Toby's damp forehead. "I'll be back to see you later, sweathead."

He was at his desk at the Shanahan late the morning when his cell rang.

"Hi, it's René Lewis."

"Good morning." His spirits lifted slightly. "Have you heard from Mark?"

"Not yet. But I've been thinking."

"Oh?"

"That woman you asked me about yesterday?"

"Roberta Kelley?"

"Yes. It kept me up all night."

"Do you know her after all?"

"I think I might."

I knew it, he thought.

"How?"

He could barely keep the eagerness out of his voice. Finally, he thought. Some movement.

She hesitated. "You're going to think I'm crazy."

"My crazy bar is set pretty high, René."

"I think she might be my sister."

He said nothing. The facts of the case abruptly realigned.

"Maybe we better talk about this in person," she said.

"Maybe we better."

They parked in front of Janey Cahill's bungalow in the Ferndale neighborhood the residents called the Dales because of the names of the streets (Flowerdale, Farmdale, Gardendale). Preuss wanted to get René in a neutral location for their talk, and he wanted Janey's take on what René was going to tell him.

On their way over Preuss didn't ask about Matt, and René didn't mention him, which made Preuss wonder what was going on between them. He was reminded of the situation between Madison Kaufman's parents, which ended when Madison's father Stanley went after his wife's lover with a gun.

Isn't there anybody with a good marriage nowadays? he thought.

As he locked the Explorer and walked René to Janey's front door, he realized most of the couples he knew, including Janey and her husband Tommy, were in marriages that were troubled at best. The couple he knew with the strongest marriage was the gay couple who lived next door to him. They had been together for over twenty years and were still devoted to each other.

The luck of the draw, he thought. The random motion pushing us through our lives happened to push together two people who vibrated at the same frequency. It didn't happen often but it did with them and they had the good sense to recognize it and embrace their good fortune.

And his neighbors couldn't even legally marry under Michigan law. One of those laws he swore to uphold.

Janey Cahill welcomed them into her home with a hug for René and an affectionate pat on the arm for Preuss.

She led them through the living and dining rooms to what she called the sun room, the all-weather addition to the house her husband put on during one of his many periods of unemployment. From downstairs came explosions and gunfire from the video game her two boys were playing.

She set a carafe of coffee with three mugs on a wrought-iron table. René's color was high, with ruddy red splotches on each cheek.

"I'll be mother," Cahill said. She poured the coffee into each mug and passed around a bowl of sugar and Splenda packets and a small jug of cream. Then she passed a small platter with napkins and spoons.

The three sat back and waited for someone to start.

"So René," Preuss began. "I told Janey what you said about Roberta Kelley. Want to start there?"

"She's my half-sister, to be perfectly accurate. I've never actually met her and I can't say for sure the woman you talked with is her."

"Wait," Cahill said, "you've never seen her? How could you recognize the photo?"

"I didn't. I noticed the name on her license, Roberta Shepherd Kelley. I spent a sleepless night and called my aunt this morning. She lives outside Chicago. My mother sent me to live with her and my uncle during my father's trial. She reminded me of the whole story."

She took a sip of coffee. "My father had a mistress while he was married to my mother, and together they had a daughter whose name was Roberta Shepherd. So it was the name, yes, but I also saw something in her face that reminded me of Jack."

"Jack?" Preuss said.

"My father, Jack Stone. Something about the shape of her jaw, the spacing of the eyes. It gave me chills, to tell you the truth."

"Your father's trial," Preuss said. "What was that about?"

"When I was four, my father went to prison."

"For what?"

"He was an embezzler. He was the CFO of Vitalife, which was a pharmaceutical company in Ann Arbor. It turned out he was working with a couple of other guys and together they skimmed millions from the company. Vitalife developed an anti-anxiety medication that was very popular back in the seventies. But these guys drove the company into bankruptcy. The family lore is, my father agreed to take the fall for the others and in return they gave him a bigger share of the money they hid in offshore accounts."

"When was this?" Preuss asked.

"Seventy-three, I think. I don't know how true it all is," René continued, "and I don't care. All I know is, my father went to prison, my mother divorced him while he was away, and we never got a dime from him."

She paused for another sip of coffee. "After the divorce she tried to make a new life for us. It wasn't easy, but my mother was an incredibly strong woman and we did it. We lived on food stamps while she went back to school and got a degree in social work."

Preuss thought of the odd correspondences between her life and her half-sister's. If Roberta Kelley really was her half-sister.

"I only saw my father one time after he got out of prison. He moved to Florida and flew me down there once. I guess to show off his lifestyle to me, so I'd understand what I was missing because of my mother."

Her continuing bitterness seared her words. "I don't even know if the bastard's still alive or not. And to tell you the truth, I couldn't care less. I haven't given him a thought in years. Not till I saw that license with the woman's name."

Through all this, the look Janey Cahill was giving René was tragic. Janey of all people knew the effects of missing parenting on the legions of lost children she dealt with every day.

René started to say something else, but couldn't. She choked up and wrung her hands.

Preuss felt terrible about provoking her sadness. But finding her missing son and the killer of two men might depend on her information.

Janey Cahill got up from her chair and sat next to René. She laid a hand on René's arm and glanced at Preuss.

What now? her look said.

"You'll have to forgive me," René got out. "This is all a bit much. For this to come out of the blue . . ."

The noise from the boys downstairs was turning into a din, so Cahill said, "Would you excuse me?" and went into the house.

René took one of the napkins and dabbed at her eyes. "Sorry. I just need a minute."

"Sure."

He went into the kitchen to give her time to collect herself. He opened cupboards till he found where Janey kept her glasses and poured himself a glass of water. The refrigerator was covered with photographs of Cahill's family, held in place by magnets advertising local plumbers and pizza carryouts. Several large photos showed groups of people at cookouts and picnics.

Their crowd, Preuss thought. All the friends and relatives who formed their kinship group. A photo of his crowd would be very small indeed. He and his peeps (or peep, as the case may be) could all fit inside one of those instant photo booths at the mall. As long as there was room for the wheelchair.

"Everything okay down there?" he asked when Janey came back upstairs.

"They're just being boys. I told them to keep it down."

"So what are you thinking about this?"

"The name isn't that unusual. It's possible this woman isn't really her half-sister."

"That was my thought, too. But it's not likely there's no connection considering the circumstances."

"No," she agreed. "Too coincidental. So we need to assume the connection is real."

"The question is, what does it mean if it is?"

"Hell if I know."

They returned to the living room.

"Sorry," René repeated. "Things just got too much there for a second."

"Okay to keep going?" Preuss asked. She nodded and took a sip of coffee. "Are you just finding out about all this now? From the phone call with your aunt?"

"I already knew most of what I just told you about my father. My aunt filled me in on my father's other family. I'd heard whisperings among the grown-ups when I was little, and I must have heard that woman's name at some point for it to register with me last night. I just didn't know all the details."

"Did your mother know about your father's other family?" Cahill asked.

"My aunt says she did. He set them up in an apartment in Southfield. Just before the trial, Jack's mistress died and the little girl went to live with her own aunt. Apparently she never had any dealings with anybody on our side of the family."

"So let me get this straight," Preuss said. "You're thinking the woman in the nursing home may be your father's *other* daughter, your half-sister."

"Yes."

"And *her* daughter may be the young woman we think your son is with."

"That would make her Mark's cousin," Cahill said.

"In a nutshell," René Lewis said.

They all took a moment to digest that.

"Assuming Roberta Kelley is who you think she is," Preuss said, "that puts the question of what Mark is doing with her daughter in a new light."

They were all silent till René said, "I don't have any explanation. Or any words to describe how this feels."

Cahill couldn't sit still so she got up to make another pot of coffee. When she returned with it and refilled their mugs, René said, "Can I ask a favor?"

"Sure," Preuss said.

"This is partly what kept me up all night. If this woman really is my half-sister, and if it's okay with her, I think I'd like to meet her."

Monday, April 20, 2009

39

On the way into the station, Preuss stopped off at Toby's to check on his progress.

He was still running a temperature so his nurse was keeping him home from school. This was particularly disappointing because today was the day of the spring program, so he'd miss appearing as a flower. The group home manager said they would try to get him in to see his physician at some point during the day.

"Keep me posted," Preuss said, and they assured him they would.

At the Shanahan he went down to the Records Bureau where the clerk, Jill Vollmer, was entering data at her desk. She was the wife of Paul Vollmer, one of the uniformed officers. She was a perky attractive woman with short bleached blonde hair in a pixie cut and glasses worn down on the bridge of her nose.

He told her what he was looking for, and she said she'd start on it right away. He hadn't eaten yet so he went to the canteen to nuke an egg sandwich from a vending machine, and by the time he got back up to his office and thrown most of the sandwich away as being inedible an email from Jill came through with an attachment.

She said the files on Jack Stone's arrest that he asked for weren't available electronically because they were so old, so she put a request through to the State Police archives. But she took the initiative to search for news articles and was able to find a few from the *Detroit Free Press* and *Detroit News*. She gave him the links and also attached some documents as PDF files.

In addition to the articles about Jack Stone's embezzlement trial, Preuss saw pieces that mentioned him in other contexts.

Among the articles describing new drugs his company was developing were several about the death of Roberta Kelley's mother. Her name was Katherine Shepherd and she died in a fall from the balcony of her apartment building in Southfield in 1972. It was a sensation. The police investigation first focused on Jack Stone, a married businessman who was, as René said, the chief financial officer for a national pharmaceutical company based in Ann Arbor.

One of the articles from the *Free Press* included photos of him. He was a paunchy, sour-looking man with a helmet of thinning blown-dry hair and the tinted aviator glasses popular at the time.

Examining the photo, Preuss saw a resemblance between the man and Roberta Kelley, especially the wide-set eyes and oval shape of their faces.

The investigators quickly cleared him of any involvement, and no one was ever charged in connection with Katherine Shepherd's death. It was deemed to be a terrible accident.

Katherine Shepherd left behind just the one child, Roberta. She was seven when her mother died. The last newspaper report he could find about her said she would be taken care of by her mother's sister and her husband.

One enterprising *News* photographer caught a photo of the child holding the hand of a woman in sunglasses. Preuss guessed it was her aunt. In the face of the child looking out from the grainy photograph, scared and overwhelmed by the events surrounding her, Preuss saw the large eyes and snub nose of Roberta Kelley at the nursing home.

As he sat thinking about the articles and what they might mean, the cell phone ping records came through for Mark and Shay. Their phones pinged off a circle of cell towers around the city of Pontiac, a city twenty miles north of Ferndale straight up Woodward. Triangulation put them close to the center of the city.

Preuss read through the case file again but found no link to Pontiac. Had the two gone to ground in a motel? Was there some other connection to Pontiac that hadn't emerged yet?

He texted Ed Blair and asked him to focus his search for Shay on Pontiac motels.

Time for another road trip, he thought.

"No!"

Roberta Kelley's scream was so loud it brought an aide running.

Preuss assured the young woman all was well, and after Roberta told her the same thing she left them alone. Roberta's roommate was somewhere else in the facility, no doubt trying to get someone to tell her where she should go.

"Never," Roberta said again, quieter but with no less passion. "I never want to have anything to do with her. Or any of that family."

"I'm just relaying a request."

"That bitch got a lot of nerve if she thinks I want to see her ugly face after all they put me and my family through."

"What do you mean by that? René told me nobody in her family ever had anything to do with you."

"She told you that?"

"Yes. But if you know something different—"

"You're goddamn right I know something different. She's the reason I'm in this shithole."

"I'm not sure what you mean by that."

"Oh, you're not?"

"No."

"Then you can just get the fuck out of here, that's what you can do! There's nothing I want to say to you!"

"If you'll just let me—"

"No!" she cried again. "Coming in here like you're my friend."

"Roberta, please. I—"

"No! Get out! Get out!"

That brought the aide again and the floor nurse too, along with a short, compact woman with tight reddish curls and an oval face the color of light brown sugar. She seemed to be the one in charge because she came into the room and said, "Is there a problem here, Roberta?" Her badge said her name was Norma Zaragoza and she was the facility's nurse manager.

"I want this asshole out of my room!"

Norma Zaragoza pointed to the door. "Would you please leave before I call the police?"

He held his hands up in surrender. "I'm leaving."

Norma Zaragoza patted Roberta's shoulder as Preuss left the room in the company of the floor nurse who made sure he kept going.

He waited at the nursing station. In retrospect, he told himself, starting out with René's request wasn't the best strategy.

When Norma Zaragoza returned he introduced himself and showed his badge.

"You're the police? What was that all about?" she demanded.

"I'm investigating a pair of murders down in Ferndale and it's starting to look like there might be a connection with Roberta."

"You can't come in here and aggravate the residents, I don't care who you are."

"I know, I'm sorry I got her upset. But this is urgent, a boy might in a lot of trouble and I'm pretty sure Roberta knows something that can help prevent another killing."

"That still doesn't give you the right to come in here and bully that poor woman."

"That was not my intent. Look, do you have a minute for some questions?"

She grumbled some more, then said, "I'm not sure what I can tell you. We're careful about patient confidentiality so I'm limited in what I can say."

"My questions aren't about her condition."

"Still, there are rules about what I can say. Come on."

She led him away from the nursing station and into a small office with a tiny round table and three chairs.

"Roberta's daughter is missing," he began, "along with a boy who's a witness to the murders. I think they're together. If I could take a look at the visitors' log for Roberta I could see who visited her and maybe get a clue about where her daughter might be."

"We don't have that back here," she said. "The visitors log is kept up front, and it's open on the receptionist's desk so you can take a look at it. It's a public document."

"Does every visitor have to sign it?"

"Yes. Our front desk manager is very conscientious. What we keep back here is the sign-out log. Whenever any of the residents go out of the facility, they have to be signed out so we know where they're going, who they're going with, and when they get back."

"Everybody signs it?"

"Most of them. Except for some of the older guys who don't like us keeping track of them. They ignore it, but most of the others go along."

"Can I look at it?"

"No, that one's not public. Michigan's Patient Bill of Rights says any patient or resident of a health care facility is entitled to confidential treatment of personal and medical records. Including the sign-out log."

He thought about it.

"I could subpoena it," he said.

"Be my guest."

He thought some more.

"The clock is ticking here. My witness is a fifteen-year-old boy who's with Roberta's daughter and maybe her son, too. And I don't think he's with them willingly. Two men were killed in Ferndale. I need to make sure more people aren't going to die."

Now it was her turn to think.

"Are you looking for something specific? I can't show you the logs, but I might be able to check something if it doesn't go too far over the line."

"I'm looking to see who signed Roberta out and where she signed out to. Especially if she ever went to Pontiac."

"How far back do you want to go?"

He pulled a number out of the air. "Three months."

"Wait here."

She left the office, closing the door behind her.

He sat back and and thought about where they might be if nothing popped here. He could ask Emma Blalock if she could find some people to make the rounds of motels in Pontiac with photos. He wasn't crazy about getting in touch with her (he suddenly remembered he never called her back on the night of the bakery killing), but if she could help find Mark then he needed to ask her despite their personal issues.

Or his personal issues, rather. She would appreciate hearing from him more than the other way around.

He checked his phone. No messages from Toby's house.

In ten minutes Norma Zaragoza came back with a legal pad on which she had written names and dates in a large round hand.

"I wrote down all the people who signed her out, the dates, and the places they signed her out to for the past three months," she said. "I can't let you have this. I can let you see it, and you can get whatever information you need to from it, but you can't walk out the door with it."

"I understand."

"I could be in a lot of trouble for doing this. But you said it's urgent and I believe you."

"It is."

"As I thought, nobody signed her out besides her children, and there weren't any trips to Pontiac. But I'll give you five minutes."

She left him alone and he copied down every bit of information on the sheet. He would think about it later.

In exactly five minutes she returned.

He thanked her gave her back the sheet she wrote out for him. She tore it into little pieces, which she stuck in the pocket of her tunic.

"We never had this conversation," she said. "And I mean never. I could lose my job."

"Depend on me."

He went back to look in on Roberta Kelley, but she refused to see him. Her roommate was in bed. She lay on her side muttering to herself and making small quick squirrelly gestures, as though telling herself secrets she didn't want to hear.

On his way out he stopped at the front desk to look at the visitors' log. He copied down the names of Roberta Kelley's visitors for the past three months, as well as the dates and times. Most of the visitors were Shay and Ronnie, but there were a half-dozen others he didn't recognize. One or two were completely illegible but he made do with the ones he could read.

He sat in his car in the visitors lot, going over the notes he just made. Most of the outings Roberta had made were to local restaurants.

He called the station and got hold of Reg Trombley. Preuss gave him the names of Roberta's visitors and asked him to match them with addresses.

Trombley said he would.

Then he said, "You left a note for me. What was that all about?"

"Let's talk about it later, all right?"

"Whatever you say."

They disconnected without saying goodbye.

He stopped for a slice of pizza at a strip mall near the nursing home, and by the time he finished it Trombley emailed him with the addresses he asked for.

One turned out to be in Pontiac.

That's it, he thought. I need to speak with Emma.

Before pulling out of the parking lot he punched in Emma Blalock's number on his cell phone.

She wasn't as glad to hear from him as he thought she might be.

40

She stepped out of one of the Oakland County Sheriff's Office black scout cars parked at the end of the block of brick duplexes dating from the 1930s. She stepped out wearing jeans and an oversized corded sweater. She gave Preuss a frosty nod.

"I was wondering when you were going to bring us in on this," Emma Blalock said.

Three other deputies in their crisp uniforms stood around them in the street. Because the City of Pontiac's financial problems decimated the city police force, the Sheriff's Office was often called to provide police services. There was talk about giving the Oakland County Sheriff complete responsibility for all public safety services but so far no decision had been made.

"So what's the deal here?" she said.

Preuss filled her in and passed around the photos of the three they were looking for.

"There's a strong possibility they're staying in this house."

"You don't know for certain they're here?"

"No," he admitted. "But this is dead center in their cell pings and the woman who lives here is the aunt of the mother of two of them. You might call it an educated guess."

"Otherwise known as a wild stab in the dark. So what do you have in mind?"

"I'm going to try and persuade her to let us inside, and if that doesn't work we'll get a warrant. Meantime we'll wait outside in case the kids are in there."

"Sounds like a recipe for a hostage situation. Why don't you have an arrest warrant right now?"

"At this point they're just persons of interest, not suspects. So I don't have anything to charge them with and don't have any evidence to base a warrant on. I just want to talk to them."

"What's the plan?"

"You and I will go to the front door, with one of your deputies as backup. The other two will go around the back in case they run."

"Are these people armed?"

"At least one of them might be. Ronnie Kelley. He may be responsible for two killings so we have to go carefully."

The five walked down the street to the duplex. It was a quiet, shabby street in a poor part of Pontiac, which itself was one of Michigan's poor post-industrial cities. Every third house on the block seemed boarded up, foreclosed and up for sale.

Preuss climbed the front stoop with Emma Blalock. Flanking them on the steps was a deputy whose name tag said LaRosa, a square-bodied, clear-eyed man with a buzzcut. He stood with his hand on the butt of his duty weapon. Emma surveyed the house and the street. The other two deputies went around the back of the house, which faced onto an alley.

Preuss rang the doorbell beside a wrought-iron security gate.

He waited a minute, then rang again. Behind him he heard LaRosa murmuring to the deputies at the rear of the house. They radioed back things were calm, with no sign of activity.

The inside front door opened.

Standing in the doorway behind the gate was a stout elderly woman in bent wire-rimmed glasses. She had stringy gray hair and wore a threadbare housecoat over a nightgown with a tattered hem hanging below the bottom of the housecoat.

Preuss held up his shield. "Detective Martin Preuss, Ferndale Police. Are you Esther Militello?"

She gave a wary nod of her head.

"Can we talk to you inside, ma'am?"

Her glance skipped to Emma Blalock and LaRosa, then back to Preuss.

Then she stepped aside so they could enter.

Preuss and Emma Blalock exchanged a glance as they stepped into a dark foyer. *Either this is a mistake,* Preuss thought, *or something else is going on here than what I expected.*

"We're inside," LaRosa told the radio. He planted himself in the front doorway as Esther Militello led Preuss and Emma Blalock into the living room. It was large and musty-smelling with two old-fashioned sofas facing each other in front of a mammoth fireplace with an intricately-tiled dark surround. Dark brocade paper spotted with stains covered the walls.

"Ms. Militello," Preuss said, "are you Roberta Shepherd Kelley's aunt?"

"Yes," the old woman said in surprise. Her voice was creaky and old. "She's my niece. Did something happen to her?"

"No, ma'am. Not since the last time you saw her. So that would make you Katherine Shepherd's sister?"

"Yes. But how do you know Katherine?"

Preuss held out photos of Shay and Ronnie. "Shay Kelley and Ronnie Kelley. You know them too, don't you, Mrs. Militello?"

She glanced at the photos and then up at Preuss with growing suspicion.

"What's this all about?"

He showed a photo of Mark Lewis. "How about this boy. Do you know him too?"

When she didn't say anything, he said, "Are they staying with you, Mrs. Militello?"

He could see a calculation going on behind her eyes.

"I have to tell you, they could be in a lot of trouble," Preuss said. "I know your first instinct is to protect them, but you have to trust me, the best thing you can do for them right now is let us talk to them. This young man's life could depend on it."

She thought about that. In the silence, Preuss could hear LaRosa whispering into his radio, "Anything moving back there?"

Preuss glanced at him and he shook his head.

"Are they here, Mrs. Militello?"

"Well," she said after another long pause, "not right this minute."

41

Preuss and Emma Blalock sprinted to his car.

Two of the deputies stayed with Esther Militello to make sure she didn't notify Shay or Ronnie, and in case the three came home before Preuss found them. As soon as she said the three young people went grocery shopping at the Pontiac Foodland on North Perry Street, Emma called in a bulletin on Shay Kelley's car and asked deputies to meet them at the store.

LaRosa and his partner followed Preuss and Emma with the gumball light flashing but no siren.

Preuss pulled into the parking lot off East Walton Boulevard with LaRosa on his tail. The market was on the far south end of a long structure that also housed a tax service, beauty supply outlet, video store, dry cleaners, and discount store. He stopped the Explorer and motioned LaRosa up beside him. They could see a deputy waiting in his car at the far end of the parking lot lane from the entrance to the market.

LaRosa's partner rolled down the window and Emma said, "You two go around the back and watch the rear of the market. Who's in the cruiser over there?"

"Williams," LaRosa said.

"Tell him to sit tight."

"Should I call for more backup out here?"

"Fine," said Emma.

"But no shooting if we can help it," Preuss said. "Make sure everybody knows that."

They all agreed.

Preuss drove on as LaRosa got on the radio to the other deputy to let him know what was happening.

He quickly spotted Shay's battered Toyota parked close in. He pulled in beside it and watched the front of the store. Business was slow at this hour of the morning. The few shoppers were mostly African Americans and Hispanics, the majority of the population in this area of Pontiac.

"We can wait here and take them when they get to their car," Emma Blalock suggested.

He considered that. "Mark knows me," he said. "He'd make me right away. We don't know if he's with them voluntarily or not. If he tips off Ronnie, and Ronnie's armed, things could get hairy. The other thing is, we don't even know for sure they're in there. They could have finished shopping and gone into the Dollar Store or the Blockbuster."

They considered their options.

"Why don't I scope out the store," he said, "and if we see them I'll withdraw and we'll take them as soon as they get outside."

"Fine. Except you're not going in alone."

He opened his mouth to protest but she stopped him with a hand. "Don't even," she said.

Keeping an eye on the electric sliding door of the front of the market, she got LaRosa on the radio.

"Are you in position?"

"Affirmative. Got eyes on the rear door."

"How about you radio Williams and tell him to pull up by the front entrance where they can't see him if they come out of the store. When he gets in position there, we're going in to have a look around."

"Will do. Want me in there, too?"

"No, just stay where you are. We need to keep everybody safe here. If they're inside, we'll take them when they exit the store."

"Copy that."

Preuss and Emma slid out of the Explorer and walked down the parking lane to the front of the store. The windows of the market were bricked-in as a security measure but from outside the sliding glass doors Preuss could see the row of cashiers. He scanned the customers but didn't see any of the three waiting in line to check out.

He waited another tense minute for Williams's cruiser to come to a rolling stop next to the market. The deputy stepped out with his hand on his gun. Preuss shook his head so the deputy would know not to draw the weapon, but he couldn't catch his eye.

Trusting the deputy would know he wasn't expected to shoot anyone, Preuss took one more look at the cashiers' row, then nodded to Emma and entered the store.

42

The clamor of voices, shopping carts, scanners, conveyor belts, cans and boxes of food packed into plastic bags.

For a crazy second, he thought of how much Toby loved this commotion.

Then he focused on examining faces for any of the three they were looking for.

Emma grabbed an empty basket and like an average happy couple they walked past the row of cashiers toward the produce section, which was the path to entering the food section of the market. Because most of the faces were black or brown, Preuss thought he would be able to spot three young white kids, but he realized he would stand out in the crowd too. With her milk chocolate complexion, Emma would be far less conspicuous. None of the three had ever seen her before, so he dawdled behind her and tried to let her block any view of him.

Mark Lewis knew what he looked like, so he was the one Preuss looked for most carefully. If Mark spotted him before Preuss saw the boy, things could go badly very quickly if he was on the side of the Kelleys.

The store was laid out like most mid-sized grocery stores, on a large rectangular grid with two horizontal aisles split by a number of vertical ones. They walked down the horizontal aisle at the base of the store and looked up each one of the vertical aisles. The aisles were wide, and because of the hour they were mostly empty. Trying to hide behind the end displays of breads and tortilla chips and chocolate sauce until they were able to see up the aisles, they proceeded slowly through the store.

By the time they got to the last aisle, the long frozen food section, they didn't see Mark or either of the Kelleys. They retraced their steps, watching both ahead and behind.

They shared a look. Each realized chances were good their targets were in the cross lane at the end of the aisle if they were anywhere, since they weren't in the other aisles.

They paused before they made the turn. Preuss signaled Emma to move out slowly. She eased out with her cart, sweeping her gaze across the area in front of her as she put a box of coffee cake in the cart. As though forgetting something she came back toward where Preuss stood.

"Ronnie and Mark," she whispered, "at the deli counter. No sign of Shay."

She came close to his ear. "You stay here, I'll see if I can spot her."

Taking the basket, she sauntered around the corner before he could ask what he really wanted to know, whether Mark looked like he was there willingly. He needed to know, so he backed around the corner so the two men wouldn't see his face and dawdled over the cheese display. He snuck a look at the two young men. Ronnie was husky, a head taller than Mark, and was certainly the one who fit into those huge clothes back at Shay's apartment.

He risked a full-on glance.

At that exact moment Mark happened to look his way.

They met each other's eyes and time stopped. They were ten feet from each other.

Preuss made a quick decision. He turned and was about to raise a finger to his lips to let Mark know to keep silent when Ronnie looked Preuss's way too.

His mother said he was slow but there was nothing sluggish about how he scoped out the situation.

Preuss moved in immediately but Ronnie was even faster, grabbing Mark and pushing him away from Preuss while he bolted in the opposite direction around the deli counter. He disappeared through a set of swinging doors into the stock room.

Preuss ran toward Mark and lunged forward to get a hand on the boy but missed and lost his balance and fell to the floor. Mark took off running down and aisle.

Struggling to his feet, Preuss felt a brief wave of vertigo wash over him. He reached for a display rack to steady himself.

He took a deep breath. After a moment his head cleared and, with his heart pounding, he went after Mark.

Who by now was sprinting up the wine aisle with a several second head start. As he ran he held out an arm to knock an entire shelf of bottles onto the floor.

Preuss hoped Ronnie would go through the store room and out the back door where he would run straight into the arms of the deputies, who should be on their toes waiting for him. So he focused on Mark.

To avoid the shards of glass and spilled wine, Preuss ducked around the next aisle and ran to the front end of the store, judder-stepping around the few carts and shoppers in his way.

Mark burst through a line of people waiting to check out, scattering them and overturning their shopping carts. When he couldn't get past the ones lined up at the register, he elbowed through as far as he could go and then pushed the cashier at the next register out of the way and clambered over the conveyor and leapt out toward the entrance. He stumbled but kept going.

Preuss was about ten paces back. In the commotion he couldn't tell if Emma was able to collar Shay Kelley anywhere.

A shopper was entering the store so the sliding doors were open as Mark sprinted out. The Sheriff's deputy who was supposed to be watching the front door happened to be looking away as Mark raced by him, and didn't figure out what was going on until he turned his head and saw Preuss in pursuit.

Mark ran down the long front of the building. He was an athlete with thirty years on Preuss and easily outdistanced him.

A high berm separated the shopping center from the next parking lot so the boy couldn't keep running straight. Instead he made a sharp right and ran around the side of the building toward the rear.

The deputy pulled up in his car and Preuss jumped in. They roared down the length of the store and around the corner in pursuit.

A brick wall separated the roadway at the rear of the stores from a residential area so Mark couldn't escape that way. He stopped, turned to see the Sheriff's car heading toward him, and kept running toward the rear of the building.

He turned the corner and ran right into the Sheriff's unit parked diagonally across the roadway behind the grocery store. The car Preuss was in squealed to a stop perpendicular to the store, blocking off Mark from retreating the way he had come.

Preuss and the deputy spilled from the car and Preuss grabbed Mark from behind in a bear hug.

Panting, they both watched Deputy LaRosa in a shooting stance with his duty weapon drawn and aimed at Ronnie Kelley.

Who was floundering among a stack of pallets and broken-down boxes in the shadows of the loading dock at the rear of the market. He was trying to get to his feet but kept slipping on the loose cardboard. In one hand he held a gun.

The gun that killed Leon Banks and probably Eddie Watkins, Preuss thought.

"I said halt!" LaRosa shouted.

Standing off to the side a few yards away was his partner, also in a shooting stance aiming at Ronnie.

"I'm warning you," LaRosa said. "Drop your weapon NOW!"

Ronnie looked around, wild-eyed. He reminded Preuss of a terrified cow in the chute of a slaughterhouse.

"Ronnie!" Preuss cried.

Ronnie looked over at him.

"Ronnie, there's a good way out of this," Preuss said. "Do what he says. This doesn't have to end badly."

"Listen to him, Ronnie," LaRosa said. "This is not a request, I'm ordering you to drop your weapon now or I *will* shoot you."

"LaRosa, be cool." Preuss let go of Mark and stepped around the cruiser with his arms up like a referee trying to keep two boxers away from each other. He took baby steps to insert himself between the two armed men.

"Ronnie, LaRosa, everybody just calm down. We can talk our way out of this."

"No!" Ronnie hollered. "You don't come any closer. You stay right there!"

His lumbering form finally got his feet under him. He stood upright. The hand holding the gun waved wildly.

"Ronnie, please," Preuss said, "you don't want to do this."

Out of the corner of his eye Preuss saw Mark Lewis coming around the Sheriff's car.

"Mark," Preuss shouted, "stay back."

"Don't nobody take another step," Ronnie said.

"Ronnie man," Mark said, "come on, don't do this."

"Mark, get back!"

"No, he'll listen to me."

"Don't come any closer!" Ronnie cried.

"Ronnie," Preuss said, "nobody needs to get hurt here. Think about your mother. Think about Mary Grace."

"Don't you talk about my daughter!"

"You don't want to leave her without a father, do you?"

"You leave her out of this," Ronnie cried. "I'll shoot *you!*"

"No you won't, Ronnie," LaRosa said. "You're going to drop your weapon. I will not tell you again."

"Ronnie," Preuss implored, "please. Put it down. Please."

"Drop it, Ronnie! Last chance!"

"You can walk out of—"

Preuss never finished his sentence.

Ronnie Kelley brought his gun up. It wasn't clear if he was going to shoot or was offering it in surrender.

It didn't matter. Deputy LaRosa and his partner opened fire.

43

Preuss dove back toward Mark. He fell on top of the boy and covered him with his body.

The shots were impossibly loud. LaRosa stood as if frozen to the ground, then with short steps moved in toward the loading dock. His partner came in behind him, gun up and edgy. Preuss kept Mark's head down. The boy beneath him was whimpering and quaking with fear.

"It's all right," Preuss told him. "I got you. You're safe."

He turned his head to see Ronnie Kelley sprawled on his back on a pile of boxes. From the awkward position of his body Preuss knew he was dead.

When LaRosa kicked Ronnie's gun away, he straightened up and yelled, "Clear!"

Mark Lewis started to bawl.

Preuss put his arms around the boy and held him tightly but it couldn't stop the wailing.

Mark's teeth were chattering as Preuss and Emma Blalock hustled him into one of the deputy's units. Emma took a blanket from the trunk and wrapped the boy in it to calm his trembling. She sat with him in the back seat of the car. Preuss stood outside the car.

"Shay must have gotten away," Emma said.

"Did you ever see her?"

"No. I was going up and down the aisles looking for her, but when I heard the gunfire I came back here to see what was going on."

"She might not have even been in the store."

She radioed the deputy who was supposed to be waiting by Ronnie's car but he turned out to be standing beside LaRosa behind the building.

"That does it," Preuss said when they both realized where the deputy was. "She probably took off in the Toyota in all the confusion. I'm sure she's long gone."

Two ambulances pulled behind the market, coming from opposite ends of the building. One team of EMTs jumped out and tended to Ronnie Kelley, though they quickly determined there wasn't much to be done. Preuss motioned the other team over to the car where Mark and Emma were sitting, and they starting seeing to the boy.

Déjà vu all over again, Preuss thought. This is how it began a week ago: one dead, one injured, one gone.

He called Paul Horvath at the Shanahan to ask for a car to sit on Shay's apartment in case she turned up there. His next call was to René Lewis.

"I have Mark," he told her. "He's shaken up but he's in one piece."

On the other end of the line he heard her sobbing in relief.

René and Matt Lewis were waiting with Janey Cahill at the sheriff's substation in Pontiac. When she saw Mark, René folded him into her arms and rocked him back and forth like an infant. He began to weep again into her shoulder. Matt stood by as if embarrassed by this display and totally clueless about what to do.

René finally pulled away and Matt took Mark in his arms, but more awkwardly than his wife and the hug was considerably shorter. His father gave him a few manly pats on the shoulder but Mark pulled free and took a step backwards.

Emma found an interview room for them and let René and Matt get some time alone with their son. While they were conferring, Emma went off to prepare a warrant request for Shay Kelley and Preuss recapped for Janey Cahill what happened.

"Are you all right?" she asked when he finished. "Because you don't look all right."

"That boy didn't have to die."

"What happens when you go waving a gun around and threatening to shoot people. Especially public safety officers."

"I know."

"You tried your best but some things you can't stop."

"I know that, too."

René appeared in the doorway to the interview room. "Mark is ready to talk to us," she said. "But first we want to know if he needs a lawyer."

Preuss and Cahill shared a look. "We're not planning to charge him with anything," Preuss said. "But he should be protected."

"What do you think, René?" Cahill asked. "You can have one if you want one."

"I just don't know. I trust your judgment about this."

"We'll need to read him his rights to protect him," Preuss said. "But how about if we start talking and if it seems like the conversation's going to go someplace risky, we'll stop. Meantime we've got about a thousand questions for him."

"I hope he has the right answers," René said.

"If he sticks to the truth, they'll be right."

"Let's start at the beginning," Preuss said.

Ashen but calmer, Mark sat between his mother and father at the interview table. His mother rested a hand on his forearm and another on his shoulder. His father sat with a hand on the back of the boy's chair but not actually touching him.

Preuss and Cahill sat on the opposite side of the table from them. Emma was in a chair against the wall. They decided this should be Preuss and Cahill's conversation, but she wanted to be in the room.

"We need to know about everything that happened that night at the store. Okay?"

The boy took a deep breath and a drink from the can of Coke they brought him. He nodded.

"What time did you get there?" Preuss asked.

"About, um, eight-thirty, maybe quarter to nine."

"Where you the first one there?"

"Yes."

"When did Eddie and Leon come?"

"Not till a little later. Around nine."

"They came in together?"

"Yes."

"While you were waiting for them, were you by yourself?"

"Yes."

"What were you doing?"

"Just playing a game on my phone."

"So they got there around nine," Preuss said. "Then what happened?"

Mark paused to take a big swallow of pop.

"We goofed around a little. Like we usually do."

"Doing what?"

"Eddie, he started to, um, talk like an Arab."

"Talk like an Arab, what's that mean?"

"You know, he started to talk with, like, an Arab accent and was running around all wide-eyed and crazy, talking about blowing shit up."

"Why did he do that?"

"Just to be funny. Because of Leon and all his terrorist conspiracies. And it made Leon go crazy. It was pretty sick."

"How long did that last?"

"Not long. We were just about to get started with the prep work for my dad's catering job when that guy I told you about before showed up."

"The guy with the dreads and the scar."

"Yes."

"Tell me about him again," Preuss said.

"Well," Mark began.

"Well?"

"It's just that we've been over this already," Mark said.

"We're going over it again," Preuss said. "How did he get in?"

"Through the back."

"What time did he get there?"

"Must have been around quarter after nine or so."

"The last time we talked, you told us you didn't remember much about what happened after he got there. Have you thought about it any more?"

"Of course. That's all I think about."

"Mark," René cautioned. "Tone it down."

"Sorry."

"Do you remember anything else besides what you've told us?" Preuss asked.

"I don't."

His mother patted his arm and Preuss said, "Okay. Let's talk about Shay and Ronnie, all right?"

"Okay."

"You need to help us understand what you were doing with them."

"I'll try."

"Why don't you start by telling us how you met her."

"Shay, you mean?"

"Yes."

"At the bakery."

"How?"

"She came in one day when I was working. I was bringing something out to put in the display case and she was in the front buying something. We started to talk and she introduced herself."

"When was this?"

"The exact date? I don't remember."

"Approximately."

Mark thought, then said, "Sometime near the beginning of March, I think."

"What did you talk about?"

"I don't remember. Just stuff. This and that. I thought she was pretty cool."

Matt Lewis squirmed in his seat. All three of the other adults in the room looked at him but he only examined the ancient network of scratches on the formica tabletop.

"And then you saw her again after that?" Preuss asked.

"Yeah. After work one day she showed up and asked me if I wanted to go get some coffee with her. I said sure, so we went to the Java Hutt down the street and talked for a while. Then she gave me her phone number and we started texting, and then a couple weeks after that she picked me up from school one day and we went to Rosie O'Grady's to get something to eat. That's when I met Ronnie."

"What happened then?"

"I don't understand what you mean."

"I mean what happened when you met Ronnie. Tell me about your relationship with these people, Mark."

"We hung out together a few times. I liked him. I liked her."

"When did she tell you about her relationship with your family?"

Mark pulled free from his mother's hands and got to his feet. He went to stand with his back against a corner of the room as though giving himself a time-out.

"Mom," he said, "could you please leave the room?"

"What?" said René Lewis.

"I have to say some stuff you're not going to want to hear. And it would be easier if you left the room for a couple of minutes."

"Honey, there's nothing you could say I wouldn't want to hear."

"Yeah there is. It's about Dad."

"I already know what you're going to tell me, sweetie."

"You do?"

She patted the chair for him to take his seat again, which he did.

She looked at her husband but said to her son, "There's nothing you could tell me about any of your father's extra-curricular activities I don't already know."

44

The bombshell rang in the tinny silence of the interview room.

Matt looked at René, whose head swiveled from her son to her husband like a gun turret sighting on its target. "I wasn't aware of this last one yet, but I knew about all the others."

She let her words sink in, then to Mark said, "Go on, honey. Finish what you're going to say."

Mark gave his father a steely glare, then continued.

"So Shay and Ronnie told me about how me and Kenny are related to them. They said we're like step-brothers and sisters or something."

"You're cousins, actually," said Cahill. "Your mother and their mother are half-sisters. They have the same father, but different mothers."

"When did they tell you this?" Preuss asked.

"After I got to know them. She also told me . . . she also told me about her and Dad . . ."

He sent a worried glance toward his mother, who nodded encouragingly.

"She said Dad . . . came on to her . . . you know."

"What did you think about all this information?" Preuss asked.

"At first when she told me we were related, I thought it was kind of cool. We don't have any other relatives, so it was nice to know there's somebody else out there we're family with. But then when she told me about my dad and her, I got really mad."

"It wasn't what it looked like," Matt said weakly.

"No?" René said. "I think it was *exactly* what it looked like."

"How could you do that to Mom?" Mark spat.

When Matt didn't say anything, René said, "Yes, would you like to answer your son's question?"

Matt couldn't bring himself to reply.

This was moving in the exact wrong direction, Preuss thought. They're losing their focus. They may need to work through these issues, but this isn't the time or place.

"Mark," he said, "let's get back to Shay and Ronnie. You were telling us what you talked about with them."

"Okay," Mark said, "so then after they told me we were related, that's when they told me they knew Grandpa Jack was loaded, and they thought Mom inherited a lot of money from him. Which I told them was totally wrong but they didn't believe me. I told them we couldn't even afford cable TV so how could we be rich? Me and Kenny never even knew Grandpa Jack. They told me they were positive there was a bunch of money somewhere in my mom's name, and they wanted their share of it."

"Oh, honey," René said. She stroked her son's hair. "You should have asked me about this. I never got a thing from my father. Grandma Ruthie divorced him and he never gave us anything."

"But Shay said you guys never told me the truth about it all because the money must have been there."

"Baby, there never was any money," René said. "We've never lied to you."

"Well, maybe *you* never did," he said, with a furious look at his father. "Shay told me she moved here to get close to us to find out about the money."

"Mark," René said, "don't you see, honey, she was doing the same thing with you as she did with your father? Getting close to you to get at the money she thinks we have. Which doesn't even exist. She was just trying to take advantage of you."

"No," the boy insisted. "She wasn't. She was my friend. She was my friend and we're *related*."

He intertwined his fingers tightly and sat looking at them as fat tears rolled down his cheeks.

His mother put a hand on the back of his head but he shook it off. His father could do nothing except sit with a thousand mile stare.

Here's our cue, Preuss thought. He said, "Let's take a short break," and looked at Cahill and Emma Blalock as he nodded toward the door.

"'Every unhappy family is unhappy in its own way,'" Preuss said as they stood in the hallway outside the interview room.

Cahill stood leaning against the wall and exhaled loudly. "You make that up yourself?"

"Not exactly."

"What a mess."

"I don't see any charges for this kid," Emma said. "Do you?"

"Nothing so far," Preuss said. "Let's give them a few minutes and see what comes out of part two."

45

In the interview room Mark hung his head. His long hair fell around his face, obscuring it from view. Which was the point.

They all resumed their seats and Preuss said, "Let's get back to what happened the night of the bakery shooting." Before this all skitters completely out of control, he thought. "When your mother told you about Eddie being shot, you figured whoever killed Leon went to kill Eddie, and was going to be after you and that's why you took off, correct?"

"Yes."

"Why did you think that?"

"Because I thought he was killing off witnesses or something."

"And you were a witness."

"Yes."

"But you still can't remember what happened after this guy got there?"

"Correct."

Preuss thought about that.

"Have you seen this guy around since then?"

"No."

"How did you wind up at Esther Militello's with Shay and Ronnie?"

"I texted Shay and told her what was going on. And she said she knew someplace I could stay that was safe."

"Did you know Esther was their mother's aunt?"

"No, but Shay told me when she picked me up."

"You mean from the building where you were hiding?"

"Yes."

"Honey, why would you go with her?" René asked. "Why didn't you tell us you were afraid? Or Detective Cahill or Detective Preuss?"

"I told you, I needed to get away."

"But why?"

He turned a withering, accusatory look on his father.

"Because of him," Mark spat. "I hated him for what he did to you. I didn't even want to be in the same house with him."

"But baby," René said, "you hurt me too when you took off. Do you see that?"

"I didn't care," Mark said. He was too angry with his father to think about such subtleties. Preuss felt for both Mark's anger and his father's inept culpability. He had been in both places.

"I hate this family," Mark said. "I can't wait till I can move out on my own."

"Now just a second!" Matt said.

"You shut up, you—"

"Mark!" René cried.

"Hold it," Preuss said. "Let's everybody just calm down, all right? Everybody just take a breath and step back."

They did as he asked but it did nothing to ease the tension in the room.

"Mark?" Preuss said. "Mark, look at me, please."

The boy turned his head toward Preuss with the same deliberate move his mother used on his father.

"So you went willingly with Shay?"

"Yes."

"And they didn't force you to stay with them?"

"Correct."

"Did either of them tell you they were involved in what happened at the bakery?"

"No! I already told you about that."

"You did," Preuss said. "But what I don't understand is why Ronnie and Shay ran today. Ronnie made me as a cop in about a second flat and then took off. Shay must have, too. Why did they do that? Innocent people don't start running full tilt boogie as soon as they spot a cop."

When Mark said nothing, Preuss said, "You can't say anything about that?"

"Have to ask them about it."

"Did you know Ronnie was armed?"

"No."

"He never showed the gun to you? You didn't know he was armed when you went to the market?"

"No."

"And what was that standoff with the deputies about? Why didn't he give himself up? You need to help me understand this."

"I can't help you," Mark said. "Maybe he was scared. You could ask him if he wasn't dead."

He started to cry again.

"We might as well let his parents take him home," Emma said. "We're not going to get anymore from him today."

Press said nothing. He watched what was going on in the interview room through the small window in the door. René was stroking Mark while Matt was sitting with his arms folded, gazing into space. Mark stopped crying but looked miserable.

"What's the matter?" Emma asked.

"I'm certain the boy still isn't telling us the whole truth," Preuss said.

"He's confused," Emma said. "He's been under a lot of stress. He's just seen two men killed right in front of him."

"Yeah, but this whole business about a white Rasta pulling the trigger . . . sounds bogus. I wish I could put my finger on why that description bothers me so much. Besides it being such an obvious lie. And Ronnie just taking off like that?" He shook his head. "Something's wrong."

"Maybe he was scared, like Mark said. You told me his mother said he was slow."

"Unless it was Ronnie who killed Eddie Watkins? And Leon Banks, for that matter."

"And Mark's lying about Dreadlocks guy? Why?"

"To protect his new cousin."

"Could be," Cahill said. "Thing is, we don't have anything that contradicts what he's telling us."

"That doesn't mean it's true."

To Emma he said, "Still no word about Shay?"

"Nothing yet."

"She wouldn't just up and leave."

"So we're agreed we should let the parents take Mark home?" Emma asked.

"No reason to hold him for now," Preuss said. Emma Blalock went off to find the substation commander.

"I'd like to get a car to sit on their house, though," Preuss said. "At least for tonight, just to make sure he doesn't slip away again."

"And just in case the Rastaman story is true and he comes looking to tie up this last loose end," Cahill said.

"We'll see Santa coming down the chimney first," Preuss said.

"Poor Matt," Cahill said. "Here he thought he was scoring with a major babe and it turns out she was just using him to get at his wife and sons."

"Yeah, sucks being him. Meantime we're back to square one with this imaginary dreadlock guy."

Preuss continued watching the three people in the interview room. Matt Lewis was trying to offer his son some comfort, or possibly apologies, but Mark wasn't having any of it. He leaned toward his mother, who looked like she was trying to pull the boy completely out of her husband's clutches.

46

"They told me I'd find you here."

René Lewis slipped into the seat across from where Preuss sat with a container of coffee in the substation canteen.

"Just trying to clear my head," he said.

"Should I leave you alone?"

"No, it's fine. Want some coffee?"

"I think my nerves are already too much on edge."

"Where's Mark?"

"He said he wanted to use the rest room before we go home."

Preuss nodded. He couldn't come up with any bromides about their situation so he stayed silent.

"Pretty awful, huh?" she said.

"It's nasty," he admitted.

"Is this what you have to see every day? No wonder you want to be a musician."

"It's not always this bad."

"Are you all right?"

"Sure. Still in one piece."

"Thanks so much for finding him. And keeping him safe."

"It's what I do."

"Bringing order out of chaos."

"A little bit of order out of a whole lot of chaos."

"Still. Baby steps. I'm glad you haven't quit just yet."

He forced a grin and raised his cup in a silent toast to the thought.

At length she said, "You're probably wondering why I stay with him."

"No," he said. "I'm really not, René. I've stopped wondering what keeps people together. Or pulls them apart, for that matter. But you don't need to explain yourself."

"It's not like I haven't known about his . . . proclivities. The thing with this girl is just the latest in a long line. He thinks he's fooling me with his good husband routine. With the others I was able to look the other way. But this one hits home in a different way."

"I can see that."

"My mother and I had an awfully hard time, just the two of us. I always promised myself I'd never subject my sons to the same hardships I faced growing up without a father in the house."

He couldn't help saying something now. "No matter the cost to yourself?"

"As long as the cost was mine to bear, and not my boys'."

"Seems like it's hitting at least one of your boys pretty hard." He suspected the younger boy also felt the tension in the house and that's why he spent so much time in his own head with his iPod.

"I wish I could have talked to him about it before everything got to this point," she said.

"You think he's old enough to understand?"

"I think so. He's pretty mature for his age."

"Okay," Preuss said. "Just asking. He'll be a lot more mature when this is over."

"We all will be."

"You know, the similarities between your early life and Roberta Kelley's are pretty remarkable."

She gave him a wry smile. "It's all connected, right? Isn't that what we were talking about before? Connected in ways we can't begin to understand."

She gave him a long look, as though she were trying to decide how they would be connected after this.

"Before," she said, "I didn't mean to barge in on you and Janey."

"You weren't interrupting anything."

"Are you two . . . together?"

"No. Good friends. And she's married."

"That doesn't always mean anything. As we've just seen."

"No," he admitted. "It doesn't."

"Are you married?"

"No. My wife died a few years ago."

"Oh, sorry."

"Don't worry about it."

"Maybe," she began, "when this is all over, we could meet for coffee and I can let you know how Mark is doing."

Preuss surprised himself by saying, "That would be nice."

She pushed her chair back and stood. "Well," she said, "I'm glad you're all right. I'm going to get back to Mark."

She reached out to squeeze his hand and said, "Thank you again."

And she was gone.

The only sound in the canteen was the hum of the vending machines. He stared around the room at the posters explaining the Heimlich maneuver, advising what to do In Case of Emergency, and encouraging confidentiality in public spaces.

All connected indeed . . . not just the personal sorrows, but everything—the sadness, the greed, the violence, the crimes large and small, all related. And so many systems of their world not only made those connections possible, but encouraged them.

And it was his job to protect these systems and allow them to function unimpeded in the guise of upholding the law.

He threw what was left of his coffee in the trash and went up to find Janey Cahill.

They finished at the Pontiac substation and he returned to the Shanahan Complex in Ferndale. He knew Mark wasn't telling them the complete truth, but he couldn't suss out where the boy was lying.

He searched his desk among the folders and empty Tim Horton's carryout cups for the envelope with the forensics report from Arnold Biederman. He didn't read it when Tanya Corcoran gave it to him—when was it? It felt like a month ago—because Chief Warnock commandeered him for his come-to-Jesus talk.

Under it was the folder with the charges Russo leveled against him, which he didn't read either.

He thought about his conversation with Warnock about the charges, and the chief's insistence that he solve the murder quickly to render the worst charges irrelevant. Unfortunately he wasn't any closer than he was when the chief talked to him.

The one thing he was more sure of was that this crime was anything but random. All appearances and Mark's story to the contrary.

He read through Biederman's report. (The other thing from Russo could wait.)

DNA wouldn't be back for a while, but the prints on the rolling pin were definitely Eddie Watkins's and the blood was from Mark Lewis. There was also some hair on the pin consistent with Mark's.

Otherwise the scenario was essentially as Biederman described it when they all met the Monday following Eddie Watkins's murder. The autopsy results on Leon Banks would not be ready for a while.

When he finished the report, he called Emma Blalock's office number in the Oakland County government office campus in Pontiac. The call went to voicemail and he left a message asking about the calibre and make of weapon Ronnie was carrying

"Also if you've run the ownership, that would be helpful, too. And ballistics when it's ready."

He paused, trying to think of something else to say. Unable to come up with anything, he said, "Thanks for your help today. We'll talk soon," and hung up.

He sat at his desk staring at his helm clock. It made him think of the grace of sailboats on the water. He flashed on an image of a sailing race he and Jeanette and the boys watched the one time they all went down to Orlando.

The thought of Florida reminded him of the business card they found in Shay's apartment. Someone in Florida . . . what was the name?

He pulled out his phone and thumbed back through the recent calls. He found the call with a 561 area code.

Leo Steinberg, that was the man's name.

Preuss never called him back. At the time he didn't know why Shay had the card of a man in Florida. But now he wondered if there could be a link between Leo Steinberg and Jack Stone, Shay Kelley's grandfather. *Stein* is German for *stone*.

All connected.

He called the number again, and got the Appliance department at the Sears in Palm Beach Gardens.

After being channeled through three different salesmen, he was put through to Leo Steinberg.

Preuss explained who he was and asked the man if he knew Jack Stone.

The weary voice on the other end of the line gave a dry chuckle.

"I'm not sure anybody ever knew Jack Stone," he said. "But in any case Jack was my brother," he added, in the same tone a man might use to admit he had inoperable cancer.

47

Preuss spent what was left of the day with Toby.

He went to the doctor's earlier that afternoon. His problem turned out to be an ear infection. Because he couldn't speak, he couldn't make it known that his ears hurt, the poor kid. The doctor prescribed antibiotics and suggested Preuss consider getting tubes for Toby's ears.

His fever was slightly lower, and he was starting to perk up.

Preuss read him another few chapters of Harry Potter, then sat chatting with his son, who was wide awake and sitting up in his chair. Preuss, sitting on Toby's bed, filled him in on the day's events, as usual taking both sides of the conversation, making what he felt were appropriate remarks to keep up Toby's end.

Preuss stopped talking and held Toby's warm hand in his own. How strong was the bond they shared . . . how could it ever be broken?

Never, except for the death of one of them.

He felt the same for his wandering son, too, even though Jason did everything he could think of to sever their connection. Preuss could never cut Jason loose, regardless of how much the boy wanted to escape what was left of his ruined family.

Jack Stone, on the other hand, seemed to have had no trouble turning his back on either René Lewis or Roberta Kelley. Preuss told Toby about his conversation with Jack Stone's brother, Leo Steinberg.

According to Leo, Shay Kelley went down to Florida at the beginning of February looking for Stone (who had, Leo said, changed his name early on to sound less ethnic once he started his business). She was able to track down Leo because years before he kept in touch with the Kelley side of the family; he was always ashamed of how Jack treated them.

Leo gave Preuss an earful about his brother. Stone died a few years before, so Shay missed her chance to meet him. Leo described Jack Stone as an intensely narcissistic and selfish man who cared only for himself and seemed to lack whatever gene was necessary to make a man care about his children. He spent his money on the toys of an affluent American male while leaving both of his children to struggle on food stamps.

Leo said Jack actually did have a secret stash of money put away by his business partners for when he got out of prison. But he never shared any of it with anybody. Leo said his brother thought the mothers of his children were both free-loaders who only wanted to get their hands on his money. He spent so wastefully on his possessions that he was actually in debt when he died.

"Did you ever meet Roberta Kelley?" Preuss had asked Leo.

"Only once, when she was an infant. I'm sure she doesn't remember me."

"So you don't know how she wound up?"

"No. But I do know what happened to her mother."

"What do you mean?"

"Katherine Shepherd. You know she died in a fall off the balcony at the apartment Jack kept for her?"

"I know what the newspaper reports said. It was ruled an accidental death. Are you saying that's not what happened?"

"That's how she died. What I'm saying is, it wasn't an accident. Somebody pushed her."

"Was it Jack?"

"He didn't kill her himself. But he was the one who arranged it."

"How do you know that?"

"He told me."

"Your brother confessed to you that he arranged to have his mistress killed?"

"After he got out of prison and moved down here, he came to visit me one night. That was unusual in and of itself. He thought I was a loser with my head in the clouds and no ambition to do anything except mooch off my successful sibling. So he never wanted anything to do with me. When he died I introduced myself to mourners at his funeral who said he never told anyone he even had a brother.

"So anyway, on this one night he came down to my house in Boca Raton. He got drunk and started bragging about his life, how good it was, how much more successful he was than I was. And that's when he told me about Katherine. He said he arranged for a guy to get the key to the apartment in Southfield, and one morning after she dropped their daughter off at school this guy snuck in and pushed her off the balcony."

"He would have been at the top of the list for the police investigation. So they must have looked at him pretty closely. But they cleared him."

"He had it all taken care of. He arranged to be out of town when it happened, and he made sure the guy who killed her was well taken care of. Everyone he knew swore up and down he loved Katherine Shepherd and planned to marry her as soon as he divorced his wife, so he couldn't have killed her."

"Why did he?"

"She was evidently going to come forward about his embezzling scheme. He said he tried everything he could to buy her silence and finally there was only one way left to keep her quiet. Of course his embezzling scheme all came out anyway."

"Why didn't you tell the police in Michigan when he told you?"

He took so long to answer Preuss was about to ask if he was still there.

"I know I should have," Steinberg said at last. "And I was going to, I really was. But then I thought, it happened such a long time ago, what good would it do to rake it all up again?"

"A woman died because of him. He needed to be brought to justice."

"'Justice.' People like my brother don't care about justice, Detective Preuss. They care about getting theirs. And getting away with whatever they want. But they don't care about justice."

"That's not an excuse for not coming forward. You don't do it because he wants justice, you do it because Katherine Shepherd requires it."

"You're right, of course. But there was another reason. I knew if I told the police, it would mean my own brother was capable of doing such a thing. And I don't think I wanted to face that."

After a long silence, Leo Steinberg said, "I know that means he got away with it. And I helped him."

When Preuss finished relating his conversation with Leo Steinberg, Toby made a high-pitched squeal, interrupting his thoughts. It was the kind of sound the boy made when he was ecstatic.

"What?"

Toby said his word, "Onion," and flashed his crooked grin. He hunched his narrow shoulders and hummed and squirmed happily in his chair.

"Either you just pooped your pants or else you figured something out for me. Which is it?"

He took a whiff of his son. "Don't smell anything," he said. "So you must have figured something out. Are you going to tell me, or make me guess?"

Toby glanced around slyly, as though looking to see if anyone was nearby before he told his father the secret he discovered.

Preuss put his ear next to Toby's mouth. "Tell me."

Toby took the opportunity to plant a sloppy kiss on his father's cheek. He opened his mouth in a wide O, like a little bird, and as Preuss leaned against his son's mouth Toby worked his lips and gave a little tongue action.

Preuss wiped his soggy face with the back of his hand. He caressed his son's cheek and Toby nuzzled his hand, then looked at him full on, something he rarely did. Once again Preuss was reminded of Jeanette's eyes.

How the people from our past continue to make their presence felt, he marveled.

Toby kept looking at him as though waiting for his father to understand fully how the past persists inside, and shapes, the present.

And especially how much the present owes to the past.

Toby kept staring at his slow-witted father, then gave his father's hand a gentle squeeze.

I'd do anything for you, he thought. At once he heard Roberta Kelley's voice in his head.

They'd do anything for me, my kids.

Preuss leaned over and threw an arm around his son's thin shoulders, drawing the boy closer to him, inhaling his sweet Toby-smell.

He leaned his forehead against his son's and said, "Sometimes it feels like you're so far ahead of me, it's not even funny."

On the way home from Toby's he pulled over and got René Lewis on the phone.

"Hi," she said. There was an expectant note in her voice that made him feel glad and sad at the same time.

"René," he said, "did Mark go to the bakery right from home on the night Leon died?"

"I'm not sure. I didn't even know he was going to the bakery. I thought he was going over to a friend's to do homework for school."

"Do you remember when he left the house?"

"No, sorry."

"Do you know the friend's name?"

"His buddy Larry Berkowitz."

"In Ferndale?"

"On Oakridge."

He thanked her and hung up, then punched in the number for Edmund Blair.

He gave Blair Berkowitz's name and asked him to pinpoint Mark's movements on Easter Sunday evening before he went to the bakery.

"As soon as you can, please," Preuss said, and rang off.

Tuesday, April 21, 2009

48

In the morning his computer chirped its musical note as an email came through.

It was from Emma Blalock, about the gun Ronnie Kelly was carrying. It was a Smith-Wesson M-6 .38 Special.

What was most interesting was the ownership. It was legally registered to Brian Kulhanek.

Preuss looked through Biederman's report to satisfy himself it was the same kind of weapon that killed Leon Banks. Ballistics would take longer but Preuss didn't doubt was the same gun.

He texted Alonzo Barber and asked about the calibre and type of weapon that killed Eddie Watkins. They both thought Watkins was killed with a larger weapon but he wanted to know for sure.

He reread Emma Blalock's email.

What was Ronnie Kelley doing with Shay's ex-husband's gun?

Before he could follow that thought through, Ed Blair called.

"Hey," Preuss said, "any luck?"

"Just got off the phone with the Berkowitz kid."

"Good deal."

"He told me Mark was at his house before he drove him to the bakery. He dropped Mark off at 7:30."

"He's sure about that?"

"Said he was."

"So then Mark was there an hour earlier than he told us."

"Looks that way."

Preuss thanked him and disconnected the call.

He went through the case file again, this time combing through the listing of Mark's phone calls. As Mark said, there were several texts back and forth between Mark and Shay on the morning of Thursday the 16th.

He went backwards in the phone listing to see what other calls Mark made and received. He found four calls to his brother Kenny's cell number within the space of ten minutes, beginning at 7:45 on the night of the bakery shooting.

He stared at the numbers.

The longest call, the first, lasted for seventeen minutes, the shortest (the last) less than a minute.

So Mark called Kenny four times in a row just after he got to the bakery.

All the times I've gone through the file looking for the key, Preuss told himself, and here it was all along.

He picked up René Lewis and together they drove to the middle school. Kenny's counselor pulled him out of his Language Arts class and let them talk in her office.

Preuss sat observing the boy as René asked how his morning was going. Watching her chatting with her younger son, he marveled at how calm she seemed for someone whose world was teetering on the edge of dissolution.

"Kenny, how are you holding up?" Preuss asked.

"Okay."

"Glad to have your brother home?"

Kenny shrugged a narrow shoulder. "I guess."

"You guess? You don't know? Are you and your brother close?"

Another shrug. Kenny began to tap his thumbs on the wooden arms of the chair he sat in.

"Kenny," Preuss said, "it looks like Mark called you a few times just before the shooting at the bakery."

"Okay."

"Can we talk about those?"

The tapping turned into a concerted rhythmic thumping of his thumbs. Something's inside this boy trying to get out, Preuss saw.

Evidently with the same thought, René reached out to put her hands over her son's to quiet the tapping and bring this out in words.

"Honey," she said. "Please."

Her son looked up at her, then looked away. He found something very interesting in the coleus plant on the windowsill in the counselor's office.

Preuss let the silence stretch for another few moments, then said, "Kenny, you were supposed to be there that night, weren't you?"

When the boy said nothing, René asked him the same question. He nodded without looking at her.

"Do you want to tell us about it?" Preuss asked.

Kenny said something in his whiny murmur and Preuss said, "Speak up, please?"

"I said Mark asked me if I would work with him to get the order ready for the morning. So I was gonna do it. But then just before it was time to go over there, I decided I didn't want to. I wanted to stay home and do my homework instead. My science project was due the next day and it wasn't finished yet. So that's what I did."

"Why didn't you tell us?" René asked.

"He told me not to."

"Who?"

"Mark."

"Why not?"

"He didn't say. He just told me to keep it between us."

He was silent for a few moments more.

Then in a small voice he said, "Was that a mistake?"

"Oh, honey, not at all."

As though his mother's words gave him the permission he was waiting for, Kenny's face dissolved and he began to cry in a high-pitched, keening sound. He seemed to be in such agony that his mother could only reach out to the child and draw his fragile body close to her own.

She offered whatever futile pretense of reassurance she could.

René asked Kenny if he wanted to come home or go back to his classroom and he said he wanted to stay at school. When they returned to the house on Earle, Preuss asked René if he could take another look at Mark's room.

The bed was unmade and the room smelled like old socks. Preuss's gaze fell on the soccer posters. He quickly saw the one that had teased his memory. It was a photograph from the last Olympics, of a goal being blocked by the American team's goaltender. He was airborne, stretched out full-length across the goal mouth, his blond dreadlocks flying out behind him as though electrified.

Even in the slight action blur of the photo, Preuss could make out the livid scar that ran down the side of his face.

Mark Lewis was in the basement watching a mixed martial arts brawl on TV.

René took the remote from her son and turned the set off.

The boy gave his mother a petulant look and turned an angry glare on Preuss.

"We need to talk," René said.

49

She didn't show till after dark.

The sodium lights of the parking lot turned her battered silver Corolla a ghostly white. The driver's profile was obscured as the car pulled into a slot near the front door. She exited the car wearing a U of M hoodie hiding her face.

She strode quickly up to the sliding doors of the nursing home. They parted and she disappeared inside.

He called Joe Curran, the sergeant in charge of the Oakland County Sheriff's substation in Brandon Township.

"She's here," Preuss said.

"Okay. Be right there."

They disconnected. Emma Blalock put him in touch with Curran earlier in the day so Preuss could act under Curran's authority. Reg Trombley emailed him earlier with the arrest warrant.

He went into the nursing home.

It was just before visiting hours ended. He saw her walk down the long hallway to the rotunda where the central nursing station was. He hugged the walls as he made his own way. He knew he should wait for Curran but he wanted to keep her in sight.

When he got to the open area at the end of the long corridor, he scanned the desks behind the counters between the nursing station and the rest of the rotunda. Norma Zaragoza looked up from her computer screen. She was about to say something but he quickly brought a finger to his lips and she caught herself. He pointed to the woman he was following and Norma caught on immediately and nodded.

He moved quickly across the area in front of the nursing station to the entrance to the long-term care wing. He glanced down the hall. In the center of the corridor the dietary aide was collecting the resident's empty dinner trays and stacking them in the meal cart. He passed her and stopped outside the door to room 264.

The bed nearest the door was empty. The woman who didn't know where to go must have found someplace, at least for now. The curtain was drawn around Roberta Kelley's bed. He tiptoed in and paused, listening. He heard the whisper of a cloth on flesh and Roberta's weak murmur.

He pulled open the curtain and saw, standing with her back against the window, Shay Kelley leaning over her mother, wiping the woman's face with a towel. Her mother was on her back in bed. Her eyelids drooped but she was awake. She turned her head lazily toward Preuss.

But it was Shay he was focused on. For all the times he showed her photograph around, this was the first time he saw her in person.

Here was the young woman who captivated both Matt and Mark Lewis. Standing there in the maize and blue sweatshirt, the hood now off her head revealing her copper-colored hair drawn back into a pony tail and bright eyes so blue they looked transparent, she seemed younger than her age, with an oval face and pouting lips.

"Who are you?" she said.

"Martin Preuss, Ferndale police. I've been looking for you."

"What are you doing in my mother's room?"

"I want to talk to you."

"What about?"

"What you and Ronnie have been up to these past few weeks."

At the sound of her son's name, Roberta smiled. "You know my Ronnie?" she asked Preuss. "Siobhan, honey, why hasn't he been to see me?"

"He's been busy, Mama."

"You don't know, do you," Preuss said.

"Know what?"

"What happened to your brother yesterday. After you ran off from the grocery store."

"What about him?" Roberta said.

"Nothing, Mama. Ronnie's fine. This guy's just—"

"Ronnie's not fine," Preuss said.

"Did you arrest him?" Shay asked.

"No, he's not under arrest."

He couldn't say more, not in front of Roberta, who lay looking from her daughter to Preuss.

Shay searched his face for more information and realized what he meant.

"No. No!" She brought a hand to her mouth.

Oblivious to what was passing between them, Roberta squinted at Preuss as though peering through a fog. "Do I know you?"

"You do. Martin Preuss. I was here a few days ago. I came looking for your daughter. And now I found her."

Roberta turned her head toward the young woman and patted her hand. "My good girl. All my children are good kids. They'd do anything for her mother, you know."

"You're right about that," Preuss said.

Then he thought, *All* my children? Why not *both* my children? How many were there?

Shay folded the washcloth she held and draped it over the guardrail of the bed. She stuck her hands in the side pockets of her sweatshirt and moved slowly away from her mother's side.

"Shay," he said, "you have to answer for Leon Banks."

"Who?"

"The guy you shot at the bakery last Sunday."

"Oh no, I didn't shoot anybody."

"I was thinking it was your brother because he's the one with the impulse control problem, and he's the one who wound up with your ex-husband's gun, which is the one that fired the bullet that killed Leon. But he didn't have the wherewithal to pull any of this off. It must have been you."

"Honey," Roberta said, "what's he talking about?"

"Nothing, ma. He's making all this up."

"But why—" Roberta began.

"Stop, ma, please!"

"It's over, Shay. You're going to have to come with me." He moved toward her and she backed into the wall behind her.

"Please, no," she said, "I can't leave my mother."

"You should have thought of that before you started all this."

"Please, it was a mistake."

"Shay," her mother said, "what's he mean, your *ex*-husband? That's not right. Honey, tell him that's not right."

Preuss looked at Roberta, then at Shay.

"You and Brian are still married?"

Shay Kelley nodded, and as she did everything he thought about the case shifted.

It explained why Mark was so afraid that whoever killed Leon would be after him that he ran away, yet willingly went with Shay and Ronnie when they offered him refuge. It wasn't Ronnie at all.

"It was Brian," Preuss said, "not Ronnie."

Shay said nothing but stood there looking miserable.

"So why did Ronnie make a stand at the——"

Before he finished the question, he saw her eyes flick behind him for an instant.

Turning, he raised his right arm as he felt rather than saw the shape rushing towards him.

His elbow took most of the force of the blow but the hard plastic dinner tray still struck his face with enough power to split the tray and stagger him.

He was able to get his arms up to protect himself from Brian Kulhanek's second blow though he lost his footing in the narrow space between the two beds and hit the floor with his back against Roberta's nightstand.

Kulhanek threw the two pieces of tray at Preuss's head and dove toward him but before he could get close Preuss swept the big man's legs from under him. He went down hard on his ass but scrambled to his knees at once. He bent forward to grab Preuss's shirt with his left hand while cocking his right fist, big and hard as a kettlebell.

Roberta screamed for him to stop.

Kulhanek was imposing but he was slow and even though Preuss was on his back and dizzy from the blow of the tray, he was able to push Kulhanek's left hand across his body so he couldn't latch onto him.

It put Kulhanek off-balance enough so that Preuss could push his right shoulder and swept Kulhanek around and into the side of Roberta's roommate's bed.

Preuss grabbed Kulhanek by the hair and forced the top of his head into the metal bed frame again. The big man went down.

With her husband momentarily out of commission, Shay made a break for the door but Preuss pushed Kulhanek off of him and lunged for her.

He caught the leg of her Levis. She kicked at his head and face furiously but he held on and wrestled her other leg out from under her and she went sprawling face-first on the hard linoleum floor.

Blood gushed from her busted nose.

Preuss got his feet under him just as Kulhanek was leaning on his arms trying to raise himself between the beds.

Preuss landed on top of him with a knee pressed into the center of his back and one hand forcing his face into the floor. He pulled his handcuffs from his jacket pocket and twisted Kulhanek's arms behind him and got the big man immobilized before he could catch his breath.

Preuss's head hurt so badly he thought he would pass out.

He struggled to his feet, the room tilting as a sickening wave of nausea passed over him, just as Joe Curran, panting, appeared in the doorway with his hand on his sidearm.

He took in the scene with eyes as wide as saucers.

Behind him stood Norma Zaragoza, her own eyes as wide as dinner plates.

50

Martin Preuss looked at Siobhan Kelley sitting across the table from him. Doctors at Crittendon Medical Center in Rochester, where the ambulances that Norma Zaragoza summoned took her and her husband, set and packed her broken nose. Now her nose was swollen and purple rings of shiners were coming up under both eyes.

She looked exhausted. Her skin was sallow and waxen.

She looked down at her hands folded in her lap.

"I didn't want it to turn out this way," she said softly. "Nobody was supposed to get hurt."

"I can't tell you how many times in my life I've heard that from people sitting in that exact chair," Preuss said.

"But it's true," she insisted weakly. "I just wanted my mother to get what she's always been owed."

"From your grandfather?"

"Yes. All I ever heard growing up was how much money he had, and how he never gave any of it to my mother."

"Not knowing his wife and other daughter never got any of it either."

"No. All Uncle Dwight ever talked about was how much money he screwed my mother out of."

"Uncle Dwight would be Esther's husband?"

"Yeah. 'He's sitting on a pile of dough, living in the lap of luxury and we ain't seeing none of it.'" Her imitation of a dumb guy was cruel and precise.

"So you went down to Florida to find your grandfather and see for yourself?"

"But when I got down there I found out it was too late, he was dead. So I talked to his brother instead. I thought he might know something about the money. I just wanted enough money to move my mom to a better nursing home. I hated her being in that place but she was on Medicaid so we couldn't afford anything nicer. But after she broke her arm because they didn't take care of her, all I could think of was moving her someplace else. I lost my job in the downturn last year so I knew I'd never get enough money to move her on my own."

"How did you know where they were?"

"When I talked to Leo Steinberg in Florida he told me they were still in Michigan, and my mom saw a thing on TV about what they were doing for veterans. She recognized them right away and told me about it. So I moved down to Ferndale to get close to them to see if all the stories about their money were true."

"You took up with Matt Lewis?"

"It wasn't really serious. I never slept with him, I just wanted him to think I was interested in him so I could find out more about the family. It didn't seem like they did have any money, but Brian didn't believe it."

"Was it his idea to kidnap Kenny Lewis?"

Her face dissolved in tears. She shook her head. It was hard to talk while crying with a packed broken nose. She snuffled uncomfortably.

After a while she said, "Yes. I told him Matt and Mark both said there wasn't any money and I was starting to believe them. But Brian wanted to make them pay us what they owed anyway. He decided the best thing was to pretend to kidnap one of their boys. We figured it would take a couple of days for them to raise money, and then we'd let the kid go and we could move my mom someplace better than where she was."

"Didn't you think they'd go to the police if you abducted their son?"

"Brian said we'd tell them we'd kill the boy if they did. But we weren't really going to. Nobody was supposed to get hurt."

"So you said. How did Mark get involved?"

"At first I just wanted to meet him to see what he was like, and also to see if maybe he'd be a good one to . . . well, for the plan, I mean. But as I got to know him I realized he was as angry with his parents as I was, especially after I told him about what his father was doing to me."

"I thought you said there wasn't anything between you."

"There wasn't. But I kind of misled him," she admitted.

"Were you at the bakery when Leon Banks was killed?"

"I wasn't," she insisted, as if he was going to contradict her though he said nothing. "Brian went. Mark arranged for his brother to be there, so Brian and Mark were supposed to grab him and then make it seem like he was kidnapped."

"But when Kenny decided not to work that night it threw the plan off."

"Yeah. Brian told me him and Mark were trying to figure out what to do next when those two guys walked in. He'd brought his gun and the one guy started to go apeshit about being restrained and having a gun stuck in his face."

"Those two guys were combat veterans, and at least one of them had mental issues. They weren't about to let a couple of wanna-be thugs push them around."

"Brian said he wouldn't shut up and finally rushed him . . ." Her voice trailed off.

"So your husband shot him in the head."

She nodded and looked down at her hands again.

"Then Eddie Watkins grabbed the dough roller and clocked Mark because he realized Brian and Mark were working together. And Brian turned the gun on Watkins but only grazed him and Eddie ran for his life."

"He said he didn't mean to do it . . . he just reacted without thinking."

That sounds about right, Preuss thought.

"How did Ronnie wind up with Brian's gun?"

"Ronnie said he'd get rid of it for Brian and for some reason Brian gave it to him. But apparently he never did dump it. My brother was always fascinated with it."

"And he paid for that fascination with his life."

Guns kill even when they're not fired, he thought.

"I'm still trying to understand why Ronnie forced that confrontation with the deputy. If he'd just stopped struggling and handed the gun over, he'd still be alive."

And Mary Grace wouldn't be another daughter growing up without her father.

She began to snuffle again. "I don't think he understood what was happening. In his mind he might have thought him and Brian were like partners or something."

She buried her head in her hands and sobbed.

As he sat watching her, the pounding of his head became unbearable. He gathered his papers together in the folder on the table in front of him.

"Well, that's all for now," he said.

"What's going to happen to me?" She stared at him with fine blue eyes that were opaque with sadness and fear.

"Nothing good, I'm afraid."

Preuss sat in his office with the door closed. He made up his mind to go home but before he could make himself move his cell phone rang.

He gazed at the screen with no enthusiasm, then pressed the Answer button.

"Martin," said Alonzo Barber. "Don't tell me you're still working?"

"I am."

"Why so late?"

Preuss sighed. Where to even start?

"It's just your basic Tuesday," he said. "I've been punched, kicked, beaten, lied to, and generally abused."

"Who did all that?"

"The couple who did the bakery killing."

"The couple? There were two of them?"

"Husband and wife."

"You got them locked up, I hope?"

"I do."

He gave Barber the short version of what happened.

"The two guys who got shot walked in on the bad guy trying to salvage the kidnapping plan," he concluded. "They tried to disrupt it but got shot for their efforts."

"But this guy, the one who killed your vic at the bakery, he didn't do Eddie Watkins."

"It doesn't look like it."

"I'm telling you, he didn't."

"You know that for a fact?"

"I do."

"How?"

"I caught the asshat who did it. Some young banger wannabe trying to impress his boss. An audition, like."

"How'd you find him?"

"You put me onto Watkins's ex-wife. I spoke with her and she directed me to his cousin, who stays in the apartment on Riopelle. He gave the guy up right away. This cousin was also the one who told the banger where Eddie was staying in the first place. Working both ends against the middle."

"Never heard that one before. "

"Turns out this cousin, he was trying to curry favor with the same bossman. They wanted to punish Watkins for stealing drugs from them. Only he didn't do it. They mixed him up with another guy who really did steal their shit."

"You're telling me Eddie Watkins's death was a mistake?"

"I asked the guy who killed him where he heard about Eddie stealing the dope. Know what he told me?"

Without waiting for an answer, Barber said, "The rumor started with the sinister minister himself, Rocellus Gaines."

"Why am I not surprised."

"I talked to Gaines, asked him why he started the rumor. Told me he was afraid Shatoya was going to fall for Eddie again when he showed up all new and improved and changed by the army. So he started spreading a story about how Eddie was back in the drug life, hoping it would put Shatoya off him. Unfortunately for Eddie, there was another guy who actually did steal some shit and Eddie's cousin thought he could score some brownie points by giving Eddie up for it."

"So the poor guy got capped by mistake."

"I tell you, these idiots, when they're not knocking each other off, they're working hard being stupid."

Preuss couldn't bring himself to respond.

"Good for the gene pool, I suppose," Barber said.

He almost made it to the Explorer.

"Martin!"

He stood in the parking lot watching Reg Trombley trotting over to him.

Exactly who Preuss didn't want to see right now.

"You were looking for me?"

"I was."

"Here I am."

I'm so not in the mood for this, Preuss thought.

Still, Trombley was here . . . might as well get this over with.

Trombley stared at Preuss's battered face. "What happened to you?"

He repeated the story he told Barber.

"Damn. You should go home."

"Trying."

"Do you want to do this another time?"

"No, let's do it now. I just wanted to apologize."

"For what?"

"Russo's bringing me up on charges again. Somebody in the squad was feeding him information about how I was screwing up the bakery investigation, among other bogus allegations. I thought he was getting it from you."

"Why would I do that?"

"I thought you were angry with me for seeing Emma Blalock."

"Well, it's true I was pissed about it."

"Damn, man, I knew something was going on."

"But I wouldn't have sunk your career over it."

"Why were you pissed? Because she's black?"

"No, because she's married."

"Excuse me?"

"She's married. You didn't know that?"

"Information she neglected to bring to my attention."

"Yeah. I'm friends with her husband. They're separated but he wants to get back with her. I knew she had her eye on you and I thought as long as you were in the picture, they'd never get together again."

"Reg, can I tell you something? I'm not interested in her. Nothing is ever going to happen between us. She's just not my type."

"Well," Trombley said. He let a few seconds pass as that sunk in.

"Then I guess it's me who owes you an apology," he said at last.

"Accepted."

"So who's giving Russo information?"

The two men sat looking at each other. At the same time they both said, "Bellamy."

"That fat fuck," Trombley said. "What are you going to do about him?"

His head began to throb again. "I don't know."

He put a hand on his crown to restrain the pounding.

"Right now I just want to go home."

Saturday, April 25, 2009

51

He pulled the Explorer to the shoulder near Flint and again outside Saginaw to adjust Toby's position. Both of the boy's hips were dislocated, so if he was sitting wrong he became uncomfortable and started to whine. It was how Preuss knew something was wrong, because otherwise Toby never complained about anything.

They stopped again around Pinconning and Preuss hooked Toby up for his lunch. The nurse at the group home had prepared his travel bag, including setting up the feeding pump with a bag of Jevity, his nutrition formula. Preuss attached the feeding line to Toby's gastrostomy button and started the pump.

On the road again, the regular drone of the pump's motor was lost in the music. Toby loved Townes Van Zandt's voice and Preuss played *The Late Great Townes Van Zandt* over and over. Whenever "Pancho and Lefty" came on, Preuss sang out the words and Toby screamed his own version, punctuated by chortles and chirps of happiness.

When they got tired of the music, he turned it off and they talked for a while. Preuss talked about the conclusion to his case and Toby listened, hummed, said his word, "Onion," and at the appropriate spots said, "Ohhhh."

"Nobody can tell me you don't understand," Preuss told him.

Toby said, "Hum."

It was another unseasonably warm day for April. The previous day the temperature topped 80 in northern Michigan, which would spell disaster for the cherry crop that would peak too soon. They seemed to be following the rain most of the way, so the pavement was wet and the passing cars spit road grime over the windshield.

He drove straight on I-75 to Grayling, three-quarters of the way up the mitten of the state. Then he turned onto M-72, which became Munson Avenue as he approached Traverse City. He took a left on East 8th Street and followed the signs for Traverse Bay Gardens.

Once inside the cemetery, he paused to get his bearings. Though the grounds were heavily wooded, the trees were only just beginning to bloom in the unseasonable weather so he easily found his way through the narrow lanes of the park.

When he found what he was looking for, he pulled as close to the verge as he could and turned the car off. The rain stopped and a delicate blue patch peeked through the cloud cover.

"We're here," he said

Toby was silent. He looked out the windows of the car, doing his characteristic double-take when he was trying extra hard to focus.

They sat for a few moments longer, then Preuss slowly and stiffly got out and went around the back to extract Toby's travel wheelchair from the rear of the Explorer. His fight left him feeling old and out of shape.

He set up the wheelchair and pushed it next to the rear passenger door. He reached in to unhook his son's seat belt, and remembered he was still plugged in from his lunch, which ended an hour ago. He unplugged the feeding tube end, fumbled in Toby's bag until he found the bottle of fresh water, and connected one of the big bolus tubes to the button. He poured four ounces of water into the tube to rinse the button and give Toby a drink.

He lowered the tube to let air burble out of Toby's tummy, then put away the bottle and tube, snapped the cap on the g-tube button, and got a firm grip around Toby's hips. He was careful to support the boy's back with his left hand and not grab him around the thighs. The long bones of Toby's legs were delicate as a bird's and would break if he wasn't handled correctly.

He swept the boy up into his arms and lifted him from the car. He twisted his body to set him as lightly as he could in the wheelchair without jarring Toby's hips. Preuss felt a distressing tinge in his lower back. It wasn't a problem now, but as he got older and Toby got heavier he knew the time would come when he could no longer toss his son around like this.

Well, something he couldn't worry about now. Instead he concentrated on making sure Toby was buckled in securely. The day was warm but he drew Toby's heavy cotton Red Wings poncho around him in case the rain started again. He pulled a watch cap down over Toby's head and ears.

"It's warm and you're mostly over your infection but we still don't want to take any chances with those ears," Preuss told him.

Toby hated anything touching his head but after trying to shake the snug cap off he gave in and let it stay.

Preuss retrieved the curved pillow in the shape of an otter from the back seat and put it around Toby's neck to keep his head from flopping when they went over the uneven surface of the grass. Preuss also put a small square pillow under his son's feet on the platform of the wheelchair so his legs wouldn't jostle.

With his son bundled in, Preuss pushed the chair over the grass to the grave they had made the four-and-a-half-hour trip up from Ferndale to visit.

They rolled past headstones until they found the one they were looking for, a plain rectangular polished granite block.

Jeanette Russo Preuss
Beloved Daughter, Mother, Wife
September 16, 1961 - June 6, 2003

Agnes Russo, Jeanette's mother, lived nearby. She insisted her daughter be buried up here and not downstate where she would be near Preuss and her ex-husband Nick Russo. Like her ex-husband, she blamed Preuss for her daughter's death; even though he wasn't driving the car that slammed into hers six years ago, she was driving with both boys in the car because she just walked out on Preuss and was making the four-and-a-half hour trip from Ferndale up to her mother's house. The drunk driver who t-boned her made sure she would never make it.

Unlike Nick, Agnes's anger at Preuss softened over the years, mostly because of Toby. She couldn't stay angry at someone who loved the boy as much as she did.

She came downstate to visit Toby every other month except in the snowiest part of winter, and he brought Toby north to spend time with Agnes and visit Jeanette's grave in the months when Agnes didn't come to Ferndale. The day before, Preuss called to tell her they were coming up. Preuss didn't want Toby to lose touch with her as he had done with his grandfather, who never saw him anymore.

"Toby, here's your mom," Preuss said. "Jeanette, here's our boy."

Toby looked at the grave out of the corner of his eye, his eyes and mouth open wide as if in surprise. And maybe he was surprised to hear his father talking to the ground.

Preuss stood beside his son, caressing the fuzzy short hair on the back of his head below the watch cap.

Suddenly Toby screwed up his face and began to wail, a loud high disconsolate cry.

Preuss bent down to put his arms around his son's narrow shoulders. Toby's whole body was tense as he screamed his anguish.

Preuss couldn't tell the boy it would be all right. He couldn't in good faith say anything would ever be all right.

Whatever he could say wouldn't calm the boy anyway. This state needed to run its course. Preuss could only murmur, "I'm here, sweetheart. Daddy's here."

He waited until his son quieted down and his muscle tone relaxed, then still with his arm around the boy he spoke thoughts Toby might have wanted to say to his mother.

"Let's tell Mom how much we miss her, okay? Say, 'I miss you very much, Mom. I miss you so much.'"

Hearing the words, in Preuss's quietest tones, Toby relaxed even more. He began to hum.

"Let's tell Mom we love her, okay? Let's say, 'We love you, Mom.'"

Toby said something that sounded like "Mmmommm."

Preuss knelt quietly beside his son for another half hour, mentally voicing his own thoughts to his wife. Toby's face was composed and serious as though communing with his mother himself. And maybe he was.

Then he felt Toby shiver as the damp air from the south end of Grand Traverse Bay worked its way into his bones.

"Okay, Toby, let's say goodbye to Mom for now. We'll be back again soon, Mom. We love you. We love and miss you very much."

Toby murmured his agreement.

Preuss wheeled his son away from the grave and bumped him over the grass back to the Explorer. Toby looked back up at him, his face calm and demure, his mother's brown eyes trying to make contact with his father. Preuss stopped and leaned down to take the boy's gorgeous face between his hands and kissed his cheeks.

"Your brother's out there somewhere, but for now it's just us."

When he got Toby buckled into his seat in the car, Preuss called Agnes Russo to let her know they would be there in about an hour.

He knew Agnes would greet him coolly when they rolled into her house in Greilickville. But she would make a huge fuss over the boy and Toby would respond with smiles and chirps of joy. It would be the perfect way to shift from the elegiac sadness they both felt so keenly at the graveyard.

Agnes was a pediatric nurse practitioner at the medical center near her house so she knew how to care for him. She built a ramp so he could get into the house, and kept a closet of supplies for him as well as a portable Hoyer lift to get him on the bed and into the tub.

Before he took his son to see Agnes, there was one more stop to make.

They drove back along M-22 toward Traverse City, where Preuss was spending the night at the Hampton Inn. What was ahead of him was predictable, what always happened when he brought his son north for a visit: dinner at one of the nearby restaurants, then hours to fill until he grew too tired to stay awake.

A night like any other.

He brought his guitar so he could pass the time playing with his pocket amp in his room if he didn't go out to hear live music, which he already knew he didn't want to do. He was not in the mood to be around people.

Driving along, his thoughts turned toward the folder with the latest salvo from Nick Russo's vendetta, still on his desk back at the station. Still unread.

"Toby," he said, "I don't know how much longer I can keep this up. Between the conflict with your grandfather and the strain of my cases, I'm not convinced it's worth what it takes out of me anymore."

Toby had no comment.

When they reached the cut-off for the East Traverse Highway, he drove west till they reached the shore of Lake Michigan. He turned north and found a spot where he could pull off the road. He parked by a deserted beach.

He removed Toby's wheelchair from the back and lifted the boy into it once again. When Preuss got him warmly wrapped in the poncho and an additional blanket against the wind off the lake, he took a sack that held a folding chair from the rear of the Explorer and found a section of beach where he could get through on the hard-packed sand.

He pushed Toby's chair to a stop about a dozen feet from the vast water spreading out before them. A brisk southeast wind kicked up and drove a chop toward the melting ice floes still piled up near shore despite the mild weather.

He unfolded the chair and sat beside his son. Toby was bundled up in his hat, Red Wings poncho, and blanket. Preuss pulled the edge of the blanket away from Toby's face.

He reached under the blankets and poncho to hold his son's hand.

After a while the chop turned to gentle rollers pushing steadily into shore. He watched as they came on without ceasing, and grew sleepy from the warmth of the day. Toby hummed gently.

Sitting there in a half-waking state, he remembered the first line of a poem he once read in college, "Like as the waves make towards the pebbled shore." He could only remember the first line, but it burned itself into his memory. He remembered the poem was about how the waves, like minutes, pass inexorably. And how, in the midst of such constancy, life itself is so fleeting.

Watching the waves making toward this particular shore with his son by his side, fresh from the cemetery, thinking about the cruel brevity of life, he could feel Jeanette's presence strongly.

He asked Toby if he felt the same. Toby turned his head dreamily and looked at his father out of the corner of his eye. "Um," he said in his foghorn voice.

Preuss took it for agreement. "Me, too."

He never believed in an afterlife, and never took consolation from people who told him Jeanette was now an angel, or in a better place, or at peace, or playing pinochle with Jesus or whatever she was supposed to be doing in other people's versions of heaven. To him Jeanette was just dead, a collection of bones in a box buried at the cemetery they just visited.

Yet now, feeling her with them, he considered the possibility that her spirit might still survive in some form as part of the endlessly changing universe around him, eternal yet constantly in motion. Like the gulls dipping over the waves. And the waves themselves.

Like Eddie Watkins and Leon Banks. Like they all would be some day.

What would she think of her husband and son now, he wondered, him sober these six years, chastened by what had torn their family apart; Toby older and more mannish; Jason lost somewhere in the cosmos. Would she be glad their precious younger son was in good hands?

Would she approve of how he was dealing with the older boy, keeping tabs from a distance and waiting till Jason felt it was time to make contact again?

If he ever would feel that way . . .

His mind eddied toward all the things the boys taught him, Toby of course but Jason too . . . about love freely given, about patience, about the need to connect and the need to let go, about what was important in life beyond scrambling for a living and accumulating prestige.

Whatever those wise children tried to teach him, he tried to learn.

He thought about parents and children whose love for each other went in the wrong directions, or nowhere at all . . . about absent fathers who passed misery down through the generations like a prized family legacy, about the cascading consequences of greed and violence, about the children who were lost or luckless or dead.

We extend the unhappiness of the world, Preuss thought, or do what we can to mitigate it.

Watching the endless roll of the lake, he asked Jeanette for forgiveness for all he had done to cause her unhappiness, and for whatever sorrow he visited on their sons.

There was no response except for the sound of the wind and the creaking of the ice floes by the shore, which he couldn't interpret.

He glanced at Toby, who sat with his eyes closed against the wind and a beatific smile on his face.

As always, Toby seemed to know.

They sat. The lake spread out before them, silver in the leaden light of the sunless day.

In a while the sky began to spit rain. Taking that as his cue, Preuss gathered up his chair and pushed Toby back over the sand to the Explorer. He buckled the boy into the back seat and wrapped him in a massive hug.

Toby couldn't return the embrace but he turned his head and put the O of his lips on his father's cheek in a sloppy kiss. Preuss let the kiss linger, then returned it with a noisy smack that made Toby laugh.

Reluctantly he released the boy and slid back into the driver's seat. He cranked up "Pancho and Lefty" one more time. When the guitar intro began, Toby sang a high note of joy at being warm, dry, and happy on a road trip with his father.

Then Preuss turned the Explorer around and drove to Agnes Russo's.

Acknowledgements

Authorship seems solitary, but is really multiple. Warm thanks for their assistance and support go to Michael J. Brady, for help with legal questions (though all resulting mistakes and misinformation are my own); Detroitblogger John (John Carlisle), whose article in the *Metro Times* ("Shut Down," February 9, 2009) provided the inspiration for the inciting action of this story; the Royal Oak and Ferndale Public Libraries, two wonderful establishments where much of this book was written; Marygrove College, for the sabbatical support that gave me time to write; Michael Kitchen, retired Chief of Police of Ferndale, for his recommendations and suggestions; Rich Carnahan from PublishPros for his design expertise; Jamie Kril, for providing the model for Toby as well as being the abiding spirit that infuses these pages; and my wife Suzanne Allen, whose love and support continue to sustain me (and whose artwork makes an appearance in Chapter 36).

Also by DONALD LEVIN

CRIMES OF LOVE | BOOK 1

One cold November night, police detective Martin Preuss joins a frantic search for a seven-year-old girl with epilepsy who has disappeared from the streets of his suburban Detroit community. Unwilling to let go after the Oakland County Sheriff's Office takes over the case from his city agency, he strikes out on his own, following leads across the entire metropolitan region. Probing deep within the anguished lives of all those who came in contact with the missing girl, Preuss must summon all his skills and resources to solve the many crimes of love he uncovers.

GUILT IN HIDING | BOOK 3

Preparing to take his beloved son Toby to a Detroit Tigers baseball game, Detective Martin Preuss instead must search for a van that has gone up in smoke along with its passenger, a young handicapped man and the woman who was driving. Working through the layers of the many mysteries surrounding their disappearances, Preuss confronts contemporary crimes intertwined with the unspeakable evils of the 20th century's darkest period. Complex, chilling, and compulsively readable, *Guilt in Hiding* has been called "both the brightest and the darkest tale in this riveting series."

CPSIA information can be obtained
at www.ICGtesting.com
Printed in the USA
LVHW092236230619
622115LV00001B/103/P